What the critics are saying...

5 CUPS: "Nibbles 'n' Bits is a wonderful anthology that features vampire themed stories by three extremely talented authors who utilize some very creative twists and turns that make this book a must read for fans of the vampire genre. I greatly enjoyed all three stories and will read them repeatedly. Nibbles 'n' Bits is most definitely a keeper!" ~ *Susan White, Coffee Time Romance*

5 ANGELS "RECOMMENDED READ: ...three stories that will have readers falling out of their chair laughing... [The authors]... will have people talking about the scenes in these books for a long time to come." ~ *Donna, Fallen Angel Reviews*

"...a witty, humorous romantic anthology... Three talented ladies embrace the night and write enticing tales of torrid sex and love."~ *Sinclair Reid, Romance Reviews Today*

4 STARS "...a wonderful collection of three steamy and amusing tales of vampire love..." ~ *Susan Biliter, eCataRomance*

4 HEARTS "I highly recommend this book and can promise readers will not be disappointed..." ~ *Angel Brewer , The Romance Studio*

"Vampires can have love lives just as screwed up as anybody else's, and here's the proof. *Nibbles and Bits* is a trio of funny, romantic horror tales of the undead." ~ *Hoot Island*

Nibbles 'n' Bits

Judy Mays

Mardi Ballou

&

Delilah Devlin

NIBBLES 'N' BITS
An Ellora's Cave Publication, December 2004

Ellora's Cave Publishing, Inc.
1337 Commerce Drive, Suite #13
Stow, Ohio 44224

ISBN #1419951432
Other available formats: ISBN MS Reader (LIT), Adobe (PDF),
Rocketbook (RB), Mobipocket (PRC) & HTML

Edited by: *Raelene Gorlinsky, Heather Osborn and Briana St. James*
Cover art by: *Christine Clavel*

Warning:

The following material contains graphic sexual content meant for mature readers. *Nibbles 'N' Bits* has been rated *E-rotic* by a minimum of three independent reviewers.

Ellora's Cave Publishing offers three levels of Romantica™ reading entertainment: S (S-ensuous), E (E-rotic), and X (X-treme).

S-*ensuous* love scenes are explicit and leave nothing to the imagination.

E-*rotic* love scenes are explicit, leave nothing to the imagination, and are high in volume per the overall word count. In addition, some E-rated titles might contain fantasy material that some readers find objectionable, such as bondage, submission, same sex encounters, forced seductions, etc. E-rated titles are the most graphic titles we carry; it is common, for instance, for an author to use words such as "fucking", "cock", "pussy", etc., within their work of literature.

X-*treme* titles differ from E-rated titles only in plot premise and storyline execution. Unlike E-rated titles, stories designated with the letter X tend to contain controversial subject matter not for the faint of heart.

Contents

Rednecks 'n' Roses

Judy Mays

Dedication

For my friend Amber, whose real life adventures gave me the idea for this story.

No, she's not a vampire—but, yes, she has a cross-eyed black cat named Midnight.

Trademarks Acknowledgement

The author acknowledges the trademarked status and trademark owners of the following wordmarks mentioned in this work of fiction:

Chevrolet (Chevy) Blazer: General Motors Corporation

Lysol: Linden Corporation

Chapter One

"You got fucked."

Amber blinked, burped, then reached for her glass. "No I didn't. I got a house and over a hundred acres of land."

Tequila, lime juice and ice sloshed as Mandi mixed another pitcher of margaritas. "In fricking Juniata County. Do you realize how far away from civilization that is? It's the middle of nowhere."

Amber shook her head. "It's only an hour away from Harrisburg." The room started to spin and she closed her eyes.

An ice cube bounced off the table and skidded across the kitchen floor.

"Harrisburg! What the hell is there to do in Harrisburg when all your friends are in Philadelphia? How can you be so...so easygoing? You should be pissed as hell that Frank got all that money. Shit, he's a fricking engineer. I'll say it again. You got fucked."

Amber gulped down the last swallow in her glass. Warmth rolled through her veins. She felt so good! Why did Mandi keep harping on and on about Aunt Ernestine? Could she be right?

Amber held out her glass. "You really think so?"

Nodding, Mandi poured both of them another drink. "Shit yeah. Your Aunt Ernestine was a real bitch not to leave you any money."

At first Amber watched Mandi's head go up and down but it made her dizzy so she stared at the drink Mandi had poured instead. It sure was a pretty yellow color—all soft and pale like a gentle spring sun. Then she frowned. Aunt Ernestine had hated any color except gray, brown, white or black. How could normal people hate pretty colors? Maybe Mandi was right. "She was a bitch, wasn't she? But Mandi, I didn't expect her to leave me anything in her will, so how can I be disappointed?"

"Christ, Amber. Would you stop being so nice!" Mandi picked a particularly bright fuchsia pillow up off the floor and threw it at an equally colorful purple sofa. "You got fucked—royally. You went to that bitch's house three or four times a week to run her errands, drag her wherever she wanted to go or see if she needed anything. And how does she thank you? By leaving all her money to your asshole cousin."

Amber swallowed more of her drink. Hmmm, but it tasted good. "Asshole cousin Frank," she agreed. Frank was an asshole. And his wife was a stuck-up snob.

"He's getting money that belongs to you."

Amber stared at the tiny, white salt crystals hugging the rim of her glass. One of those itty-bitty umbrellas, a bright orange or green one, would really look nice in it.

"Are you listening to me, Amber. Frank got your money."

Still smiling at her glass, Amber shook her head and repeated, "Nope. Not my money. I knew Aunt Ernestine wouldn't leave me any so why should I be disappointed?"

Mandi gaped. "Why? Because you're the one who took care of the old tightwad for the last three years. Because you're almost broke. You got downsized out of your job two months ago, remember?"

That reminder momentarily cleared Amber's mind. "How could I forget?" She gulped the rest of her drink and held out her glass. "More."

Mandi poured. "Your aunt knew that. Did she ever offer to help you? To even pay for gas when you ran her errands?"

Squinting as she swayed in her chair, Amber stared at the blur that was her friend. Mandi was making more and more sense. Aunt Ernestine never did offer to help her. Hell, she rarely ever said "thank you." "You're right. She was a bitch, a stingy, penny-pinching, sour-faced bitch."

Mandi grinned. "Now you're talking."

Another swallow. Amber hiccuped. "Tight-fisted, dried-up old biddy."

Mandi nodded. "She treated you like dirt."

Blinking, Amber concentrated harder on her friend's face—both of them. "Did I ever tell you what she thought of my stories?"

Mandi tossed back a shot of tequila and almost fell out of her chair. She grabbed the table and steadied herself. "No, you never did."

Leaning forward, Amber leaned her elbows on the table. They slipped off; she caught herself and planted them more firmly. In a low voice she said, "She called them 'dirty' books. She said I was 'lacking morals' and that decent people would be offended by what I was writing." She frowned. "Are you offended by what I write, Mandi?" She belched a deep belch.

After answering Amber's belch with one of her own, Mandi gulped another shot. "Your aunt was a narrow-minded prude and a sanctimonious bitch. Hard to believe she was ever married. Bet she did it with the lights out, wearing a high-necked, long-sleeved nightgown, missionary position with her eyes screwed shut, stiff as a board until your uncle was finished. She wouldn't know good sex if it bit her in the ass. So what if your stories have a little sex in them. Sex sells."

Amber giggled. "Maybe Uncle Henry should have bitten her in the ass."

Pale yellow liquid squirted across the table as Mandi tried to swallow and laugh at the same time.

Nodding, Amber grabbed the bottle and poured a shot of tequila—and got most of it in the glass. "Yep, he should have bitten her in the ass. She called me a 'loose woman', you know." Amber lifted the shot glass and tossed its contents into her mouth. After an involuntary shake, she continued. "Me! A loose woman. Ha! I haven't had a date in six months, let alone sex. The last time I had sex was with that investment banker I was dating last year."

Wiping away the liquid she'd snorted out of her nose, Mandi grabbed the bottle from Amber and poured herself another shot. "Oh yeah, Mini-dick, right?"

Amber nodded. "Yep, good, old Mini-dick. Mini-est dick in the East. His dick would slip out every time he'd really start pumping. Most unsatisfying sex I ever had." She sighed. "The last sex I ever had."

Giggling, Mandi poured, missed her glass, and tequila rolled across the table. "You sure do attract the losers. Remember Buggy Cal?"

Amber watched the stream of tequila cascade down over the side of the table and splash onto the floor. Did it always splash straight back up again? She swayed to the left then caught herself and focused on Mandi. "Well shit, I didn't know he collected bugs until after we'd been dating for a couple of months."

Finally managing to fill her shot glass, Mandi shook her head—and swayed from one side of her chair to the other. "Amber, Amber, Amber. You should have known when he wouldn't kill that spider for you."

"Spiders! Yuk." Shuddering, Amber leaned forward and lowered her voice. "Did I ever tell you he had this huge spider he kept as a pet? He wanted me to hold it! Can you believe it? Me? Hold a spider? Ha! That's the last time he saw me. I was out that door so fast he didn't know what happened."

Guffawing, Mandi finger-combed her hair back from her face then lifted the pitcher and poured another margarita into Amber's glass. "Here, have another drink."

Amber picked up her glass, sipped, and swirled the delicious liquid around her mouth. Mmmmmmmmmm. Mandi definitely knew how to make good margaritas. How many pitchers had they drunk? And when was the last time they had something to eat? She swallowed some more and giggled. Liquid dribbled down her chin and splattered her blouse.

Mandi blinked a few times. "Did we have anything to eat today?"

Tilting her head to the side, Amber grinned. "Nope. You dragged me home right after the reading of the will and starting mixing drinks and pouring shots."

Mandi grinned back. "Oh yeah. Want me to make another pitcher?"

* * * * *

A bullhorn blared in Amber's ear. "Wake up."

Groaning, she rolled over. "Who turned the TV up so loud?"

Mandi shook her again. "Wake up. There's some guy at the door with a certified letter and a package for you. He won't let me sign for it."

Amber dragged her eyes open, squinting into the sunlight exploding through the window. Her head pounded in time with her heartbeat. "Oh God! Who hit me?"

Hands covering her eyes, Mandi fell across Amber's bed and moaned with her. "I shouldn't have made that fourth pitcher of margaritas. Or maybe it was that last shot."

Dragging herself up, Amber sat on the edge of the bed and held her head in her hands. "Coffee. I need coffee."

"One step ahead of you. It's on your night stand." Mandi mumbled into the sheets. "Aspirin too."

Amber grabbed the mug with shaking hands and lifted it to her lips. "God, that tastes good." Grabbing the bottle, she popped the lid off and dumped three aspirin into her hand. She swallowed them with a gulp of coffee.

A few minutes later, after the room stopped spinning, she felt steady enough to heave herself up off of bed and shuffle to the living room. She set her coffee mug on the end table— wincing at the sonic boom that reverberated around the room as she did so—and very carefully opened the front door. "You have a package for me?"

The postman slid a medium-sized box across the threshold, handed her a gray envelope and shouted, "Sign here." At least it seemed like he shouted.

Stomach rolling from the aftershave engulfing his body, Amber blinked a few times to clear her vision then scribbled her signature on the paper he held out to her. She closed the door in his grinning face.

Mandi was sprawled on the couch, holding a mug against her forehead. She winced at the sound to the door closing. "What is it?"

Pushing the box across the floor with her foot—it wasn't heavy—Amber collapsed onto the raspberry-colored chair. "Give me a chance to open it, already. Fuck, but I feel like shit. And it's your fault."

Mandi groaned. "I didn't hold your mouth open and pour the drinks in, you know."

Amber glanced toward the mirror hanging on the wall. Bloodshot eyes stared back at her. "You many as well have. The margaritas were your idea."

Mandi slid further down the couch. "Oh, quit complaining and open the damn letter."

Taking a deep breath, hoping it would still the throbbing in her head, Amber perused the envelope. "It's from Aunt Ernestine's lawyer."

Mandi moved closer then groaned. Closing her eyes, she leaned her head against the back of the sofa. "So what does it say?" She groaned again. "Oh, who gives a rat's ass what it says. Open the package first."

After struggling with and cursing at the packing tape for five minutes, Amber tore open the box and lifted out a silver urn. "What the hell…"

Tearing open the envelope, Amber blinked to focus her eyes then quickly scanned the missive.

"Is there something valuable in it?"

Amber gaped at the letter then laughed until tears rolled down her cheeks, simultaneously wincing at the pounding in her head. "Hell no. It's Aunt Ernestine."

Chapter Two

Amber ducked involuntarily as a sheet of muddy water pelted the windshield. Her eight-year-old Chevy Blazer rattled as it lurched through another pothole in the unpaved road.

Leaning forward, she gripped the wheel tighter as the wipers smeared the muddy water from that morning's thunderstorm across the windshield. "Damn puddle was the size of Rhode Island."

The urn lying between the bucket seats banged off one seat and slammed into the console as the left side of the car dipped into an especially deep rut.

"Don't you dare say a word, Aunt Ernestine. You wanted to come on this trip."

Amber jerked the wheel to the left, swerving to miss a tree branch that was lying partway across the road. The right wheel dropped into an especially deep pothole, rocking the vehicle first from one side then to the other as the tire crawled back onto a more level surface.

"Merroooooooow!" The fluffy, black cat curled up on the passenger seat bounced a foot into the air as the urn rolled toward the back seat.

Amber eased her foot off the accelerator. "Oh, shit! Sorry Midnight, but this road sucks."

Blinking twice, Midnight pulled her claws out of the seat and settled back down, curling her paws underneath her chest.

They bounced through another set of ruts.

The possessions loaded in the back started to shift.

The urn rolled back to the front of the car.

Hissing, Midnight pushed herself against the backrest and

dug her claws into the seat again.

Amber screwed up her face as she clenched the steering wheel tighter. "Damn it. How much farther do we have to go? This is the right road, isn't it?" Blinking at a ray of afternoon sunlight that escaped from behind a cloud, Amber jerked the visor down. "I swear this is the right road. I remember turning at that pink house when I came here with Uncle Henry and Aunt Ernestine years ago."

She jerked the wheel to the right to miss another pothole.

Amber blew some straggling wisps of hair out of her eyes and glanced down at the urn that now lay between the two front seats again. "Don't worry, Auntie, I'll spread your ashes on that hillside of wild roses—eventually. I think I'll keep you around a while first and let you help me with my novel. So, how much more sex should I add to my story, dear Aunt Ernestine? That's what that last editor said, you know. She liked my style. I just need to take out the secret baby, the amnesia, make my hero a vampire instead of a cowboy, and not have my heroine be a virgin the first time she has sex with the hero. Oh, also, add more sex, more sex, more sex." Amber chuckled then grinned. "Lots more sex, Auntie. And I'll describe every bit of it to you as I write it."

The silver urn bounced off the side of Amber's seat again.

She glanced down at it. "You know, this is going to work out okay. I have the money I saved and the money in that maintenance account for the property. I don't know how he did it but Uncle Henry managed to keep that account secret from you so I don't have to worry about making repairs or paying taxes. It's even okay for me to withdraw money for food. I'm all set. I can spend the next year or so just writing. And I bet I could find a part-time job here if I really need it. I'll even waitress if I have to. I did it in college, I can do it again."

The urn thunked against the side of the passenger seat.

Amber squinted through the windshield, the afternoon sunlight half blinding her as it slipped below the visor.

The urn rolled and thunked against her seat.

As she rounded a turn, the sun outlined a small, white, two-story house.

"Looks like we're here, Midnight."

After driving through one more puddle that sent more sheets of water flying into the air on both sides of the car, Amber braked to a slow halt before the six steps that led up to the front porch. Shifting into park, she sighed, tightened her hands on the wheel, then let go. She glanced over at her cat.

Midnight stared back, her head tilted slightly to the left.

Amber smiled and stroked her head. "I bet there'll be lots of mice for you to chase. Come on, let's go check the place out."

Gathering Midnight against her chest, she elbowed the door latch, pushed the door open and slid out of the car.

Her nose wrinkling, Midnight swiveled her head and scented the air.

A few steps away, a rabbit flinched then sprang away to disappear under the porch.

"Meeerrroooowww!" Twisting and turning, the cat dug her claws into Amber's stomach and squirmed out of her arms.

Amber let her fall to the ground. "Ouch! Damn it, Midnight! You didn't have to scratch me!"

The cat scrambled after the rabbit, stumbling up a porch step then squeezing between it and the next one to disappear after the rabbit.

Hands on hips, Amber glared at the steps. "Oh great. Midnight, you're supposed to chase mice, not rabbits. Come out from under there right now!"

A faint meow answered her.

Raking her hair back from her forehead, Amber stomped to the steps and squatted. Squinting, she tried to see into the darkness.

Midnight meowed again.

Mumbling under her breath, Amber grabbed a step and pulled it.

It didn't give. The steps were solid.

Another meow.

"Well what do you expect me to do? You're the one who got yourself into this mess. Find your own way out."

Midnight's meows became more plaintive.

Rising, Amber wiped her hands on the seat of her jeans. "I swear, I've never had a cat that got herself into so many predicaments. How am I going to get you out from under there?"

Looking around, she spied a dark opening at the end of the porch.

"You're lucky somebody or something pulled the latticework away, Midnight," she muttered as she settled onto her hands and knees and wiggled her way through the opening. "Now where are you?"

"Meeeeooooow."

Blinking, Amber grimaced as damp moisture seeped into the knees of her jeans and soft dirt sifted through her fingers. She held her breath against the musty, moldy smell emanating from the damp soil, waited for her eyes to adjust to the darkness, then looked around trying to find her cat. "I would have to have a black cat. Midnight, where are you?"

Something soft tickled her right cheek.

She turned her head, trying to see her cat. "Well, come on out of here."

Midnight meowed off to her left.

A feathery caress brushed her cheek again.

Whatever was touching her wasn't Midnight's fur. Only one other thing could be that soft — cobwebs.

"Ahhhhhhhh! Spiders! Oh my God, there's a spider on me!" Amber jerked back, banging her head against the dark wood above her head. Eyes watering, she pushed herself back out the hole. Leaping to her feet, she immediately began shaking her head and brushing her clothing, all the while jumping from one foot to the other. "Ahhhhhh. Get it off me. Get it off me!"

"Problem, Ma'am?"

Chapter Three

Fingers buried in her hair, Amber froze.

That was a man's voice.

Slowly, she turned and peered through the strands of hair dangling before her eyes.

The man who faced her wore what looked like a police uniform. A white car trimmed in green and yellow with "Juniata County Sheriff" printed on the side was parked next to her muddy Blazer.

"Umm…"

The sheriff planted his hands on his hips.

"My cat is stuck under the porch?"

He tilted his head to the side. "Stuck?"

Blowing the hair out of her face, Amber straightened to her full five-feet-eleven-inches and crossed her arms over her chest. "Okay, so there was a spider. I hate spiders. Is there something I can do for you?"

"Name's Brad Keister." He nodded toward his car. "I'm the sheriff. Who are you? This is private property, you know."

She lifted her chin. "I'm Amber Blake and this is my property."

Pursing his lips, he nodded. "Heard Mrs. Myers finally passed on and left the property to a niece. You intend to live here?"

Amber sighed. Nosy sheriff. But he was the law and she'd be better off not irritating him at their first meeting. "Yes, for the next six months or so. I got downsized out of my job and it seemed like coming here for a while was a good idea."

"What you gonna do?"

"I beg your pardon?"

The sheriff scowled. "What you gonna do all day? You aren't one of those city-slicker types who want to party all night then sleep all day, are you? Neighbors won't take kindly to it."

Amber blinked. "Neighbors?" She lifted her arm and pointed to the woods surrounding the property. "What neighbors? Nobody even knows I'm here except you."

He shook his head. "Everybody knows you're here now. Sadie Dunkelburger, the woman who lives across the road from your driveway, phoned my office and said a strange car had turned in here. I was close so figured I'd just drive in to make sure no one was up to any mischief. You can be sure that as soon as Sadie hung up from my office, she was calling everyone she knew to tell them about someone driving in to the Myers' place."

"Great, a nosy old lady is my closest neighbor," Amber mumbled mostly to herself.

He opened his mouth but before he could answer, a sharp crack exploded from the woods in front of the house.

Amber jumped. "What was that?"

The sheriff spun toward his car. "Damn Nipples poking around where they aren't supposed to be again."

Amber started. Nipples? She looked down at her tee-shirt. Nothing. Her nipples weren't poking out. What the hell was this crazy sheriff talking about?

"What's going on?"

"Poachers. Guys hunting out of season," he answered over his shoulder as he yanked open the car door.

Amber's stomach dropped to the ground. "Poaching? Somebody is shooting a gun? Here?" Flinching, she scrunched down and jerked her head from side to side.

Another gunshot. This one sounded closer.

She scrabbled after the sheriff. "You can't leave me here

alone! There's someone with a gun out there."

Half in his car, the sheriff took the time to grin at her. "Don't worry. Nobody is going to shoot at you. But if it makes you feel better, there are three shotguns and a deer rifle in the closet of the front bedroom. Ammunition is in the top dresser drawer." He slid into the car, slammed the door, gunned the engine and tore away down the driveway.

Small chunks of mud bombarded the ground at Amber's feet and she jumped back. *Guns? Ammunition? In my house? And how the hell does he know?* Shuddering, she flopped down on her behind and gaped at the now-empty driveway.

"Meeeeeerrroooooow?" Midnight rubbed her head against Amber's knee.

Leaning over, she gathered the cat into her arms. "Sure, now you come out." Tilting her head back, she looked up at the sky and closed her eyes. "Some moron is out there shooting a gun, the sheriff thinks I'm an idiot and the local busybody is already spying on me. Maybe Mandi was right and I should have stayed in Philadelphia."

Dampness seeped into the seat of her pants.

Shivering, she struggled to her feet, the fluffy cat held firmly in her arms. "Well, we're here now." She looked down into Midnight's face. "No more running after rabbits. What in the world would you do with it if you caught it anyway?" She shook her head. "Come on, let's see what our new home looks like."

With one last sigh, Amber cuddled her cat in her arms and marched up the steps.

Tucking one hand under Midnight's stomach, she balanced the cat on her arm and pulled the rusty screen door open.

It squeaked.

"At least I know how to oil a door," she mumbled to the cat. Then she grabbed the doorknob of the inner door. "Oh, shit. The key's in my purse."

She rattled the knob.

The door swung open.

She shifted the heavy cat to her other arm. "Oh great. It wasn't even locked. I wouldn't be surprised if everything has been stolen."

Pushing the door open, she stepped partway into the living room.

The screen door hit her in the ass as it swung shut.

"Ouch! Damn it." Slapping her hand against the wall, she found the light switch and flipped it up.

Soft light from a ceiling fixture flooded the room.

"The lawyer said the electricity would be turned on. I'll have to contact the phone company, though. Good thing I have a cell phone."

Dropping Midnight at her feet, she stepped further into the room. A comfortable-looking sofa sat before a huge fireplace that stretched across the back wall of the room. Two leather chairs flanked a table in front of a large window. To her left, a carved staircase led to a small landing then turned at a right angle toward the second floor.

Amber stepped further into the room and pulled the heavy blue curtains apart. A large, dusty picture window with an intricate stained glass design bordering the top and two sides appeared.

"Oh my. This window is beautiful."

After a quick look outside—she didn't see anything except trees -- Amber turned and headed toward the door to the left of the fireplace. "Guess the kitchen is this way. Come on, Midnight." Her cat pacing behind her, she strode toward the back of the house. "I sure hope there's a bathroom back here."

The kitchen was surprisingly large, the appliances not too old. The door on the left led to a small dining room. The one on the right to a smaller laundry room that contained an almost new washer and dryer—and a sink and toilet.

"Thank goodness! And there's even toilet paper."

A few minutes later, Amber was back in the kitchen. She looked down at her cat. "Guess I should unload before it gets any later."

Half an hour later, all the possessions she'd brought with her were piled on the living room floor—except for Aunt Ernestine's urn. That sat on the table next to the front door.

Amber stared at it and sighed.

Midnight meowed and danced a little dance.

She looked around the room, then at her pile of belongings. "Litter box. I better set that up in the laundry room right away, huh? It will fit under that table. Cat food stays down here too, and the supplies I brought. Guess I should get the stuff out of the cooler and put it in the fridge. She tucked the litter box under her arm and grabbed the bag of cat litter with her left hand. Grasping the handle of the cooler with her right, she lifted the end and wheeled it into the kitchen.

Midnight was curled on top of one of her suitcases when she returned fifteen minutes later.

"Are you just going to sit there and watch me? I thought you wanted to use your litter box."

Midnight yawned then licked her paw.

Mumbling something about cats, Amber lifted the case holding her laptop. "I'm going to turn that small dining room off the kitchen into an office. There's a nice view of the hill with the wild roses and the forest behind it from there. It should be a good place to write." She frowned and shook her head. "A vampire hero. Who would have thought they could ever be so popular. Lord knows, thanks to Mandi, I've seen enough of Buffy, Spike and Angel, not to mention every Dracula movie ever made, so that I should be able to figure out how to write one."

Midnight yawned again.

Amber stared at the case in her hand then looked out the window. The front of the house faced east, and she could barely make out her car in the fading light. The kitchen wasn't much brighter even though it faced west. Once the sun slipped down behind the woods, the darkness spread quickly. "This can wait. I'm tired. There's supposed to be a modern bathroom upstairs. I'm going to take a hot shower and go to bed." She bent and stroked Midnight. "Your bowls of food and water are in the kitchen."

Grabbing her overnight bag — and the broom she'd brought with her — she headed up the steps, grimacing as dust rose when she grabbed the stair rail. "I'll be spending the next week cleaning. I hate to clean."

At the top of the steps, she flipped the light switch and stepped into the small hallway. Four doors stood open.

Turning right, she walked the short distance to the doorway at the end of the hall, felt inside and flipped the light switch. The room was small and contained only an unmade single bed and a small dresser. Broom extended before her, she eyed the corners of the ceiling. No spiders. Good.

She turned off the light and turned left and reached in that doorway for the light switch. A slightly larger room, bare except for a large, old-fashioned trunk. She checked the corners. No spiders here either. Maybe this wouldn't be so bad.

Sneezing, Amber turned off the light and walked to the other end of the hallway. Stepping into the doorway on the right, she jumped, flailing her hands around when something bumped against her forehead. "Bats! There better not be bats in this house."

Her fingers brushed against a swinging chain and she chuckled weakly. Grabbing it, she pulled. Light flooded the room and a ceiling fan began to spin slowly. This room was larger. A double bed, draped with a dust cover, was pushed against the wall. A matching bureau and dresser were pushed against another. Sliding doors on the left wall indicated a good sized closet.

"Thank goodness for the dust cover," Amber muttered as she set the broom against the wall and carefully removed the dust cover from the bed, folding it over on itself. At least she wouldn't spend the night sneezing. And she didn't have to worry about sheets either. She'd brought her own, but if she didn't feel like making the bed, she could always use her sleeping bag. She'd see how she felt after her shower.

Leaving the light on, she headed for the last doorway. It had to be the bathroom.

Again, the light switch was just inside the door. After flipping it on, Amber looked around. Obviously a converted bedroom, the bathroom was larger than she'd thought it would be.

"Mmmm. I can put some plants in here. But that shower curtain has got to go. Dark blue with green fish. Yuck. Who picked that out?"

Grabbing the curtain, she yanked it back.

A bushy-bearded, long-haired, redheaded man wearing a brown flannel shirt and bib overalls lay in the old claw-footed tub.

Speechless, Amber stared.

He didn't move and he was very pale.

Realization dawned.

"Oh my God! There's a dead man in my bathtub!"

Chapter Four

Amber stumbled back, tripped against the toilet—which had the seat up—and fell in. Water splashed as her legs flailed. She grabbed the toilet paper dispenser and pulled herself out. More water slopped onto the floor and soaked into the seat of her jeans.

Her gaze never left the body in the tub. "Oh my God! Oh my God! He's dead. There's a dead man in my bathtub. What do I do? What do I do? Think, Amber, think. 911. I have to call 911. Purse. I need my purse. Downstairs. My cell is in my purse."

Sneakers squishing, she sprinted out of the bathroom and down the stairs and skidded to a stop before the belongings she had piled at the bottom of the staircase. Clammy jeans sticking to her thighs and ass, she tossed boxes and bags willy-nilly. "It's here somewhere. I know it is. I set it right next to the steps. Come on. Come on. Come on. I need my damn phone!"

As the last box bounced off the wall, Amber grabbed her purse and upended it. Everything inside clattered to the floor and bounced or skidded in all directions off the hardwood. Her phone slid toward the kitchen.

She dove after it, banging her elbow against the floor, leaving a thin streak of water behind her. When she grabbed the phone, it slipped out of her hand. She caught it in her left hand and punched in 911 with her right. Struggling to her knees, she held the phone to her ear.

Nothing.

"No! The battery can't be dead. I just charged it."

She glared at the screen. No signal.

"Fuck! What am I supposed to do now? There's a dead man

in my bathtub."

He woke the same way he had awakened for the last month and a half. One minute he was dead to the world, the next he was wide awake.

This time, something was different.

A heavy weight had settled on his chest.

Slowly, he opened his eyes.

A large, hairy, black blob with a pair of yellow eyes stared back at him—crossed eyes.

Below the eyes, a pair of pointy, ivory teeth stuck up at a slight angle—like a vee.

"Jesus H. Christ!"

As he leaped to his feet, the hairy blob flew through the air and landed in a puddle of water in front of the toilet.

"Meeeeerrrooooooooowwwlllllll!" it yowled as it scrabbled through the puddle and shot toward the door. It bounced off the jamb, shook its head and scooted out the door.

"A cat. A fucking, cross-eyed, black cat! With goofy teeth. What the hell is going on here?"

Stepping out of the tub, he strode through the door and headed for the stairs.

Amber continued to punch 911 into her cell phone, hold it to her ear, then punch in 911 again. "Work, damn it. You have to work. What the hell am I supposed to do? My God. There's a dead man in my bathtub. I can't stay here. I can't stay with a dead man."

Caterwauling, Midnight tumbled down the steps and leaped into her arms—well, almost. Because of her crossed eyes, she misjudged her leap again and landed to Amber's left. Digging her claws into her human's leg, she scrambled into her lap.

The phone bounced across the floor when Amber dropped it to grab her thigh. "Eyooow! Midnight! Stop that. I have enough problems without you skinning me alive."

"Who the hell are you and what the hell are you doing in my house?"

At the sound of the angry male voice, Amber froze. Then she pushed Midnight off her lap, rolled to the fireplace and grabbed the poker. Grasping it in both hands, she rose to face her assailant.

The dead man from the bathtub stood on the bottom step and stared at her.

Her mouth dropped open.

She snapped it shut and raised the poker. "You're dead."

He crossed his arms over his bushy beard and stepped down. "Do I look dead?"

Amber's knuckles whitened as she clasped the poker more tightly. "Who the hell are you and what are you doing in my house?"

Green fire flashed in his emerald eyes as he stroked his beard. "I live here."

"No you don't. This house belongs to my Aunt Ernestine. Er, it did before she died. Now it belongs to me."

He frowned. "You mean old lady Myers finally kicked the bucket?"

Amber swallowed. "Last month. This property was left to me. I'm her niece."

He raked his long hair behind his ears. "Well, fuck."

Amber nodded. He was listening to her. That was good. Right? "I told you the house is mine."

He glared first at her then down at her belongings. "You can't move in here. I live here."

Beside her, Midnight hissed, arched her back and fluffed out her already fluffy fur.

"Not anymore. Now get lost before I call the cops."

He crossed his arms over his chest and grinned. "Phone's not hooked up."

Reaching out with her foot, she pulled her cell phone toward her. "I have one of my own."

His grin widened. "No signal here."

Amber swallowed then gritted her teeth. If he was going to attack her, he'd have done it by now? Right? Her gaze drifted to his mouth. Damn but he had beautiful white teeth and a nice smile. His eyes were nice too, an absolutely gorgeous green. But all that hair all over his face—yuk!

Her subconscious slapped her attention away from his face. *Holy shit, Amber. What are you thinking? There's a man, a big man, in your house. For all you know he's an ax murderer or rapist or serial killer or something. You have to get him out of here.* "Listen. You leave now and there won't be any trouble. The sheriff was just here, you know. He knows I'm living here."

He cocked his head to the side. "Brad was here?"

Amber blinked. *He calls the sheriff by his first name? What was he, a relative or something?* "Who are you anyway?"

He scratched under his beard. "Rusty Nipple."

Amber stared. *Did he just say what she thought he said.* "I beg your pardon?"

"Rusty Nipple."

She gulped then choked. The poker wavered as her shoulders began to shake. She coughed and choked again. "Nipple? Rusty Nipple?" Another gulp and choke. "Your name is Rusty Nipple? What kind of name is that?" A gurgling snort and a hiccup. "It sounds like a really bad mixed drink. Oh my God. I'm dreaming, aren't I? I was in an accident, wasn't I? I'm lying in a hospital in a coma. Rusty Nipple! What real person would admit to the name Rusty Nipple? This isn't real. I'm in the *Twilight Zone.*" The poker clattered to the floor. Amber followed, laughing until the tears ran down her cheeks.

Rusty stared at the tall blonde who lay on the floor with her back to him, arms wrapped around her sides, laughing hysterically. Soaked jeans were plastered to her thighs, hips and butt. He focused on her ass. It was a nice ass, the kind a man could grab hold of while he was burying his cock deep inside. Did the rest of her look as good?

He caught hold of his thoughts. Hell, Nipple, get your mind off of her ass and back on the important stuff—like what the fuck she's doing here. You need a place to stay and you can't go back home. And there aren't that many unoccupied houses around here. You gotta get rid of her.

He looked around at the boxes and suitcases. Lots of them.

And her cat glared at him out of those goofy crossed eyes. The tip of its pink tongue was wedged in the vee of its teeth. Fuckin' spooky, that cat. Shit, but he hated cats. Give him a good old hound dog any day.

Rusty looked around the room again. Yep, she looked like she was moving in to stay. He had to get rid of both of the cat and her. Best way would be to let her see what he really was. First though, he had to get her attention. She had to stop laughing.

"Hey lady, you gonna lay there laughing all night or what? And what the hell is the matter with my name, anyway?"

At the sound of his voice, Amber rolled over. His name might be ridiculous but he had a nice tenor voice.

After sucking in a few deep breaths of air, she pushed herself to her feet.

"Listen, Mr.-er-Nipple." A few giggles escaped. "This is my house, not yours."

He crossed his arms over his chest and grinned widely. "How about a compromise? I live here now. You come back in about six months or so." His teeth seemed to get whiter.

At her side, Midnight's hiss became a high-pitched growl.

Amber shook her head. "Nope. I was downsized out of my job. I don't have anywhere else to go. Besides, I need a nice quiet place to write my novel."

His grin widened. "A novel? About what?"

Amber stared. How could anyone's teeth get brighter—no,

longer—and pointier?

She leaned closer and stared at his teeth, his very long, very sharp, canine teeth. The ones that were curling down over his bottom lip.

What the hell? Then, realization dawned and she forgot to breathe. Holy shit! The dead man in her bathtub was a vampire.

How lucky could a girl get?

Chapter Five

Concentrating on his teeth, she leaned closer. "Are you really a vampire?"

He opened his mouth wider. His teeth were very long and very pointy. "Yep. And if you don't get out of here right now, I'm going to suck all of the blood out of your body."

Amber shivered — with excitement. A real vampire lived in her house! Had any other author ever been so lucky? She shook her head. "Bullshit. No way is your stomach big enough to hold all the blood in my body. I've been researching vampires for the last month. That's what I'm writing about."

He snapped his mouth closed. "You're writing a book about vampires?"

Again Amber shook her head. "No, I'm writing a romance and the vampire is the hero."

Lines appeared on his forehead. "Hero? I thought vampires were always the bad guys."

Excitement danced its way up Amber's spine. *I'm talking to a real vampire. Oh wow! Just think of the information I can get for my book!* "Oh no. Vampires are very popular as heroes now. Would you mind answering a few questions for me?" She stepped forward.

Rusty stepped back. The woman had a really strange look on her face — like she'd just found a long-lost friend or something. And what kind of questions did she want to ask him?"

"How much blood do you drink when you bite people? Do you lap it or suck it? Do you prefer the neck or some other part of the body?"

He scratched under his beard again. "Ah…"

"Who do you prefer to bite, men or women?"

He stopped scratching. "What the hell kind of question is that?"

She stepped closer, her eyes sparkling with some kind of fanatic blue light. "Does biting someone make you horny? Do you get a hard-on? Do you like to have sex when you bite people?"

He edged toward the front door. Horny! Hard-on! "Jesus, lady, you're crazy."

She came closer. "But I can get such good information from you. No other author has ever had this kind opportunity—at least I don't think so, anyway. Please, say you'll help me. I'll let you stay here. Please?"

"Look, lady…"

Smiling broadly, she stuck out her hand. "Amber. Amber Blake. Pleased to meet you. You have no idea how pleased I am to meet you."

Staring at her proffered hand, Rusty continued to back away. "Ah, thanks, I think. Ah, I gotta go now."

A brighter smile lit her face. "That's right. You just woke up. You have to hunt for blood."

He reached behind the door and pulled out a rifle. "Ah, yeah. That's right. I have to go hunt."

Frowning, she stared at the rifle. "What's that for?"

He glanced at it then her. "To shoot a deer."

"Shoot a deer. Why?"

He shrugged. "Like you said, I'm hungry." Turning, he strode out the door.

She followed him. "No. That's not right. You can't go hunting deer."

"Why not?"

"Because vampires drink human blood."

"Not this one. I like deer," he yelled over his shoulder. Without a backward glance, he hurried across the porch, vaulted over the railing and disappeared around the side of the house.

Grinning, her mind dancing with ideas, Amber hugged herself as she stared at the spot where Rusty had disappeared. A vampire. A real vampire. Her nipples puckered as she shivered and orgasmic satisfaction surged through her body. Her very own flesh and blood vampire. A best seller. She was going to write a best seller. The publishing companies would be begging to buy her book.

Turning, she headed back into the house, her mind spinning with possibilities. Of course she was going to have to cure him of this stupid taste for deer blood and get him to bite some humans. And she would have to do something about that beard. It would have to come off. His long hair would be okay, after a trim. She wrinkled her nose. But those clothes would have to go. Vampires were debonair and well-dressed. A plaid flannel shirt and bib overalls weren't going to cut it.

She grabbed a suitcase and started up the stairs. No, she'd go to Harrisburg — there were bound to be some decent men's stores there — and get him appropriate clothing. Once that beard was shaved off, his hair was pulled back in a ponytail and he was dressed in appropriate clothing, he'd look much more vampirish.

As her foot settled on the top step, Amber frowned and bit the inside of her cheek. He had red hair. Did vampires have red hair? Her mind ran back through all the "Buffy" episodes she'd watched. Angel had dark hair. Spike was a blond. And all the other vampires always seemed to have dark hair, the male ones anyway.

Midnight sat in the middle of the hallway and stared at her.

Amber stopped chewing her cheek. "I know. We can dye his hair black. Yeah, that's a good idea. There are a lot of good hair dyes for men available. Yeah, I'll dye his hair. He'll look like a real vampire then."

Humming happily, followed closely by her cross-eyed cat, she sauntered into her bedroom—and closed the door firmly behind her.

Once inside, Amber leaned back against the door and stared at her cat. "My very own vampire hero. Aunt Ernestine—thank you."

Pushing away from the door, she sashayed across the room wrinkling her nose as her wet sneakers squished and her clammy jeans chafed her thighs. "Ugh. I need a shower. And these clothes need to be washed. But that bathroom has to be cleaned up first."

Momentarily she paused. There was a puddle of water from the toilet on the floor. What's more, did she really want to take a shower in a bathtub where a vampire had been sleeping? All those whiskers. She wrinkled her nose. The tub was probably filthy and the drain probably blocked. At least the water in the toilet was just water. Vampires didn't pee.

Sighing, she toed off her wet shoes, unfastened her jeans and shimmied out of them and her clinging underwear. "Yuk. Falling into the toilet. Mandi will never let me forget it."

She pulled her tee shirt over her head, reached behind her and unhooked her bra. Naked, she grabbed her suitcase and lifted it onto the bed. Her robe was in this one.

Hot pink robe belted tightly about her waist, she headed for the bathroom. Once there, she planted her hands on her hips. First, the puddle of water. In a cabinet on the other side of the room, she found some old towels.

Midnight sat in front of the, her head turning this way and that as she attempted to watch her human.

Amber tsked. "Figures they'd be threadbare, Midnight. Aunt Ernestine never threw anything away—even if it had holes in it. Glad I brought my own towels, but these are good enough to soak up this mess for now. I'll scrub the floor tomorrow.

Grabbing a metal bucket she found under the sink, she dropped the sopping towels into the puddle and continued wiping up the floor until all the water was gone. Then she turned to the tub. She pulled back the shower curtain and stared into the tub.

Midnight padded into the room and meowed.

Amber put the lid down on the toilet and lifted the cat onto it. "The tub isn't as bad as I thought, Sweets. A couple of hairs here and there. I can give it a quick rinse and a spray with Lysol and it will be okay for a fast shower. I'll scrub it tomorrow."

Fifteen minutes later, she was relaxing under a hot shower.

Chapter Six

The old bird dog whined and wagged her tail as Rusty hung the dead deer from the hook sticking out from the corner of the porch roof. He'd had as much blood as he wanted and had even chewed up a couple of chunks of meat—nothing like the taste of fresh venison. But there was no reason to let all that good meat go to waste. Ted Musser had been laid off for over a year now and his family could use the extra meat.

After patting the dog on the head, he grabbed his rifle, turned and loped across the field and into the forest. Home was thirty miles away but now he was able to travel a lot faster than he used to.

Rusty frowned. Home. She was there—the goofy author lady. What was her name? Alice—Amy—no, Amber. Yeah, Amber, that was it. He shook his head. Fool woman wasn't afraid of him at all. Why the hell not?

His mother had sobbed and run away from him when she'd seen his teeth. His father had suggested he go live somewhere else. And his grandmother. Fuck. She'd started a prayer circle to drive out the devil in his soul. All the old ladies at her church were still praying. He shrugged. Not that it had done any good.

But this writer, this Amber. She wasn't afraid of him. No, the exact opposite. She was happy because she was writing one of those crappy romance books with the half-naked people on the cover that a lot of women seemed to like.

As he loped along, he stroked his beard. Christ, those freaking questions she asked were personal. Did biting people make him horny! Where did she get off asking a question like that? He didn't even know her.

A smile tickled the corner of his lips as he trotted along. She was kinda pretty. Blonde hair, blue eyes. Her nose was a little bit pointy but at least it wasn't big. She had a nice smile, too. And not only were her teeth straight, but she wasn't missing any. Seemed like most of the women around here were missing a tooth or two. Rusty grinned. His father had always told him to make sure a woman had a mouth full of teeth before he spent any real amount of time with her.

The rest of Amber was really nice, too. Her breasts had been hidden under her baggy tee shirt but they were two very noticeable bumps. She was tall, almost as tall as he was, with legs that seemed to reach to her neck. Rusty sighed. How he loved women with long legs. Amber naked would be a sight to see.

"Not like I could do anything with her if I wanted to. Fuckin' dick doesn't do anything but hang there now anyway," he growled to the empty night.

Still, he could pretend. Pulling a picture of Amber to his mind, he stripped her naked—high, pert breasts with pink nipples, flat stomach, golden curls between her legs. Yep, mighty fine woman to look at.

As Rusty hurdled a fallen log, his stomach rolled. His stomach muscles rippled and clenched as heat flooded his groin. Blood surged into his cock. When he landed on the other side of the log, he staggered and almost fell flat on his face. Groaning, he jerked his zipper down and his cock leaped free—hard, throbbing, aching. He reached down and touched the head. It jerked. Dropping his rifle, Rusty fell to his knees. A single tear rolled down his cheek and disappeared into his beard. "Buddy, you're back!" He fisted his cock and slowly began to pump.

Joyful warmth permeated his body. He felt his canines lengthen but he ignored them, concentrating on the sheer pleasure of the first hard-on he'd had ever since he'd become a vampire, of the total bliss he felt from his warm hand massaging and sliding the soft skin of his cock up and down over the engorged muscle beneath it. Fuck, but this felt good. How he'd missed the aching need. Moaning, he pumped harder. If only he had a woman.

Just the thought of burying his cock inside a slick, tight woman hardened it even more.

Sitting down, he leaned back against a tree and spread his legs further apart. Arching his back, he thrust his hips forward and closed his eyes. A woman. What woman?

Amber appeared in his mind again—this time, naked. Oh yeah, baby. Long legs. Golden curls there between them. Would she play with herself? Come on, sit down honey. Spread those legs for me.

Rusty's teeth began to ache as she sat, spread her legs and cupped her breasts. He sucked in his breath and held it as she pinched her nipples to hard points. So white, so round. Her nipples were so pink. Oh, to be able to suck those sweet buds into his mouth.

When drops of cum dribbled out of his cock, he stopped pumping and smeared them over the head. Not quite the same as a woman's cum but now he was slipperier. He began to pump again.

Eyes still closed, he watched as both of Amber's hands slid from her breasts, down over her stomach and into the golden curls between her legs.

He began to pant. "Yes, baby. Let me see you do yourself."

She smiled at him then looked down at herself. With her left hand, she spread her lips. "Do you like what you see?"

Rusty began to pant. "Oh, yeah, honey. Let me see more. Dip your fingers in."

Her chuckle was low. The fingers of her right hand slid between her lips. They dipped and swirled then circled her clit then dipped and swirled again. She shifted and moaned. "Hmmmm. This feels good. Do you like it, Rusty?"

He ran his tongue along his teeth. Blood seeped from the shallow cuts. His cock got even harder. He pumped faster. "More, baby. Finger-fuck yourself."

She leaned back against the log that appeared out of nowhere and he had a clear view of her cunt. It was red and moist and swollen. She slid her fingers inside and moaned. Her hips jerked. She slid her fingers back out and rubbed her clit. She slipped her fingers back inside again. She pulled them out and rubbed her clit harder. "I'm going to come, Rusty. I'm going to come."

His teeth ached. His cock ached. He wanted to bury all of them inside her. "Come, baby. Come for me. Now!"

His orgasm exploded. Opening his eyes, he watched his cum shoot out before him, splatter against a tree a good four feet away. Sweat cooled on his body.

In his mind, he heard Amber shriek, then something popped and his vision of her disappeared.

When his breathing finally returned to normal, Rusty gazed in the direction of the house. Had she experienced the same thing he had? Had he connected with her mentally? "Christ, Amber. I sure hope it was as good for you as it was for me."

Now, if only his teeth would stop aching.

* * * * *

Amber tossed and turned on her bed. If the humidity was this bad now, what would it be like in August?

The window was open but no breeze stirred the curtains.

Rising on her elbow, she punched her pillow and flipped it over. "I need to get an air conditioner." The silky nightgown she wore was plastered to her body.

She was hot.

She was sweaty.

She was horny.

Amber flopped onto her stomach. "I am not horny. It's just hot. I asked my vampire those questions and I got ideas about what I wanted to write. That's all. I'm not really horny. I'm just thinking about what to write."

Her nipples ached.

Moisture seeped between her legs.

Her clit ached.

She flopped onto her back. "Okay, I'm horny. It's been a long time. I've been so busy…" Closing her eyes, she touched herself. "Okay. Just a quickie."

She slid her fingers between her thighs, nudged the crotch of her silk panties aside and brushed her aching clit.

Immediately she was sucked into a scarlet vortex of passion. Her fingers seemed to take on a life of their own as they swirled and dipped and rubbed. Her nipples tightened more and bolts of tingling pain seemed to burst from the tips. Moisture drenched her fingers as pressure built.

She arched her back. "Oh God! What's happening? I'm so hot!"

Was there a voice in her ear? A man's voice? Spread her legs?

She complied, slipping her fingers in and out, pinching and rubbing. Body slick with sweat, she let her free hand drift up her rib cage to knead her breast then pinch her nipple. Tender pain surged straight to her groin. "Ahhhh!" She pumped her hips against her fingers. When her orgasm finally exploded, tears rolled down her cheeks.

"Ahhhhhhhhhhhaaaahhhhh." Rolls of pleasure rolled over her as her internal muscles shuddered

Slowly, her muscles relaxed, her breathing slowed and the final shiver danced down her spine. She opened her eyes and sighed. Never had she experienced an orgasm like that, neither alone nor with someone. Her entire body was limp with satisfaction and she was physically sated as she had never been before.

Except—her neck itched.

Chapter Seven

The bedroom curtains billowed with a gentle breeze.

Birds sang jubilant songs.

Amber dragged her eyes open and looked at the clock sitting on the nightstand. She blinked to focus and looked again. Six o'clock! She rolled over and stared at the window. Against the white blossoms of the dogwood tree sat a bright red cardinal, singing happily.

"Hey, you stupid bird, shut up. It's only six o'clock. I don't want to get up yet."

Ignoring her, the cardinal continued to chirp.

The warm bump against Amber's back moved. Midnight planted her hind feet against Amber's ass and pushed herself into a long stretch. Her claws dug into Amber's left cheek.

Amber rolled away very quickly. "Ouch! Midnight! How often have I told you not to use me for your stretching board?"

Rubbing her ass, Amber pushed herself into a sitting position and yawned. Six o'clock in the morning. Damn, but she was spoiled. Even when she was working, she'd been able to sleep until seven, or seven-thirty if she rushed. She blinked. Oh well. The whole house had to be cleaned, so getting up early was probably a good thing. Once she had two or three cups of coffee, she'd be okay.

Standing, she stretched, slipped on her bedroom slippers and shuffled out the door to the bathroom. When she pushed the door open, she stopped short. The shower curtain was drawn completely around the tub. Was her vampire sleeping there again? She stepped closer to the tub and pulled the curtain back.

Rusty lay as he had yesterday, on his back, his red-gold

beard spread over his chest.

Bending over, Amber took the time to study him more closely. Really, once the beard was gone, he wouldn't look half bad. He had high cheekbones and a very nice nose. No bumps, no arches, no hairs growing out of it. And, considering how bushy his beard was, his eyebrows were much neater — and not even close to meeting over the bridge of his nose. His mouth was nice, firm lips, not too full, not too thin.

Her attention returned to his beard and she shook her head. When he woke tonight, she'd tell him he had to shave it off. No self-respecting vampire had a beard. She pursed her lips. What if he had a weak chin? Or a receding chin? Well, she'd worry about that after he shaved off his beard.

And tonight was the last night he slept here. What kind of vampire slept in a bathtub?

Pressure on her bladder interrupted her thoughts. Amber pushed the shower curtain shut and felt her cheeks grow warm. She really had to pee. She knew her vampire couldn't see through the curtain but what if he could hear? She bit her lower lip and chewed. Could vampires hear while they were in their sleep mode? The pressure on her bladder increased and she glanced over her shoulder at the toilet. She could pee here or run downstairs to the toilet in the laundry room. After a muttered curse, she spun around and sprinted for the staircase. No way was a vampire going to listen to her pee.

* * * * *

Six hours later, Amber flopped onto the living room sofa with a groan. Breathing deeply, she inhaled the sweet scent of the bouquet of wild roses she'd gathered from the hill behind the house and placed on the coffee table.

What a morning! But the downstairs was clean. Every floor was scrubbed or vacuumed, every nook and cranny was dusted and the few dishes in the kitchen cupboards had been washed — thanks to the portable dishwasher she found hidden behind the ironing board and a pile of empty cardboard boxes in a corner of the laundry room. Not that she'd been surprised to find it hidden away like that. Aunt Ernestine always refused to use the dishwasher in her own kitchen. Said her electric and water bills would go up.

Amber closed her eyes and leaned her head back. "God, but she was cheap. Uncle Henry must have bought this dishwasher."

Midnight scrambled up into her lap and began to purr.

A blaring horn—and Midnight's claws—jarred Amber back to consciousness. "What? Who?"

The cat yowled, leaped from her lap, bumped into the leg of the coffee table, then disappeared beneath the chair that sat diagonal to the sofa.

A knock sounded on the front door just as Amber had gathered her senses. Pushing herself to her feet, she hurried to the door.

The sheriff was standing on her porch, staring off into the distance.

"Good—ah," she checked her watch, "—afternoon, Sheriff. What can I do for you?"

He turned, took off his hat and nodded. "Afternoon, Miss Blake. Was driving by and thought I'd stop and make sure you were okay."

Is this normal? "I'm fine, thanks. You really didn't need to drive back here, you know," she said through the screen door.

He nodded. "Just making sure." He turned, then stopped and turned back to her. "Ah, just wanted to mention. There's this Nipple…"

Amber glanced down at her chest then looked into his face.

"I beg your pardon."

His flush rose all the way to his hairline. "Ah, no not your… Ah, I mean these Nipples. Ah hell. Look. Nipple is a pretty common family name around here."

"Oh. So that's what you meant yesterday. You were talking

about people."

His face reddened even more. "Yeah. Some of the Nipples like to hunt out of season. Anyway, there's this other Nipple, Rusty. Tall fella, bushy beard. He likes to take walks at night. Just wanted to tell you he's not dangerous or nothing. You don't need to be scared if you see him wandering around. He won't hurt you."

Amber stared at the sheriff. Rusty was sleeping in her bathtub as they spoke but the sheriff obviously didn't know that. Good. Rusty was her vampire and she wasn't sharing him with anybody else. "Thanks for letting me know. I won't worry if I see him."

"Good. I'll be on my way then. Have a good day."

"Thanks, Sheriff."

Frowning, Amber watched as his car disappeared down the driveway. What was that all about? Did he know Rusty was a vampire? If he knew, how many other people knew? Nobody was supposed to know if a vampire lived nearby. They kept their presence secret from everyone. What the hell was Rusty doing telling people what he was?

Spinning on her heel, Amber headed for the kitchen, mumbling. "Damn it. What's wrong with Rusty? What is he, too far out in the woods to know how he's supposed to act?" That thought brought her up short. He mustn't have been a vampire very long. That's why he still wore those terrible clothes and went hunting for deer with a rifle when he could just as easily catch one with his bare hands. She smiled. She'd teach him everything he had to know about being a vampire. What a great novel this would make!

Chapter Eight

The heavy weight was on his chest again.

He cracked his eyes open.

That cross-eyed cat was staring down her nose. The pink tip of its tongue was wedged between those upside-down fangs again. A drop of saliva rolled off its tongue and plopped onto his beard.

Rusty erupted upward. "Jesus H. Christ. There's cat spit in my beard!"

The cat dug four sets of claws into his chest and held on.

Amber had just put the last plate on its shelf when a high, keening yowl by Midnight, accompanied by a very colorful string of obscenities, rattled the rafters. Dropping her dishtowel, she turned and sprinted for the staircase.

Arms waving, a howling, cursing mass of red and black hair stumbled, slid and skidded down the staircase to land in a heap on the floor.

Fisting her hands on her hips, Amber nudged the jean-clad leg closest to her with her foot. "What the hell is going on?"

"Your freakin' weirdo cat attacked me, that's what!" Rusty shouted as he grabbed Midnight with both hands and tried to pull her off his chest.

Midnight dug her claws in deeper.

"Eeeeooow! It's skinning me alive. Get it off! Get it off!"

Bending, Amber stuck her hand under Midnight's nose. "If you'd stop screaming, she'd let go. You're scaring her to death, you idiot."

Rusty let go of the cat and tried to push himself to his feet.

"I'm scaring her? I'm scaring her! She's the one who was sitting on my chest when I woke up."

Amber pushed him back down. "Stay still and stop yelling and she'll let go. Come on, Midnight. Come to Mommy. Here kitty, kitty."

"Meeeoooow!" Midnight sheathed her claws, spun around, used Rusty's chest for a springboard and leaped into Amber's arms—almost. She misjudged again and completely missed Amber, landing instead on the floor to her right. Claws scratching the hardwood floor, she shot across the room, bounced off the corner of the sofa and disappeared beneath it.

"Now look what you've done. You scared Midnight."

Legs stretched out before him, Rusty sat at the bottom of the stairs and gaped at her. "That demon spawn you call a cat started it. She shouldn't have been sitting on my chest. Where the devil did you get that monster anyway?"

Straightening, she stared down at him, her hands on her hips. "Monster! Midnight isn't a monster. It's not her fault she has crossed eyes and weird teeth. And I got her at an animal shelter. What was I supposed to do, leave her there so she could be euthanized? No way, buster."

"Ever heard of survival of the fittest?" he grumbled as he rolled to his hands and knees then pushed himself to his feet.

Amber had a very nice view of his ass in his threadbare bibs—and a very nice ass it was, too.

Once on his feet, he turned to face her. A hunk of whiskers drifted to the floor, an obvious fatality of Midnight's claws.

Rusty rubbed his chin. "Damn cat was pulling my whiskers out by the roots."

Amber crossed her arms over her chest. Now was as good a time as any to start teaching him how to be a proper vampire. "You have to shave it off anyway."

He stiffened. "What the fuck are you talking about, lady?"

"You haven't been a vampire very long, have you?"

He began to edge away.

Amber stepped in front of him. No way was he getting away this time.

Rusty stopped when she placed herself between him and the door. He flared his nostrils. She smelled like sweat, cleaning products and woman—hot woman.

His canines began to ache and his cock stirred.

He wanted her.

He closed his eyes, willing his cock to remain where it was and his teeth to stay put in his gums. The one time he'd stolen a kiss from Sue Ellen Keiser, his daddy had whomped him good. Never force a woman—not even for a kiss. He wasn't about to start now, even if he was a vampire.

He heard her foot stamp against the floor. "Are you listening to me?"

Rusty opened his eyes. Damn, she was even prettier now that she was getting mad. "What?"

"You haven't been listening to me, have you? Look. I'm willing to help you but you have to cooperate."

"What?" He tried to concentrate on her words but the faint pulse beating at the base of her throat was so...delectable. He clenched his jaws to keep his fangs from erupting.

"I said, you need a coffin. You can't sleep in the bathtub anymore. I checked out the cellar. There's a nice place for a coffin in the one corner."

The word coffin sank into his subconscious and the fantasy of having her buck-ass naked beneath him winked out. "Coffin? What the hell are you talking about?"

"You're a vampire, right? Vampires sleep in coffins during the day."

"Are you freaking crazy? I ain't dead."

A superior smile on her face, Amber nodded. "Of course you are. You're a vampire, one of the living dead."

He rose to his full height and leaned closer. "No way am I

getting into a frickin' coffin, lady, no matter what you say. I ain't gonna wake up some morning underneath six feet of dirt. I like the bathtub and that's where I'm staying."

She rose on her tiptoes and looked him straight in the eye. "Okay, I'm willing to compromise on the coffin but you are not sleeping in the bathtub anymore. What if I want to take a bath?"

Amber naked, squirming around on top of him while she took a bath? Hot damn. "I don't mind. Not like I'll drown or anything like that."

Her mouth dropped open. She snapped it shut. Then she sputtered a bit. Finally she shut up, glared at him and said, "Okay. And every night when you wake up, Midnight will be sitting on your chest."

Rusty clenched his fists. She knew how to fight dirty. Frickin' cat.

Holding up her hands, palms outward, she took a step back. "Look, I don't want to fight. Why don't you just sleep in the front bedroom. There's only one window with a tree in front of it to help block the sun. And the drapes are pretty heavy. They won't let any sun in. Don't worry, I won't let you burn to a crisp and evaporate."

"Evaporate? What the hell are you talking about?"

She shook her head and the look on her face was the one his mother used when she was trying to explain something to her little Sunday school kids who didn't quite understand what she was talking about. "If you stay out in the sun, you'll burn up to ashes."

He snorted. "Will not. I'll get a hell of a sunburn that'll take a couple of weeks to heal and my eyes will water so much I won't be able to see. But I won't 'burn up to ashes'."

Her lips faded into a thin line and she shook her head. "Yes you will. Everybody knows that vampires burn up if they get caught out in the sun."

He threw his hands up. "Shit, lady. I'm the vampire here. I know damn well what happens if I stay out in the sun."

She shook her head again. "But…"

"Enough. I'm going hunting." He reached behind the door for his rifle.

It was gone.

"Where's my gun?"

"Vampires don't use guns and they don't drink deer blood."

"I like my gun and I like deer blood."

She shook her head—again. "No. You have to learn to drink human blood. You have to stalk humans, not deer. And you have to get rid of that beard. Vampires don't have beards. And it would probably be a good idea to dye your hair black—unless you'd prefer blonde. Spike is blonde and he's pretty cool. I don't think there are any redheaded vampires—at least none that are male."

At first, Rusty just stared at her. The longer she rambled on, though, listing one thing after another he had to do to become a 'proper vampire' , the tighter his chest felt. Shave off his beard. No more hunting deer. Spike? Who the hell was Spike? Dye his hair. Sleep in a bed. Do this. Do that. Who the hell did she think she was, his wife?

When he had to fight the urge to put his hands around her throat and strangle her, he stepped around her, slammed the screen door open and stomped across the porch.

She followed him, her list of dos and don'ts going on and on.

A few steps from the edge, a sharp, stabbing pain in his bladder drove the breath from his lungs.

Tears rolling down his cheeks, he ripped his fly open and pulled out his cock. No sooner did he have it in hand, than urine streamed over the side of the porch.

She followed and finished her list with "And you're going to have to change your name. Rusty Nipple is not a good vampire name."

Silence — except for the splatter of urine on loose stones.

She stepped to his side and gasped. "What are you doing!

He closed his eyes. God, what a relief. "Pissing." Every muscle in his body sagged with relief. This was the first time he'd pissed in a month. He'd been feeling more and more bloated as the days passed. First a hard-on, now a good piss. Maybe having this woman around would be a good thing.

"Off the porch! You can't do that off the porch. It's...it's...uncivilized. Besides, vampires don't piss — er, urinate."

Grinning, he turned and stuffed his cock back in his pants. "This one does."

Chapter Nine

Amber blinked and gasped and gulped and stuttered as warmth surged into her cheeks. Her vampire had just peed in front of her—off the edge of the porch, no less. He peed! Vampires didn't pee. Did they?

"And I'm not changing my name," he said as he pulled up his zipper. "My grandpap's name was Rusty Nipple just like his grandpap's. It's a family tradition. So forget it. Now, I'm going hunting. See you later."

"But…"

He disappeared into the darkness.

Nails digging into her palms, Amber glared at the spot where he'd disappeared. "Stiff-necked, narrow-minded, uneducated, bad-mannered…hick! All I'm trying to do is help you, you…you…moron," she yelled into the darkness. Spinning, she stomped into the house and slammed the door shut behind her. "Ungrateful ass," she muttered as she paced back and forth. "Doesn't he realize how ridiculous he's acting? He's a vampire, one of the hottest, sexiest beings there is, not some redneck hick. I'm just trying to help him."

She continued to pace, arguing with him as if he were pacing next to her.

Finally she stopped and settled onto the couch. "Okay, deep breaths, Amber. Take deep breaths. You've got yourself all worked up over nothing. You've already figured out he hasn't been a vampire long. Patience. You just need to be more patient. He'll come around."

Outside the window, Rusty stood in the shadows and watched Amber pace back and forth. Even though the window was closed, with his enhanced hearing, he had no trouble hearing every muttered word. He grinned and even laughed out loud once. What were the odds she'd use those particular words in her novel?

As he watched, she lifted her hand and shook her finger at the sofa.

He chuckled. She sure was a spitfire.

Finally she raked her honey-blond hair back from her face and flopped down on the soft cushions.

Then the fiend from hell she called a cat staggered across the room to sit at her feet. Amber reached down and picked her up. It settled on her lap, her purr rumbling.

She lifted the cat and cuddled her to her chest. "What am I going to do, Midnight? My vampire doesn't want to cooperate with me. All I want to do is write my book so I can make some money and support myself. Is that such a bad thing?"

The cat continued to purr.

Rusty wished he was the one being stroked.

Amber looked down at her cat. "Well, sitting here bitching isn't going to do me any good. I'm going to take a bath and you're going to guard the door in case Rusty comes back." She shook her head. "Rusty Nipple. How in the world am I going to make a decent vampire out of a man named Rusty Nipple? Who will take him seriously?"

As she disappeared from sight, Rusty checked out the tree growing next to the house. Yep, nice solid branch just where he wanted it. The ten-foot jump required little effort and he was comfortably ensconced against the wide trunk with a clear view through the bathroom window when Amber walked in and started to strip off her clothing.

"Oh yeah, baby," he muttered. His cock rose to attention before her tee shirt hit the floor. "Damn, do you wear bras like that every day?"

Instead of a utilitarian, white cotton bra, Amber's was hot pink satin with lace edging. Around here, women only wore bras like that when they had somewhere special to go to, like a wedding or demolition derby. If Amber wore one this fancy just to clean the house, what did she wear for special occasions?

Her jeans followed her tee shirt. Rusty yanked down his zipper and let his cock spring free. Hell, she was wearing one of those thong things instead of white cotton panties. Just a bitty piece of pink satin barely covering the golden triangle between her legs and when she turned around and bent over...

Rusty swallowed to prevent drool from dribbling into his beard. His cock jerked and his fangs exploded out of his gums. Nothing but a tiny pink string between her ass cheeks. And what an ass it was! Last night it had looked good in wet denim, but bare, decorated with a couple of pink strings! Holy shit. That was an ass meant for a man's hands to grab and squeeze as he shoved his cock into her from behind. Did those cheeks feel as smooth and tight as they looked?

When she lifted her hair off her neck and pinned it up on her head, his already elongated canines began to ache. More than anything he wanted to sink his fangs into her as he buried his cock deep.

"And she'd probably club me with the fireplace poker as soon as she got her hands on it," he mumbled. "Can't force her." Then he grinned and patted the head of his cock. "Don't worry, buddy, I'll just slip into her head again once she's in the tub."

"Oh, bother. I forgot to scrub the tub." Amber leaned over the side of the old-fashioned, claw-foot tub and scrutinized the inside. Except for some stray red hairs, it looked clean. "A quick swipe with some disinfectant won't hurt." She a pulled bottle of tub cleaner from under the sink, sprayed it liberally inside the tub, scrubbed it out with another old towel, then opened the hot water spigot full blast. Opening the cupboard, she pulled out first one bottle then another.

"Which bubble bath should I use, Midnight?"

The cat ignored her and continued washing her paw.

Amber chuckled. "Eau de garlic, maybe? To keep the big bad vampire away?" She chuckled some more. "No garlic.

Guess I'll have to go with lily of the valley. I have a lily scented candle I can light, too."

As moist, delicately scented steam rose and frothy, white bubbles filled the tub, Amber turned on the cold water spigot. She pinned up her hair then stripped out of her bra and panties. "God, but I'm tired. I can't remember when I worked so hard. A good, long soak in the tub and then I'm going to bed. I'll deal with Rusty tomorrow night. I'll have all day to figure out how to convince him to listen to me."

After turning off the water, she sank into the tub. "Ahhhhhhhhh. This feels so good."

Leaning her head back against a washcloth she'd folded over the edge of the tub earlier, she closed her eyes and inhaled the delicate floral fragrance wafting from the burning candle.

Rusty craned his neck, trying to get a better view. For a few brief seconds, she's stood before him buck-naked. She looked even sexier than he'd imagined last night. Then she'd stepped into the tub and sunk into water and bubbles that covered her to her neck.

"Why did she put so many damn bubbles in the tub? I can't see a thing," he muttered to the owl sitting in the upper branches of the tree.

His cock jerked and he settled back against the tree. Okay, time to play head games—he looked down—so to speak. He looked back through the window. "Are you just lying there, Amber honey, or are your hands busy underneath all those bubbles? Are you as wet and slippery right now on the inside as you are on the outside? Are your fingers playing with that little nub between your legs? Is it hard? Does it ache? Like me?"

Rusty stroked his cock, sliding his hand up and down as he imagined Amber fingering herself, stroking herself, plucking her sensitive clit. He began to pump faster, squeezing his cock as he imagined her hips arching. He slid his tongue along his fangs, eagerly swallowing the blood that oozed out. He kept his gaze locked on her, leaning forward when he heard her moan.

She arched and her breasts rose out of the water. Bubbles caressed them and dripped off her pebbled nipples. She moaned again. Water swirled lazily at first then splashed. Her foot appeared and she rested it on the side of the tub.

Blood thudded along the length of his cock. His balls tightened and drew closer to his body. His fangs lengthened even more. "Ah hell, honey, I wish I could see you."

Her head was thrown back, her mouth open. A groaning sob rose from deep in her throat. More water splashed on the floor.

Rusty ran a finger along his fangs and sucked the blood into his mouth. He squeezed and pumped his cock harder. "That's it, baby. Come for me. Come hard."

As her sob became a keen, cum erupted from Rusty's cock, spurting high into the air, splattering white droplets against the leaves. Groaning, he collapsed against the tree trunk. Damn, if jerking off while he watched her take a bath was that good, what would it be like when he finally buried his cock between her legs as deeply as he could while her hot, sweet blood seeped into his mouth?

He shuddered as more cum spurted.

When his body finally became still, he opened his eyes and stared in the window.

Panting, Amber was still lying back in the tub, the fingers of both hands buried in her hair. Enough water and bubbles had splashed out of the tub for him to have a clear view of her rosy nipples as her breasts rose and fell with her deep breaths. Both were still pebbled tightly.

Licking his lips, Rusty raked the hair off his forehead and grinned. Maybe tomorrow he would listen to what she had to say. Who knew what kind of ideas she'd have about how vampires make love.

Chapter Ten

Hands braced on the edge of the tub, Amber stood, knees wobbling. Sudsy bubbles meandered down her body, teasing still-sensitive nerves. As her internal muscles clenched with a final spasm of pleasure, she closed her eyes and moaned. Only her vise-like grip on the rounded tub kept her from collapsing back into the water.

She sucked in a huge breath and exhaled slowly. "My God. That was…was…unbelievable. If I could find a man who made me feel that good…"

Another deep breath. Then another.

Strength returned to her legs.

Slowly, she lifted her right leg over the side of the tub, made sure it was planted firmly on the nubby throw rug, then lifted the other out. Grabbing her towel, she wrapped around herself, held it with one hand and grabbed the towel rack to steady herself as her knees wobbled again.

A shiver danced up her spine. Her nipples still tingled. "Shit, if I can do this to myself, maybe I don't need a man."

"Meeeerowww?"

Amber chuckled. "Yeah, you're right. Having somebody around to kill the spiders would be a good idea."

Another deep breath and she finally stood without support. She dried off slowly, pausing every now and then to sigh or shiver. Finally, she slipped into her nightgown. The satiny material caressed her still-sensitive body. Delicate pin-pricks of passion danced up her spine and she shivered yet again. Why was she still so aroused? The orgasm she'd just experienced was more satisfying than any she could remember. Yet her body was still hot, still aching. Why? For what? Or for whom?

Rusty's form appeared in her mind and she shook her head and snorted. "No way, Jose. Not him. My God, he's got leaves stuck in his beard!"

Grabbing her brush, she pulled it through her damp hair. Rusty Nipple—appealing? What a joke. No, it wasn't any man she'd met recently. She was just horny from writing the love scenes in her book. After all, she hadn't made love with a man in what—over a year. No wonder her body was going crazy.

Amber nodded. Yep, that was her problem. Writing hot sex when she'd been too long without it herself.

After a few quick strokes for her hair, she patted Midnight on the head. Then she let the water drain from the tub and rinsed out the bubbles. Once it was empty, she blew out the candle then grabbed a box she'd set just inside the door earlier that day. "No way is Rusty sleeping in here tonight." She place the wooden cross she found in one of the extra bedrooms at one end of the tub and spread garlic cloves along the bottom. "There. That will keep him out. I'll leave the door to the front bedroom open. He should be smart enough to figure out he should sleep in there."

After brushing her teeth, she headed for her bedroom followed by Midnight—scratching that pesky itch on her neck.

Outside, Rusty pumped his cock twice more. Groaning, he leaned back as he came again. Who was this woman that she could have such an effect on him? Since he'd become a vampire, he hadn't been able to get a hard-on for any woman—not even Jolene, the hairdresser who'd sleep with anything that had a cock between his legs. But just watching Amber dry off after her bath had had him hard and aching again—only minutes after he'd shot his load. He'd never recovered so quickly after sex. But Amber—all she had to do was brush her hair and his little buddy roared to life. Something wasn't right about all this. Was it because he was a vampire now? Maybe Amber could tell him. She was the expert on vampires, wasn't she?

What's more, his fangs still literally ached.

After stuffing his still semi-erect cock back in his jeans, he jumped lightly to the ground. He needed blood, and he needed it now. Cocking his head to the side, he listened carefully. There, north, deer. A shiver raced up his back at the thought hot blood sliding down his throat.

After one last glance toward the now dark bathroom window, he leaped away. Once he satisfied his craving for blood, he'd be able to walk into the house where Amber slept—without worrying about whether he'd attack her or not.

Somehow, he didn't think she was the type of woman who just submitted to a man without a fuss. Nope. She was liable to hit him up alongside the head with an iron skillet.

* * * * *

Faint light was edging above the woods to the east by the time Rusty returned home. Stopping only long enough to pick a couple of rose buds, he silently stepped onto the back porch and let himself in, cringing when the hinges on the old screen door squeaked.

The owl hooted.

Other than that, it remained quiet.

As he stepped into the kitchen, the scent of brewing coffee teased his nose. He stopped, then stepped to the automatic coffee maker. Water bubbled and dripped.

He inhaled and smiled. Coffee. When was the last time he had a cup of coffee?

Laying the roses on the counter, he grabbed a mug from the cupboard, then he drummed his fingers on the countertop as he watched the thin stream of dark liquid cascade into the pot. Damn it! How long was this going to take?

Tired of waiting, Rusty grabbed the pot and filled his mug, ignoring the hot sizzle of evaporating coffee as it hit the hot pad of the brewer. He shrugged as he set the pot back. Only a little bit missed the pot. There was still plenty for Amber.

Lifting the mug, he sipped. As the fragrant odor and smooth, sharp taste of the strong, hot coffee slid over his tongue, he sighed with pleasure. He sipped some more and sighed again. Damn, but this was good.

"What are you doing?"

Slowly, Rusty turned.

Amber stood in the doorway wearing nothing but that little silk nightie she'd put on the night before. He gulped a mouthful of the hot coffee and yelped. The sharp ache of his burned tongue replaced the beginning ache in his now-soft cock.

She stomped into the kitchen.

Her cross-eyed cat scuttled after her.

"Vampires do not drink coffee. Now put that down!"

He cupped his mug with both hands, pulled it against his chest and shook his head. "No, ma'am. This is the first cup of coffee I've had in almost two months and I'm not giving it up." Then he winked. "You do make a good cup of coffee, you know. Just the way I like it, nice and strong." He swallowed more and smiled.

Taken aback at the compliment, Amber stared at the bushy-bearded vampire standing in her kitchen. Was he right? Did vampires drink coffee? Frowning, she searched her mind. Did Angel ever drink coffee? Did Spike? There was that episode where Spike was tied to the chair and Willow stuck a chocolate chip cookie in his mouth. He ate that. And he liked cornflakes with his bowl of blood. And there were those episodes of "Buffy" where Spike drank beer. Maybe vampires could drink coffee—or other liquids besides blood.

She pursed her lips.

Rusty grinned at her.

At least she thought he grinned. He had so much hair around his mouth it was hard to tell.

She sniffed. "Well, it is liquid. So I guess you're allowed to drink it."

He tossed back the last of the coffee and nodded. "Thanks for letting me know. Now, I really need to get some sleep. See you tonight."

Amber quickly stepped away from the door.

Still, Rusty's arm brushed against hers. The soft flannel of his shirt raised goosebumps on her arms.

Her nipples tingled.

And he was gone.

"Meoooooooow?"

Amber shivered, bent, picked up her cat and cuddled Midnight against her chest.

"Nothing. I'm just cold, that's all." I'm not attracted to a...a redneck vampire.

She turned and spied the roses lying on the counter. Where did they come from?

Chapter Eleven

Yawning, Rusty pushed the bathroom door shut and headed for the tub. At first it had seemed strange—sleeping in this bathtub. But it was big and deep and he was more comfortable here than anywhere else.

Lifting his arms above his head, he stretched then scratched his chin through his whiskers—and pulled a leaf out of his beard. He stared at it and snorted. Maybe he did need a trim.

He reached the side of the tub and lifted his foot over the side. Something skittered along the bottom of the tub. Frowning, he looked in. A wooden cross lay amidst dozens of cloves of garlic.

"What the hell?" He picked up the cross and set it on the back of the toilet. Then he cocked his head to the side and contemplated the garlic. "Now what the hell did she put all this garlic in the tub for? Is it supposed to make it cleaner? I never heard of that. Shit, there's enough garlic in here to make a whole tub full of deer sausage. If I'd a known she had all this, I'd a brought that deer home last night. Nothing like deer sausage with lots of garlic."

Leaning down, he pushed all the garlic toward the back of the tub. Grabbing two handfuls, he looked around. A small basket holding a bunch of little soaps in different colors sat on the counter next to the sink. That would do. There was enough room in the basket for the garlic. He dropped both handfuls on top of the soap and gathered up the rest. Once all of the garlic, except for a stray clove or two here and there, was out of the tub, Rusty climbed in, settled himself and closed his eyes. In seconds, he slept deeply.

Still mumbling to herself, Amber stuck the roses in water

and rinsed the coffee pot and the two mugs. "Roses? He's impossible! Why is he giving me such a hard time? I only want to help him. But does he listen to anything I say? No." Leaving the pot and mugs in the sink, she headed back to her bedroom to get dressed. "The house is clean so I should get some writing done today." She climbed the stairs. "I should take a drive and find the nearest grocery store, too. Midnight will soon need more cat food." She reached the top of the stairs and headed for her bedroom. She passed the bathroom, stopped and turned back. "What's this door doing shut? I didn't shut it."

Amber turned the knob and walked in. The shower curtain was drawn.

"No. He can't be in there."

Jerking the curtain back, she stared into the serene face of Rusty.

"What? How? He can't sleep on garlic. And the cross! That should have had him running out of here!"

She spotted the cross on the back of the toilet. Her nose followed the scent of garlic to her soap basket. "He put the garlic here! My soaps are ruined! What's the matter with him?"

Gritting her teeth, she swung back to face him.

He remained deathly still.

"Hey!" Reaching down, she grabbed his beard and yanked it. "Hey. Moron. You ruined my hand-dipped soaps."

Rusty slept on.

She jerked his beard again—harder.

His head lifted then thunked down against the back of the tub. He didn't stir.

"Ooooooooo!" Frustrated, she jerked his beard a third time.

As his head thumped against the tub again, Amber froze. Slowly, she opened her hand and stared at the chunk of beard in her hand. Vampires weren't supposed to have beards.

A slow smiled teased the muscles of her cheeks.

Rusty was going to lose this beard—right now.

"Shears. I know I saw some shears somewhere. Bedroom—yeah. I put them in my bedroom." Hurrying to her room, she paused long enough to throw on a pair of old jeans and a tee shirt. Then she grabbed the shears and returned to the bathroom.

"Boy, am I glad you kept all these ratty towels, Aunt Ernestine." She placed the old towel under Rusty's chin and beard and went to work with the shears.

Fifteen minutes later, Amber carefully folded the four ends of the towel over and lifted it from Rusty's chest. She stuffed it into the wastebasket, grabbed the ends of the plastic liner and pulled the entire bag out. After tying the ends shut, she set it in the hall. She'd drop it in the garbage when she went back down stairs.

Chuckling, she turned back to Rusty. Unevenly cut whiskers stuck out from his chin and cheeks in varying lengths. "I told you vampires didn't have beards. Now, to get the rest of those whiskers off." She grabbed the shaving cream and razor she normally used on her legs and went to work.

"Damn, but bending over the edge of a tub is hard on the back," Amber said as she straightened, put her hands on her hips and leaned backwards. Then she twisted from one side to the other. Her back cracked and she sighed with pleasure.

She bent back over the tub. "Now, let's see how you really look." She wiped the excess shaving cream from Rusty's face, brushed his hair back off his forehead and stared down at him. She blinked. "Wow! You're handsome. Why did you hide behind that hideous beard?"

Amber continued to stare. Oh, yeah. This could work. Her redneck vampire was a good-looking guy. Wide forehead, high cheekbones, straight nose, firm chin. And lips. Well, damn. His lips sure looked kissable. And she already knew he had beautiful green eyes. Yeah, this was definitely going to work. He would make a good vampire hero—as long as he listened to her and followed her instructions.

Sighing—he'd already proved he was stubborn as a mule—Amber turned away and left the bathroom. He'd sleep all day as usual. She had things to do.

* * * * *

Late that afternoon, Midnight strolled into the bathroom. Her human had bustled from room to room part of the day, disappeared in her moving box for part of the day, and now sat before the shiny box making clicking noises with her fingers. This was the perfect time for a catnap.

Midnight stuck her tongue out between her teeth, stared at both blurry toilets and decided to leap onto the one on the right. A slight purr seeped from her throat as she landed on the closed lid. Then she turned toward the tub. As big as it was, it was much harder to miss. After a couple of jerky, false starts, she leaped and landed on the still form of the man lying inside.

She stopped and sniffed. Something was different. She minced delicately up over his chest and sniffed his chin. Where was all that soft, comfortable, warm hair? She sniffed again. Didn't her human's legs smell like this sometimes?

Midnight licked his chin. Yes, Amber's legs tasted like this sometimes.

She rubbed her cheek against his chin, turned, kneaded his chest a bit, turned again and snuggled down. Her fluffy tail wrapped around her and her paws tucked into her chest.

She closed her eyes and began to purr.

Chapter Twelve

A loud bellow followed by an equally loud yowl completely destroyed Amber's train of thought and she stopped typing. Pushing her chair back, she glared at the urn that held Aunt Ernestine. "You'd think he'd be used to waking up with Midnight on his chest." Still grumbling, she stomped through the kitchen and living room and up the stairs.

Another bellow greeted her at the top or the steps. "My beard! Where the fuck's my beard! Damn you, woman. What did you do to me?"

When Amber walked into the bathroom, Rusty was staring into the medicine cabinet mirror with a look of horror on his face.

Amber glared at him. "What do you think you're doing looking into that mirror? You can't see yourself."

He turned, his eyes flashing with green fire. "Like hell I can't. What the fuck did you do to my beard?"

She fisted her hands on her hips. "I shaved it off. I told you vampires didn't have beards. And they can't see themselves in mirrors, either."

He stepped closer. "Says who?"

She didn't back down. "Everybody knows that vampires can't see themselves in mirrors because they don't have souls."

He threw up his hands. "Of all the fuckin' bullshit." Grabbing her toothbrush, he held it up. "Does this have a soul?"

"Of course not."

"Can you see it in a mirror?'

"Of course."

He crossed his arms over his chest, a superior grin on his

now hairless face.

Amber opened her mouth, bit back what she was going to say and snapped it shut. Damn know-it-all. She frowned. "Can you really see yourself in the mirror?"

Jerking his head in the mirror's direction, he turned and stepped in front of it.

Amber stepped behind him and looked over his shoulder.

Both their reflections stared back at her.

"Well, shit. I'm going to have to rewrite an entire chapter."

As she turned to leave, Rusty grabbed her upper arm. "Who said you could shave off my beard?"

Amber jerked her arm.

He let her go.

She didn't hide the irritation in her voice. "Take a good look at yourself, Rusty. You look a hell of a lot better without the beard. Didn't anyone ever tell you you were handsome? Or is this the first time you've been shaved since you started growing whiskers?"

As her words sank in, Rusty smiled. She thought he was handsome. What else did she think about him? "Women have told me I'm handsome — with and without the beard."

She snorted. "Well, whoever told you you were handsome with the beard needs glasses — or her head examined. Do you know there were leaves in it? And sticks? Don't you groom yourself?"

Rusty kept his attention focused on Amber. Yep. She got prettier as she got angrier. So there were sticks in his beard. It was her fault. Ever since she'd arrived, he'd been running around ass backwards.

"And when was the last time you changed your clothes? You've been wearing those same bibs and same shirt since I got here three days ago. You can't do that. Vampires are suave and debonair — sharp dressers. They don't wear old bib overalls and holey flannel shirts."

Rusty absently fingered the hole in the elbow of his shirt. He had been in these same clothes for three days. Shit, this woman really had him screwed up. He lifted his arm and sniffed. Damn, but he needed a shower.

Quickly, he unfastened the top of his bibs. As they fell to his waist, he began to unbutton his shirt.

He grinned as Amber stopped issuing orders in mid-sentence.

His shirt dropped to the floor and he stood before her bare-chested, his bibs slipping down to his hips.

What was that gurgling in her throat? What she choking?

She opened her mouth and squeaked. Snapping her mouth shut, she cleared her throat then said, "What are you doing?"

"Taking off my clothes." He hooked his fingers under his bibs at his hips.

Another gurgle. "Why?"

"You're right. I need a shower. Want to scrub my back?" He pushed them to the floor. He never did like wearing underwear.

Her face turned bright red. "Scrub your back? Are you nuts? Scrub your own back."

Spinning, she left the bathroom a lot faster than she'd entered.

Chuckling, Rusty turned on the water. His cock stirred and he looked down. "Don't worry, little buddy. You'll be making Amber's acquaintance as soon as I can coax her into bed."

Amber galloped down the steps, heat burning in her cheeks.

He'd stripped. Right in front of her. Just like that! Without any embarrassment.

Her lips twitched. Guess he could act like a vampire if he wanted to.

When she reached the small room off the kitchen that she'd turned into her study, she shut the door behind her and leaned back against it. Taking a deep breath, she sighed. Who'd have thought Rusty would look so good naked. That bushy beard and those baggy clothes had certainly fooled her.

Broad shoulders and a wide chest with only a sprinkling of reddish-gold hair. A flat stomach, lean hips, and firm thighs. And between those thighs more red-gold hair—and a nice, thick cock.

Amber shivered. Just how large could that cock get?

"Meow?" Midnight stared at her from the old leather chair on the other side of the room. She rolled to the floor and minced across the room. After bumping into Amber's leg, she twined herself between them, rubbing her cheek against Amber's shins.

Picking Midnight up and cuddling the cat against her chest, Amber sauntered across the room. Setting the cat on the table she was using for a desk, she sat down in front of her computer. A vampire hero with red-gold hair was a definite possibility now. Besides, what other author had ever written about a auburn-haired vampire? Being different was a good thing.

Midnight sat next to Aunt Ernestine's urn and meowed.

Amber flipped her hair back over her shoulder. "Don't use that tone of voice with me, Midnight. Everybody writes about dark-haired vampires with a blonde thrown in here and there. Now that he's cleaning himself up, Rusty is turning into a good model. Why not use him?"

Chapter Thirteen

Engrossed in her writing, Amber never heard the door open.

"What are you doing?"

The entire table rattled as she leaped from her chair. "Didn't your mother ever teach you to knock!"

Rusty shrugged. "Nope."

Muttering something about hicks and no manners, Amber glared at him. "Do you want something?"

He shrugged. "Just being neighborly since we are living together." He grinned. "Sort of."

Amber simply stared and swallowed. This was one redneck who cleaned up nice.

His hair was pulled back into a pony tail. And without his beard, Rusty's grin was devastating.

Her gaze left his mouth and roamed down his body. "Where did you get those clothes?"

His grin remained. "They're mine. Keep them stored in the spare bedroom. I don't wear the same clothes all the time, you know."

She blinked. Tight jeans clung to his legs and hips. The pine-colored golf shirt he wore brought out the green of his eyes. It also stretched quite nicely over his shoulders and chest. And he was wearing cowboy boots. Cowboy boots! A vampire who wore cowboy boots?

Leaning back against the door, he crossed his arms over his chest.

She swallowed again and cleared her throat. "Ah, may I ask

you some questions?"

His grin never wavered. "Shoot."

She grabbed a tablet and pencil. "How do you go about biting people? Ah, I mean, do you hypnotize them or overpower them or what?"

When she didn't get an answer, she looked up.

Was Rusty blushing? Vampires couldn't blush, could they? Her gaze slid down his body again. Were those jeans painted on?

His grin had faded and he was looking down at the floor. "To tell the truth, I haven't bitten any humans."

Amber wrenched her gaze from his crotch to his face. "You've never bitten anybody? What kind of vampire are you, anyway?"

He looked up and chuckled. "Not a very good one, according to you."

Amber bit back the words that were about to erupt from her mouth. Insulting him wouldn't get her anywhere. She swallowed then, in a softer voice, asked, "How long have you been a vampire?"

"About a month and a half."

"A month and a half? That's all?"

He nodded and smiled sheepishly.

"Didn't your sire explain anything to you?" Amber failed to keep the surprise from her voice.

He frowned. "Don't think my dad really knows anything about being a vampire."

She shook her head. "Not your father, your sire. The vampire who turned you."

Disgust and anger appeared on his face. "That son of a bitch? If I could get my hands on him, I'd rip his guts out."

Amber took a step back. All of a sudden, Rusty didn't look so — tame. Green heat flared in his eyes. His voice was low and tight. And he was blocking the only way out of the room.

She took another step back and her butt bumped the table. "What happened?"

Rusty began to pace. "I was out for a late walk—I always liked walking at night—when somebody jumped me. I got in a few good licks but then I felt him bite my neck. Hurt like hell but I figured if he was gonna fight dirty, I would too. So I bit his arm until I drew blood. That's when everything got fuzzy. I could hear this voice in my head telling me to let go, but I didn't. As long as he was gonna hold onto my neck, I was gonna keep my teeth buried in his arm."

"Did you swallow his blood?"

He nodded. "Damn stuff gushed into my mouth. It was swallow it or let go. And I sure as hell wasn't letting go before he did."

Blinking, Amber nodded. Poor guy.

"When he finally let go of my neck, I let go of his arm. I was really feeling woozy by then but managed to plant my fist in his groin. Fucker screamed and doubled over," Rusty continued in a satisfied voice, "but I was so weak, I passed out. Woke up under a hemlock tree the next night sick as a dog with a craving for blood. Found a rabbit and drained the blood from its body. Felt better after that and went home."

"That's it?"

He stopped pacing and shrugged. "More or less. Once I discovered going out in the sun was painful and regular food didn't satisfy me, I knew something was wrong. My grandmother caught me sucking blood out of a cow and pretty much explained things to me."

Amber sank onto her chair. "She did?"

His grin was amused. "Yeah, well sort of. After I explained what had happened, she told me I had become a child of Satan who would be damned for all eternity. She promised to get a prayer circle started and finished with 'Get out of my house, blood-sucker.' That's when I figured out what had happened. I was a vampire. Who'd a thought it could happen?"

Fingers curled around the back of her chair, Amber watched Rusty as he wandered around the room, examining small items she'd set here and there. No wonder he didn't know what he was doing. The vampire who'd bit him had never meant to turn him. Rusty had more or less sired himself.

She glanced at his face.

He didn't seem to be angry any more.

"Ummm. Don't you want to be a real vampire?"

He looked up, smiled and shrugged. "I guess. What should I do?"

Amber smiled. Oh yeah. Things were definitely starting to look up. "I guess the first thing you should learn how to do is bite people."

His green eyes began to sparkle. "Do you think you could help me learn how?"

Amber grabbed her chair more tightly to keep from shivering with excitement. Yes! Perfect! She'd mold him into the perfect vampire. Her book would shoot right to the top of the *New York Times'* best seller list.

"Of course, I'll help you. What are friends for?"

Rusty smiled and nodded. Before he was finished with Amber, they'd be much more than friends.

"Go change your clothes."

That brought her up short. "Why?"

"I need blood. Figured now was as good a time as any to go people hunting. Thought you might like to change since that shirt has dirt on it but you don't have to. I mean, I could bite you."

"Me! No! I mean, I have to make sure you're doing it right so I have to be able to watch, right?"

He grinned wider. "So go change your clothes."

Amber looked down. Brown streaks slashed horizontally

across her yellow tee shirt. Those boxes she'd moved had been pretty dirty. "Sure. Hang on. I'll only be a minute."

Rusty smiled as she hurried from the room then stepped toward her computer.

Midnight rose from where she was lying next to it and hissed at him.

"Stupid cat. I only want to see what she's written." He reached toward the keyboard.

Midnight's paw shot out, claws extended.

Rusty jerked his hand to the side and knocked a silver vase off the table.

It rattled to the floor, bounced once, twice, and banged against the wall. The lid popped off as it started to roll the other way. Gray dust sprinkled the floor as the urn careened back against the table.

"Now look what you made me do, you stupid cat."

Midnight hissed and jumped off the table. Of course, she misjudged her leap and landed under Rusty's feet. He tripped. Trying to maintain his balance, he stepped on the neck of the urn, flattening it.

Yowling, Midnight scuttled from the room.

Cursing the cat, Rusty headed for the laundry room and the brush and dust pan he knew he'd find there. Returning, he quickly brushed up the mess. Then he grabbed the urn, planning on dumping everything back in.

Because he'd flattened the neck, the opening was completely closed.

"Jesus H. Christ. Now what?" He glanced at the gray dust in the dust pan. Sure looked a lot like the stuff in that damn cat's litter box.

A door closed upstairs. Now or never.

Far more quickly than any human, Rusty slipped into the laundry room, emptied the dust pan into the litter box and returned to the other room. There he picked the urn up off the floor and set it back where it had been. With a little luck, Amber would never notice.

"I'm ready if you are," Amber said from the doorway.

Rusty turned from looking out the window and smiled. "Let's go then." Taking her arm, he led her through the living room and out the door.

Chapter Fourteen

Amber pulled into an empty parking space. Neon lights of various colors shone through dusty windows of the rustic log building. How quaint. "What a great idea, Rusty. A bar. The perfect place to hunt your first human. Most of them will be drunk and won't realize what you're doing."

He shrugged as he slid out. "If you say so. Personally, I could use a beer first. What about you?"

"Sure," she answered as she opened her door and slid out. "You probably need to relax a little anyway."

"Yeah," Rusty answered with a grin. He glanced down at his crotch. *You hear that buddy? Relax.*

Amber tucked her hand under Rusty's arm and dragged him toward the door. "Come on."

They were about five yards from the door when it slammed open and a man stumbled out. The door bounced closed and the man staggered toward them, singing a somebody-done-somebody-wrong song totally off key at the top of his lungs.

Amber jerked Rusty to a stop. "There. Him. He's so drunk, he won't remember a thing."

A look of shock and disgust appeared on Rusty's face. "You want me to bite him? A guy? Are you fucking nuts?"

Frowning, Amber jerked her head around and stared at Rusty. "What are you babbling about?"

He took a step back, shaking his head. "No way am I gonna suck on a guy's neck. What kind of man do you think I am?"

Amber allowed her mouth to fall open for a moment. Then she snapped it shut. "You have got to be kidding me."

He continued to shake his head. "Nope. Not kidding. I like

women, not men. I ain't nibbling no guy's neck and that's final."

"Vampires don't care who they bite."

"This one sure as hell does. I like women, not men."

Amber stamped her foot. "Fine. Stick to women. Just make sure you bite somebody!"

Spinning on her heel, she stomped to the front door and jerked it open.

Blue cigarette smoke billowed toward her along with the scents of cheap perfume, stale beer and old grease. Every pair of eyes in the place turned toward her. Conversations died. Even the song on the jukebox ended.

A short, squat man sitting at the table closest to the door spit tobacco juice onto the floor, smiled a gap-tooth smile and shoved his chair back. "Hello there, honey. What can we do for you?"

Amber's gaze was still glued to the gob of tobacco spit on the dirt floor. Dirt floor?

A hand cupped her elbow and pushed her into the room.

"Hello, Dave. How ya been?"

Dave's smile broadened. "Rusty? How the hell are ya? Where you been hidin'? Haven't seen you in a month of Sundays."

"I been around," Rusty answered as he steered Amber toward two empty stools at the end bar. "Just keepin' to myself."

Dave slapped him on the back as they passed him and snickered. "Keepin' to yerself, huh? I can see why." After another louder snicker, Dave sat back down and laughed with the other men sitting at his table.

Amber slid onto an empty stool and looked around. This bar was certainly…rustic.

As Rusty settled in beside her, the big-bellied bartender ambled over. "Hey Rusty, the usual?"

Rusty nodded.

"Beer for you too, honey?"

Amber whipped her head around and glared at the bartender. Honey?

The bartender was smiling innocuously. He was only missing three teeth.

"I'll have a margarita," she snapped.

His smile disappeared. "A what?"

"A margarita. You know, tequila…"

He started shaking his head before she finished. "We don't have none of that. We got beer, whiskey, and bourbon. Which do you want?"

Amber blinked. Just how far out in the sticks was she? "Okay, I'll have a light beer."

Bartender shook his head again.

"Fine. Just give me what Rusty is having."

The bartender smiled. "Sure thing. Two drafts."

Gritting her teeth, Amber looked around. An old man and woman sitting at a nearby table stared at her. When the old man grinned, the woman screeched like a banshee and hit him over the head with her purse.

Amber quickly turned away. Good God. She was in redneck never never land.

"Here you go, Rusty. That'll be two bucks."

Lights flashed in a dark corner and a Johnny Cash song blared from the jukebox.

Amber stared at the beer before her. "Is that a Mason jar?"

Rusty lifted his and took a long swallow. "Yep," he finally answered. "Josh got tired of everybody always breaking his glasses. These jars are harder to break. Of course, they hurt a lot more if you get hit on the head with one."

"Get hit on the head…"

Before she could finish, a deafening boom reverberated around the room.

Grasping the edge of the bar, Amber swung her head around. "That sounded like a gunshot."

Rusty continued to sip his beer. "It was. Josh has a shotgun he's been trying to sell for three years now. He let's anyone interested shoot it out the back door."

Amber sputtered then grabbed her beer and gulped half of it down. Never never land? Hell, she was in redneck crazy land.

A female voice screeched across the room. "Rusty! Rusty Nipple! Where have you been, honey?"

A buxom, bleached blonde with her bright yellow hair teased and sprayed into a towering bouffant grabbed the back of Rusty's stool and spun it around. Then she threw her arms around his neck and pulled his mouth down to hers.

Amber brightened. If this woman was this eager to kiss Rusty, she'd be perfect for his first victim.

As the kiss dragged on and Rusty slid his hands down her sides and rested them on her plump hips, heat began to crawl up Amber's neck and face. Who did this slut think she was, anyway? Rusty was her vampire.

Finally, Rusty raised his head and pulled the woman's hands from around his neck. He moved his jaw back and forth. "Hell, Jolene. You 'bout sucked my tongue right out of my mouth. How ya been?"

Wiggling her plump ass, she stepped closer between his spread legs. "I could suck a couple other things, too, Rusty," she said in a low voice. Her hand slid down his stomach to his thigh.

"Ahemmm."

Smiling, Rusty glanced at Amber. "Jolene, honey. This is Amber. Her granny and mine are old friends."

Jolene glanced at Amber, smirked and turned her full attention back to Rusty. "Let's say you and me get out of here and go somewhere nice and quiet."

Rusty's smiled widened.

Amber's temper flared. Bleached-blonde slut.

Rusty chucked Jolene under the chin. "Sure thing honey. Just let me finish my beer."

Her hand slipped between his thighs and cupped him. "Sure thing, Rusty. Gotta go powder my nose first anyway. Be right back."

He squeezed her ass cheek. "Meet me outside, okay honey?"

She squeezed his groin. "Sure thing, honey." Turning, she zig-zagged between the patrons, chairs and tables.

Almost gagging on all the 'honeys' that had been flying around, Amber grabbed Rusty's arm. "What do you think you're doing?"

Eyes wide, an innocent expression on his face, he stared at her. His voice was low. "I'm doing just what you want me to, finding my first victim."

Damn it. That was what he was supposed to be doing. Amber wanted to wipe his bemused smile right off his face.

He grabbed her hand and pulled her from her seat. "Come on. You watch and make sure I'm doing this right."

Chapter Fifteen

Watch him. Was he nuts? "Are you crazy? She'll get suspicious if she sees me."

He snorted. An audience never stopped Jolene before. He stopped behind a beat-up pickup truck. "You said you were going to watch and make sure I did this right. You can stay here, behind this pickup. I'll be right over there. If I'm doing something wrong, you can signal me."

"If you're doing something wrong! But…"

He shoved her behind the truck. "Shhh. Here she comes. Now stay there and be quiet."

Rusty pushed Amber against the back of the pickup and sauntered to where Jolene could see him. He hoped to hell he was right and Amber was a lot more interested in him than she let on. Earlier, the combination of fish and cigarettes on Jolene's breath had almost gagged him. Only the irritation that had quickly changed to anger radiating from Amber had kept him locked in that kiss.

"There you are, honey. Thought you left with that skinny-ass bitch."

Rusty smiled. He was sure Jolene thought he was smiling at her but he was really smiling at Amber's reaction to being called a skinny ass bitch. Jolene could learn a few new curses if she had hearing good as his.

"I'm right here like I said I'd be."

Jolene grabbed his hand. "My car's over here. We can go back to my place. Daddy's gone off with his fishin' buddies."

He pulled her back into his arms. "Let's just stay here, honey."

She looked up at him. "Here?"

Rusty pushed her up against the front of a car and cradled her hips between his legs. "Come on, honey. I remember when you used to like the thrill of almost getting caught." He squeezed her breast. "What do you say?"

Caressing his upper arms, Jolene laughed low in her throat. "Why, Rusty, honey. Didn't think you had it in you anymore. You ain't been the same since you came back from that fancy college." Then she grabbed the hem of her shirt and pulled it over her head. Her bra disappeared just as quickly. She cupped her breasts, her thumbs twirling around on her nipples. "Bet you didn't see tits this nice at that fancy college, did you?"

Amber leaned back against the truck. *College? Rusty went to college? Rednecks don't go to college.*

Wrapping her brain around that bit of information, Amber shook her head and peered back around the side of the truck only to be greeted with the sight of Jolene's naked, melon-sized breasts. That Jolene woman was standing half-naked in her vampire's arms! She stiffened. The slut didn't have to be naked for Rusty to bite her.

The sound of a zipper ripped through the air and Amber gasped as Rusty wiggled his hips and half-turned toward her. She saw his cock spring free of his jeans. His cock! Just what the hell was going on over there? Rusty was supposed to bite her, not hump her. Enough was enough.

She exploded from behind the pick-up. "Hey! What the hell do you think you're doing?"

Rusty let his forehead fall forward onto Jolene's. Thank God. Just the thought of biting Jolene much less making love to her had his stomach roiling. Only the picture of Amber he held firmly in his mind had kept him from gagging. He wanted blood. His body craved it. But not Jolene's. He wanted Amber — both blood and body.

No reason to let her know that, though, at least not yet.

Beneath him, Jolene was moaning and squirming,

frantically trying to unbutton her tight jeans. As Amber reached him, he stepped away from her.

Without his support, Jolene slid off the hood of the car and landed on her ass at his feet.

Amber grabbed his arm and spun him to face her.

Eyeing the angry pulse at her throat, Rusty let his fangs drop. Damn, but he wanted her.

Passion-filled anger and heat radiated from her body. "What are you doing?"

He made no attempt to hide his cock as it jerked. He bared his fangs in a toothy grin. "I'm doing just what you told me to."

"All you have to do is bite her. I didn't say anything about sex."

He stepped closer and loomed over her.

The pulse in her throat jumped erratically.

"The first day you met me you asked if biting people made me horny. Guess it does."

She jerked her chin up and spat. "How would you know? You haven't even bitten anyone yet."

Rusty stepped closer.

Her distended nipples brushed against his chest.

His voice was low. "Not for lack of trying. You just stopped me. Why?'

His cock brushed her belly.

She sucked in a breath and didn't let it out.

"Hey. Rusty, honey. What's going on? We gonna do it or what?"

Spinning, he glared at Jolene.

She was reclining against the hood of the car behind her, cupping and fondling her breasts, her jeans unbuttoned and unzipped, a splash of white cotton displayed by the vee of the folded back flaps.

Rusty stepped closer and let her get a good look at his face.

When her gaze drifted to his fangs, the blood drained from her face.

"Are you sure you want to hang around, Jolene?"

A small squeak escaped from her throat as she darted away. A minute later a car roared to life. Gravel flew as the car squealed out of the parking lot.

Rusty turned to face Amber again. "You chased my victim away."

She raised her chin. "I did not. You did."

Grabbing her upper arms, he pulled her toward him.

She didn't resist.

"I'm a vampire. I need blood."

She shivered in his grasp. "There's a whole bar full of people over there."

He rubbed his cheek against hers, slid his tongue along her ear, carefully scraped a fang along her neck. "I don't want any of them."

She moaned.

"I want you." Pulling her against his chest, he reached down, cupped her ass and pulled her against his aching cock. "Kiss me." He covered her mouth with his, forced her lips apart, stabbed his tongue into her mouth.

She slid her hands up his chest and wrapped her arms around his neck. She moaned and twirled her tongue around his, shuddering slightly whenever she grazed his fangs.

A drop of her blood slid from her tongue to his. Need more powerful than he had ever experienced exploded in his body. He pushed her back against a car. "I need you. I need to take you here. Now."

Fire and desire raced though Amber's body. She was locked in Rusty's arms, pinned against a car by his hard body and there was nowhere else in the world she'd rather be.

"Yes, now, please. I ache."

Buttons popped as he ripped her shirt from her. Her bra followed. When his head dipped to her breasts, she buried her hands in his hair, releasing it from the ponytail. The silky strands fell forward against her breasts, teasing and caressing whichever nipple Rusty didn't have in his mouth. She arched into him. "Oh God, yes."

His hand slid down the front of her jeans and yanked them. The material parted like wet paper. His voice was tight with command. "Off, get them off."

As she hooked her thumbs under the waistband, he jerked at them again. More material ripped and her jeans slid down her legs.

In a flash, he was on his knees before her, kissing and lapping her stomach and navel, being careful not to scratch her with his fangs. "Fuck, but you're the most beautiful woman I've ever seen."

He ripped her black panties away and buried his face between her legs.

Chapter Sixteen

A hollow, metallic thud echoed around the parking lot as Amber pounded her fist against the hood of the car. She wiggled as her ass made contact with cold metal. In contrast, Rusty's breath between her legs was hot, and she arched into his mouth. His tongue was magic, stabbing into her and lapping her clit. And his fangs—she moaned again. Razor sharp, he wielded them with a delicate touch that tantalized and teased but never hurt.

She wanted to explode! "Oh my God, I'm going to come."

When Amber tightened her thighs and arched herself against further his mouth, Rusty pulled away. "No. Not yet. Not without me."

Pinning her body beneath his, he captured her wrists in one hand and pulled her arms above her head. Lifting his body, he kept her thighs pinned with his and looked down. Stretched taut beneath him, she was completely at his mercy. Lust surged through his body. She was his and soon his cock and fangs would seal his claim.

"Rusty, please." She tried to arch her breasts toward his mouth.

He tightened his grip and slid a thigh between her legs. Leaning over, he dragged his tongue along her neck and followed it with a gently scraping fang. "You're mine," he whispered in her ear. "I'm going to fuck you so hard that nothing but me will exist for you. And then I'll take your blood." He captured her chin with his free hand and stared into her face. "Do you understand me, Amber? I'm going to bite you, sink my fangs into you. If you don't want me to do this, tell me now. Once I start, once I slide my cock into you, I won't be able to stop."

Panting, Amber focused on the piercing green gaze staring down at her. Stop. He wanted to stop? Now? What was he crazy? "If you stop now, I swear I'll find a pair of pliers and yank your fangs out next time you fall asleep."

Lifting her head, she nipped his chin — hard.

As Amber's sharp teeth scraped his chin, the lust Rusty had been holding at bay exploded within him. Settling his hips between hers, he rammed his cock into her as deeply as he could. "Fuck, but you're tight." Flexing his hips, he pulled back and pounded into her again.

She lifted her long legs and wrapped them around his waist.

"Oh baby, you're so hot. So wet," he groaned as he sank deeper. Moist, clinging muscles enveloped his cock.

He scraped a fang along her neck again. A thin line of blood appeared and he lapped it up.

Excitement roared through his body. His, she was his. He dipped his head and suckled first one nipple then the other — back and forth, dragging his tongue from one to the other, lapping and kissing the valley between them.

Heat and desire burned straight to his groin and his cock hardened even more. He twisted his hips and buried himself deeper.

He nipped her neck. Blood. He needed more blood. Her blood. His body burned for her blood.

His balls contracted.

Rusty dragged his tongue across her left breast, nuzzled her collarbone, then lapped Amber's neck once more.

Finally, when the ache in his balls became unbearable and exploded up through his cock, he buried his fangs where her neck and shoulder met. As the warm blood filled his mouth, he shuddered and shook with the most powerful orgasm he'd ever experienced.

"Deeper, Rusty, deeper," Amber moaned as he twisted and pumped his hips, driving his rock-hard cock against and past her slippery flesh. As she lifted her hips to meet his, her internal muscles clenched and grasped. "Oh God, you're hard. You feel so good."

He mumbled something against her neck. When his fang scraped her sensitive skin, she shuddered. More heat pooled in her groin; her nipples tightened to points of pleasure-pain.

She tried to pull her wrists free but he only tightened his grip.

Amber shivered and sucked his tongue into her mouth when his lips found hers again. He was dominating her, mastering her, and she loved it.

His mouth left hers and she gasped for breath as he sucked first one nipple into his mouth, then the other. She arched her back. When had her breasts ever been this sensitive?

Pressure was building in her groin.

He twisted his hips again and the tension against her clit increased.

Her entire body shuddered. "Please, Rusty. Harder. I need…"

He sank his fangs into her and her entire body exploded.

Stars sparkled and whirled. Then, darkness claimed her.

"Amber. Amber, love, talk to me. I'm sorry. I'll never do it again."

She dragged her eyes open and smiled into his worried face. "You never do that again and I will pull your fangs." Then she sighed and stretched. Her body ached in all the right places. And that irritating itch on her neck was finally gone.

Rusty's chuckle pulled her attention back to him. "Well, ho…"

"If you call me honey…"

He grinned. "Sweetheart. I promise to do this lots more." A small frowned creased his brow. "I didn't hurt you?" He traced a gentle finger along the side of her neck and down onto her shoulder.

She reached up and probed gently. A scab was already forming.

Rusty lifted her hand and kissed her palm. "I think there must be something in my saliva that heals it. The scab will be gone by morning and there won't be a scar."

Amber looked up into Rusty's face and a feeling of contentment such as she'd never experienced blossomed inside of her. She smiled. "I think I could fall in love with you."

The surprise on his face was easy to read. "Are you sure?"

She pushed herself up to a sitting position. "That's the one thing I am sure about. Now don't you have something to say to me?"

He grinned. "Nice night?"

When her fist connected with his stomach, pain shot up her arm. "Ouch, damn it."

Laughing, he pulled her off the car and into his arms. After a long tender kiss, he cupped her face in his hands. "I definitely love you, Amber Blake." He kissed her again. "That cat, though..."

Amber wrapped her arms around his chest and hugged him. "Sorry, we're a package deal. You don't get one without the other."

He kissed her forehead. "I was afraid of that."

A cool breeze meandered between the parked cars and caressed Amber's bare ass

She shivered.

Rusty chuckled. "You aren't exactly dressed to be wandering around a parking lot."

Her hand slid down his stomach.

His cock rose to meet it.

Amber grinned and caressed the head. "Whose fault is

that?"

She sank to her knees and kissed the head of his cock. "Doesn't take long for a vampire to get a second hard-on."

He buried his fingers in her hair. "Sweetheart, I've been semi-hard ever since I saw that cute ass of yours in those sopping wet jeans."

Her answer was to suck his cock into her mouth.

As Amber rolled her tongue at the base of the head, Rusty groaned. "That's it, baby. Suck me deep."

She complied, alternately sucking, nibbling and lapping on his cock.

He tightened his fingers on her head and thrust his hips.

She opened her throat and swallowed him deeper. "Hmmmmmmmm."

Rusty groaned and his fangs began to ache all over again.

She raked her teeth along his cock as he pulled it out of her mouth.

"Fuck." Lifting her, he turned her and pushed her down on the hood of the car. He slid a knee between hers. "Spread your legs, Amber. I'm going to ride you until you scream."

Elbows bent, her arms braced against the car, she lifted her ass further into the air. "Yes, Rusty, yes."

Slipping his hand between her legs, he fondled and probed. "Wet. So wet." Grabbing her hips, he steadied her. Slowly he entered her, watching his cock as it disappeared inside her body.

"Ohhhh, yes. Deeper, Rusty. You're so hard. Deeper."

He complied, bucking against her ass, shoving himself into her as deeply as he could.

When he pulled out, she thrust her ass back against him.

"Fuck. You have me so hot, I'm ready to come. I ache, Amber. I ache all over for you."

"Yes, come, Rusty. Come inside me—hot and hard."

"Christ, Amber. How did I ever live without you?"

Reaching around her waist, he pinched her clit.

She moaned and bucked harder.

He pinched it again, then rolled the pad of his finger against it.

She sobbed.

"Are you ready to come, love? I need you to come." He leaned over her back and nipped the back of her neck.

Fiery heat rolled and swirled in Amber's stomach and groin. She rubbed her aching nipples against the cold metal beneath them and shivered.

Rusty pinched her clit again and she shuddered.

He rubbed harder and nipped her neck.

"Come for me, love. Come for me."

Every muscle in her body clenched and froze for what seemed like an eternity. Then, the final thrust of Rusty's cock into her body and the sharp pleasure-pain of his fangs entering her shoulder released the heat dammed in her body. If he hadn't clapped his hand over her mouth, her scream would have brought every patron in the bar running to see what happened.

He collapsed on top of her, both of them panting with satisfaction.

"Well, it looks as if my latest creation managed to teach itself a few things."

Chapter Seventeen

In the blink of an eye, Rusty was up on his feet with Amber shoved behind him.

"What the hell do you want?" Never taking his eyes off the other man, he stuffed his cock in his jeans, pulled up his zipper and snapped the snap.

Amber peeked out from under his arm.

The man that faced them was everything she'd ever read a vampire should be. Tall, broad-shouldered and impeccably dressed, he looked like a dark angel. His black hair was combed back from his forehead and fell behind his ears to just brush his collar. Well-formed black eyebrows slashed the paleness of his skin above equally dark eyes that glittered with hostility. His lips were parted in a cruel smile and his white teeth gleamed in the faint light from the neon signs in the bar's windows.

As Amber watched, his fangs erupted. She shivered.

His voice was full of superiority and arrogance. "Move aside, fool. She's mine now."

Rusty didn't move. "Touch her and I'll rip your balls completely off this time."

A hiss slipped from between the other man's lips. "Claude, come here."

A second, shorter vampire joined the first. He hesitated then moved a few steps to his master's left.

"You can't fight the two of us," the first vampire sneered.

Rusty flexed his arms and hands. "Won't be the first time I was outnumbered in a fight. Won most of them too." He nodded toward the shorter vampire. "That Claude fella doesn't look too sure of himself." He cocked his head to the side and stared into the taller vampire's face. "What the hell is your name anyway?"

Cruel fangs flashed as he laughed. "Vincent. Vincent Stephen Moreau, your sire and master."

Rusty snorted and crossed his arms over his chest. "Like hell. Ain't no man my master."

Curling his lip, Vincent sneered. "You uneducated, backwoods fool. Do you honestly think you can defeat me? I'm three hundred years old and have killed far more humans and vampires than you can imagine."

Rusty shrugged. "So?"

Behind him, Amber shivered. Vincent was exactly what she'd pictured a vampire to be—tall, dark, masterful...dangerous.

Thank God, Rusty wasn't anything like him. She'd have been dead that first day in her house. But Rusty was going to need some help. He may have beaten Vincent before but he couldn't fight both him and Claude. Slowly she edged away from Rusty. The pick-up truck parked next to them had a broom sticking out the back of it. A stake in the heart would stop any vampire, including Vincent.

Vincent chuckled. "Yes, run, little bird. I do so love the chase."

Little bird? Boy, this Vincent guy was a real asshole.

Before Amber reached the truck, Vincent moved.

So did Rusty.

He tackled the older man to the ground before he could reach her.

As Amber grabbed the broomstick, a heavy hand fell on her shoulder. Jerking the broom sideways, she almost cheered when she heard a sharp crack. Spinning around, she faced Claude with the broken broomstick in her hand, the sharp, broken end pointed toward him.

Claude looked at it, then at her. Holding up his hands, he backed away.

"Smart vamp," she mumbled. Not turning her back to him, she edged her way back toward Rusty.

Vincent may have been a few hundred years older but Rusty knew how to fight dirty better. No matter how the older man twisted, turned and attacked, Rusty was always waiting for him.

Blood dripped from cuts on both men.

"There's more to you than I thought, bumpkin," Vincent growled as he licked blood from the back of his hand.

"That's the trouble with arrogant, overconfident men such as yourself. You tend to underestimate everyone else." Rusty shifted to the left.

"No more than uneducated fools like to believe they can out-think men like me." Vincent feinted left then leaped to the right. Straight toward Amber.

As he reached her, she pulled the broomstick from behind her back.

He impaled himself on it.

She twisted the stick and attempted to push it in further. "Rusty's been to college and I've got an MBA, asshole."

Screaming with rage, Vincent grabbed Amber's hair, wrenched her head back and buried his fangs in her throat.

"Amber!" In the blink of an eye, Rusty reached her side. Clasping the stick, he shoved it so far into Vincent's heart the point slid all the way through his chest and out his back. Then he wrenched the dead man's jaws apart and hurled him away from Amber.

She slowly sank to the ground, blood spurting from the mortal wound in her throat.

"Here, stanch the bleeding with this."

Rusty took the wad of cloth Claude offered, a small part of his brain registering the fact that it was the blouse he'd stripped from Amber earlier. It quickly became soaked with her blood.

Rusty sank to the ground and cradled her in his arms.

"Amber, sweetie. Look at me. Come on, love. Open your eyes."

"You can save her."

Ignoring Claude, Rusty pulled Amber closer to his chest. Tears slid down his cheeks.

A weak voice reached his ears. "Vampires can't cry."

The light was fading in Amber's eyes as she smiled at him. "I—love you."

Claude grabbed his shoulder. "Damn it, man. You can save her. Give her your blood. That and your saliva will heal even a wound such as hers."

Rusty snapped his head around. "If you're lying to me, I'll tear you into little pieces."

Claude ignored the threat. "Open the vein in your wrist and make her drink it. You'll have to alternate drinking her blood, too. You have to replace what she'll take from you, and your saliva will help the cut in her throat heal.

Without a second thought, Rusty slashed his fangs across his wrist and held it to Amber's lips. "Here, love. Take this. Drink it."

Amber lay, surrounded by darkness and warmth. A bright light appeared. She smiled and began to float toward it. A buzzing in her ears stopped her. Irritated, she frowned.

The light began to dim.

Warm liquid seeped between her lips. She swallowed.

The light disappeared.

More liquid. She sucked greedily.

Someone nuzzled her throat. The sharp pain there eased then disappeared.

Darkness embraced her.

Tired and weak, Rusty leaned back against the wheel of a car, Amber cradled in his arms. "Are you sure she'll live?"

Claude nodded. "As much as those such as we live." He swung his head to the left and listened. "Someone's coming."

Rusty groaned. "I can't believe no one came out of the bar before this. Just isn't normal."

"It was Vincent. He coerced whoever was inside to stay there until he called them out. Too many humans wandering about can mean trouble." Claude looked toward Vincent's body and chuckled. "Seems like you were more trouble than even Vincent could handle. A lot of vampires will sleep easier now that he's dead. He gave our kind a bad name."

Gravel crunched under boots.

Claude looked over his shoulder. "Goodbye, Rusty. Again, thank you."

Claude faded into the darkness as Brad Keister emerged. He looked first at Rusty, then Amber. Without saying a word, he stepped over to the body and shined his flashlight in its face. Fangs gleamed.

Brad looked back at Rusty. "This the one that bit you?"

Rusty nodded. "He tried to kill both me and Amber."

"She gonna be alright?"

Rusty nodded. "Yeah."

"Okay, then. Don't worry about it. I'll take care of everything." He nudged the body with his toe. "You sure he's dead?"

Rusty sighed. "Brad, you stick a three-foot piece of broomstick into anything's heart and it's gonna die. But, if it will make you feel better, don't pull it out."

Brad nodded. "I'll borrow Josh's truck and run the body down to Uncle Dan's. He can cremate it and no one will ever know the difference."

Rusty smiled. Sure was nice having a cousin who was the sheriff and an uncle who was not only the coroner but also owned the only crematorium in a three-county area.

Brad looked back at him. "You need any help?"

Rusty shook his head. "I'll manage. Thanks." Taking a deep breath, he rose slowly to his feet, Amber cuddled in his arms.

Once he had her in her car, he drove them home. Deep, healing sleep would be good for both of them.

Chapter Eighteen

Amber woke suddenly.

Midnight was sitting on her chest staring down at her.

"Meoooow?"

Amber lifted her hand to her throat—nothing but smooth skin. She frowned. Vincent had bitten her. She remembered that.

A rich, flowery scent enveloped her. Turning her head, she focused on the pale pink roses that lay on the pillow next to hers.

"Evening, sleepyhead. How do you feel?" Rusty sat down on the bed, a coffee mug in his hand.

She nudged Midnight from her chest and pushed herself up. "What's that?"

"Blood." He held it out.

The rich, coppery scent reached her nostrils.

Instead of the nausea she expected, her mouth immediately began to ache. A sharp pain stabbed both sides of upper gums. As she stared at her reflection in the dresser mirror, a pair of fangs slid from beneath her upper lip.

She stared. "What happened?"

Rusty set the mug on the nightstand and gathered her into his arms. "I'm sorry. I never would have done this to you if I'd had any other choice." He slipped his finger under her chin and lifted it. "You were dying. I couldn't lose you, not after I'd just found you. I love you too much."

Amber blinked. "You mean I'm a vampire now, too?"

He nodded. "Yes. Will you forgive me?"

"Forgive you?" Grabbing two handfuls of hair, she pulled his face down to hers and kissed him soundly. Then she sank her fangs into his chest.

As his hot, sweet blood hit her stomach, energy exploded through her veins.

"Wow!" she said, then bit him again.

"That's enough," he said with a laugh as he pulled her mouth away, "or you'll be nursing me. You really don't mind being a vampire?"

"Mind? Are you kidding? This is so cool!" She leaped from his lap and stretched. "I'll be the only author with an intimate knowledge of vampires. I'll write a best seller. I can't wait to get started." Throwing on a tee shirt and pair of jeans, she disappeared through the door.

Leaning back, Rusty grabbed the mug and sipped the deer blood. Life just kept getting better and better. Once she got over her initial excitement, he'd go down there, strip off his clothes, and let her have her evil way with him.

Midnight stared down her nose at him and meowed.

An angry bellow from downstairs interrupted his thoughts. In an instant, Amber was standing in the doorway with the silver urn in her hands.

"Damn it, Rusty! Where the hell is Aunt Ernestine?"

About the author:

Living in a small town in Central Pennsylvania, Judy Mays spends the time she isn't teaching English to tenth graders as a wife and mother. Family is very important to Judy, and she spends a lot of time with her husband and children. Judy's pets are a very important part of her life, and she's had many over the years. Currently, Zoe the cat and Boomer the Lab mix help keep things hopping around the house.

Judy loves reading—especially romance, the spicier the better. After reading for more years than she cares to admit, Judy decided to try her hand at writing romantica—and her wonderful husband of seventeen years provides plenty of motivation and ideas.

In the upcoming months, the tales by Judy Mays will contain werewolves, vampires, witches, and aliens from five planets on the other side of the galaxy. All of the heroes or heroines will fall madly in love and demonstrate their love in so very, very many ways.

Enjoy Judy's books, and after you've read one, she would love to hear what you think. Either stop by her website at www.judymays.com and sign her guest book or contact her directly at writermays@yahoo.com. She can't wait to hear from you.

Judy welcomes mail from readers. You can write to her c/o Ellora's Cave Publishing at 1337 Commerce Drive, #13, Stow, Ohio 44224.

Also by Judy Mays:

Fangs 'n' Foxes

Mardi Ballou

Prologue

From time immemorial, vampires and garlic didn't mix. So, of course, there could be no vampires in Trenton, New Jersey, where the scent of garlic is second only to oxygen in the air. But then there arose a newer, tougher breed of vampire — a vampire who not only could tolerate garlic but learned to love the fragrant, multi-layered bulb. As fate and Darwin might have it, not one but two distinct subspecies of vampire evolved. Alas, their tolerance to garlic did not extend to each other...

"Wanda, get your friggin' ass on down here now," a harsh voice bellowed, interrupting Wanda the Wise Muller's careful writing. She bit her lip. Determined as she was to write the full chronicles of the Trenton vampires, working for a demanding boss made it difficult to snatch the time she needed. But the tone in Darnell DeLouis's voice alerted her that he meant business. With a sigh she saved her file, put the computer to sleep, and hurried off to see what he wanted.

Despite all her efforts, she had a long way to go to get him trained right. She'd probably have given up on him already if she didn't know, sure as she knew her own name, that Darnell cloaked his finer self under the thick armor required of vampire leaders. Not to mention, Darnell was hot — movie star tall, dark and gorgeous. No surprise that the ladies lined up at his door. Lucky Wanda was immune to his charms.

Lucky also, she had good friends in high places. Soon, it would be time to join forces with them and get Darnell to evolve and commit his considerable powers to their mission.

But first things first. Assuming her haughtiest don't-mess-with-me look, she made her way to Darnell's office.

Chapter One

As night descended after another hot, muggy August day in Trenton, bright lights and the get-down beat of gangsta rap, heavy on the bass, glared and roared from the Black Guards' Social Hall, just off Perry Street. Even really tough dudes scurried on by. The place had a certain rep...

Inside his private, personal quarters, Darnell D. DeLouis, chief Black Guard and the fiercest of the fierce, rose from his coffin and growled. After looking around to make sure he was totally alone, he began to perform his nightly secret ritual. First he reached under the silk lining of his coffin and extracted a small square box. After another visual sweep of the room, he drew out a stack of paper attached to a plastic base. His voice a hoarse whisper, he proceeded to read from his "365 Love Poems" calendar, one to start off each night of the year.

No one knew he read these poems. If anyone ever found out...well, Darnell's ass would be total grass. But the poems reminded him of his first girlfriend, Maralise. The two of them would sneak behind the trash cans in the alley between their buildings, and she'd kiss him, recite a poem for him. Once he'd even told her one, and she showed her appreciation in a way that still got his cock throbbin'. But Black Guards didn't do no poetry. So each night, soon as he read his poem, he'd tear the page into a zillion pieces and set his lighter to it. Then he shoved the calendar back down into its hiding spot. If anyone ever found it, he'd have to kill them...

Talk about killing. He felt a piercing pain on the left side of his face like someone was staking him. He'd ignore it. He had to. He dressed and slapped on some of that cologne the ladies loved.

Just in time. A knock at his door. His first two ladies of the night were waiting to come in. Darnell groaned as the pain began to flare out on the left side of his face. Shit. His waking up ritual that the public knew about included a quick roll in the hay with the lucky ladies who'd won the night's lottery. He couldn't let anything distract him from his people's expectations. "Come in," he said, with a flourish of his hand.

The ladies giggled, probably from nerves and excitement about finally getting their chance to be with him. Darnell had to get his shit together, pronto, and pleasure them good. But his face was starting to ache with a grinding pain that made him think less about banging these chicks and more about banging his cheek against a slab of cement. Most any night he'd knock off hotties like these two before he fully woke up. Not that he was bragging or nothing, but he always rose from his coffin with ten inches of prime cock—round, firm, and loaded for action. He'd feed on his lovelies and fuck them a dozen or so times before he got down to the business of the night.

But tonight sucked in all the wrong ways. Darnell identified the source of his agony, and it wasn't pretty. He had the fuckin' granddaddy of all toothaches. A killer pain in his left fang that would've shriveled up his pecker—if Darnell was any other guy. But Darnell didn't get to be head Black Guard by being soft. He heroically managed to get and keep that fucker up.

The two babes, Viveca and Clarissa, dressed like harem chicks in some see-through chiffon pants and itty-bitty beaded tops just barely covering their sweet tits. The two of them sat down together on his king-size bed with the black satin sheets— a bed used just for loving the ladies—and giggled some more, just waiting on him. 'Cause they knew they were gonna have a good time. Old Darnell never left no chick high and dry, and he wasn't about to start just 'cause he was in enough pain to blow his fuckin' head off his shoulders.

"You ladies here to see me?" he said real low in his sexy voice.

"Oh, Darnell," Viveca said, batting her lids like she had some garbage caught in her eye, "we been waiting on you for *hours.*"

"Well, I'm gonna make it worth your while. You all gonna leave here happy."

"Oh, Darnell," Clarissa giggled. He winced. That stupid cackle came near to being a deal breaker even when he wasn't in head-crushing pain, but tonight it set his friggin' nerves on edge. Still, chivalry was not dead, and all that shit. She came to him to come, and she'd come and come and come, or his name wasn't Darnell D. DeLouis.

"You ladies ready to make a Darnell sandwich?" he said, chuckling less than his usual big laugh. He stripped off his cream-colored linen designer suit, custom-made shirt, and fine Italian silk tie. Black silk boxers, seven hundred dollar shoes. Hell, even his socks were elegant. They didn't call him Dapper Darnell for nothing. Normally, Darnell grooved on taking off his fine threads so the ladies could feast their eyes. Tonight, his strip and flex provided barely a moment's relief from the friggin', unrelenting agony.

Viveca and Clarissa did a little dance as they stripped off their nothing by nothing costumes, and Darnell had to remind himself to admire their movements. Viveca was the tall one, almost too skinny. But sexy with her café au lait skin and her close-cut henna hair. Chick must've took ballet lessons or some shit like that, the way she moved. Despite his pain, Darnell's cock started to join in the dance.

Clarissa was a little, round thing. Skin like cinnamon, boobs with dark brown nipples begging to be suckled. She opened her legs as she wiggled, and he could see her pussy lips gleaming with her readiness to take him in. Both of them had such pretty cunts—made him wish he had two cocks. Well, with his one he'd still have them singing the high notes before they went on home.

Darnell kissed Viveca, his tongue probing deep inside her.

"Me too," Clarissa demanded.

"Of course, baby," he said, fastening his mouth onto her generous lips. She tasted like chocolate and coffee, with a hint of wine. Man, he wished he could forget his tooth and really get into being with her.

"Let's all get comfy," Darnell said, indicating his bed. Still fully erect, he hoped he could make them happy with a double quickie because he didn't really know how long he could ignore his pain to do the wild thing with them.

He took Clarissa in his arms and buried his face in her big sweet chest. He wanted to rub his aching fang on her nipples, but he settled for kissing and licking those babies instead. Clarissa was delicious, tasting and smelling like the spice her skin reminded him of. From the way the chick was writhing and trying to maneuver her luscious pussy lips to the head of his cock, Darnell knew she wanted it bad. He ran his fingers down her slit and got all slick with her juices, which he sucked off his fingers.

Viveca had her arms around him from behind. He could feel her little breasts pressed into his back, the nipples sticking into him like marbles while she nibbled on the back of his neck. That Viveca had her legs 'round his thigh and was humping him like a bitch in heat, her pussy even wetter than Clarissa's. Damn, if she didn't hold on tight, she'd slide on down off the bed. The way the woman was panting and breathing hard, she must've been waiting all day to get her cunt lips around him.

Despite his pain, Darnell gave a little smile. For a man in agony, he was starting to feel a little bit okay. Just had to keep diverting his focus down to where the action was. Clarissa had her hand on his cock and she was rubbing him just right. She had some shiny blue polish on her long, fancy nails. Little sparkles gleamed and glittered when she moved her fingers. Yeah. A little cup-the-balls action. The fox knew how to manipulate them babies Darnell groaned, half-pain, half-lust. He needed to get into Clarissa now.

Pounding her pussy against his thigh, Viveca screamed some nasty words and came all over his leg. She sighed and pulled back. Darnell rolled on top of Clarissa.

"Can I be on top?" Clarissa whispered.

"You got it, baby," Darnell said, rolling onto his back. Clarissa stretched out on top of him and put his cock right where she wanted. Oh, baby. Tight, hot, sweet, and oh-so wet. Darnell arched his hips up and felt all her slick surfaces clutching on to him as he went deep, deep inside her.

Clarissa put her sweet little hands down on the bed next to him and pushed herself up so she was sitting right there on top of his cock. On top of the world, he laughed to himself, looking up at her sitting on him like the queen of the mother fuckin' universe. She rotated her fine brown bottom and, *have mercy*, his cock throbbed in gratitude. He arched into her, and she closed her eyes and purred.

Just then Viveca demanded his attention again. She whispered something in Clarissa's ear, and Clarissa nodded. Next thing he knew, Viveca was sitting on his face with her cunt right on his mouth. An experience in fine dining. Darnell darted his tongue into Viveca's pussy, lapping up her happy juices. Yeah. She had a strong, sultry scent of spice and woman, and she tasted like the finest nectar. Oh yeah, a little nibble on her clit, some tongue action on her lips. She held his head to her and breathed out his name. Damn, she was riding him like the Cavalry coming out of Fort Something-or-other. Yeah, yeah, yeah. That horse was stampeding and she wasn't about to let go.

Darnell was licking and tasting and eating one while he screwed the other, and all his senses were running 'round like crazy. Toothache? What friggin' toothache? Hell, a little bone-crushing agony couldn't keep a good man down. Clarissa sped up and was letting them know that, oh yeah, she was almost there, almost there, almost there. Then she *was* there, shrieking to bring down the house.

Soon as one stopped, the other started. *Shit*. Darnell was going now.

And then they both stopped. What the fuck?

"I want it up the ass," Viveca said.

Well, damn. Who could turn down an invitation like that? He got on his side behind Viveca, and Clarissa got behind him. He kissed Viveca's sweet little bud of a hole, then rubbed her pussy cream into her crack. But not too long. He needed to get into her. He eased his way in, and she wiggled her ass, getting her cheeks close to his flat, muscular hips.

Clarissa was kissing him from behind and humping his leg just like her friend had. It all felt so amazing. Viveca's ass sheathed his cock like it was custom-made. He pistoned his cock into her gorgeous butt, and she rammed her cheeks back against him. "Oh, baby," she said.

She gave one more giggle, and he exploded. The cum shot outta him like she was a fire and he was a high pressure hose. Oh, yeah. He was coming from somewhere down in his toes.

And then it was over, and he had them two hot foxes, satisfied but drooling for more, in his bed. His fang woke up and began to holler. It was about to kill him. He needed to get outta bed and take care of it fast. But first he had to make sure the two babes were okay.

'Cause Darnell heard tell, not that he'd know firsthand, how bad disappointing two sweet foxes like Viveca and Clarissa would be. Bad for them, bad for him. Hell, they'd probably develop one of them damn inferiority complexes Oprah was always yapping about on her show, which he taped 'cause it came on too damn early. Or worse, they'd talk about him and spread nasty rumors. Some of the young guys might start smelling blood. Not that anyone would believe Viveca or Clarissa. Darnell's reputation as a lady pleaser was as solid as his cock, and two lying chicks making up stories wouldn't change that none. No, he could take care of any stuff they tried to spread. Damage control.

But that was all what people called "hypothetical". 'Cause he'd gotten it up, on, in, and over. And he'd fucked them 'til their pussies put up a white flag and hollered "Uncle!" So keeping his reputation intact was not his biggest headache of the moment. Now he just had to get them two foxes outta his face so he could call Wanda, his advisor, and get her to find a goddamn dentist with night hours.

Darnell groaned, and it wasn't from Viveca wanting to suck his sleeping cock while Clarissa tongued his ass crack. She looked up at him with hope in her big dark eyes, but Darnell knew nothing those chicks could do with their magic tongues and fingers could bring back the dead. Not after he'd fucked them every which way but loose, despite his pain. Nah. Far faster than usual, he extricated himself from the chicks' sticky embraces. Darnell put his hands on Viveca's shoulders and nudged her away as he gave a butt wiggle to get Clarissa off.

"I'm calling it a night," he said.

"Does this mean you ain't gonna feed off me?" Viveca protested.

"Or me?" Clarissa chimed in.

Darnell winced. Viveca was a major fox, but tonight her voice grated on him like a garbage can lid being dragged across the sidewalk. And, except during sex, her sidekick Clarissa always sounded like she sucked helium. "Maybe later, darlings," he said, using all his self-control to sound cool. "Now I got some important business that can't wait. Why don't you two ladies go watch some DVDs from my private collection? I'll catch up with y'all later."

Viveca and Clarissa looked at each other. "I think we better go now," Clarissa said. "Night's still young. I heard them Cosa Nostra vampires been hangin' around, promising a good time. Maybe we can catch us some of that."

Crap. That was the last shit Darnell wanted to hear. The notion of his chicks going to look for satisfaction from the Cosa Nostras struck hard, like a stake to a vital organ. He had to get his heads together, the one on his shoulders and the one at the end of his cock. He was not about to let any of his women out there for the delectation and entertainment of the Mafia vampires. 'Specially not now.

The word wasn't out on the street yet, so these two wouldn't know. Three nights from now, Darnell would face off against Vinny the Mooch Miccio, head Cosa Nostra vampire, for control of Trenton. This 'burg wasn't big enough for two major vampire groups—and the Black Guards were here first. They'd tried to coexist with the Mafiosos infiltrating their turf. But those mother fuckers didn't share. And the time had come to face them down and send them the hell back across the Delaware.

Actually, Darnell and Miccio had been primed for a full-out rumble, the Black Guards against the Cosa Nostras, man to man. That was before Darnell and Wanda met in war council with Miccio and his *consigliore*, and they'd set up this deal, to have the leaders be designated warriors. Civilized like. Wanda's way. And the *consigliore's*. No sense killing each other off in a turf war, she'd said. They'd all been there and done that. This time one guy from each side. Each leader could use chains, knives, guns. Whatever weapons they could come up with except stakes or silver, which the vampire code forbade. The first guy down for more than two minutes as timed by the advisors lost. Winner take all, meaning control of Trenton and Mercer County. Loser…well, Darnell couldn't let his head go there. Normally the word *loser* wasn't even in his vocabulary. But with this friggin' toothache… Darnell ran his hand over his aching jaw. Wanda'd better come up with a way to fix what was wrong with him or they'd all be dead meat. Banished to the boonies.

"Now don't you girls go running off half-cocked to them Cosa Nostras. Rumor has it they only got two-inch peckers. That's what makes them so mean."

Viveca and Clarissa tittered. "We know better than that," they chorused.

He scowled at them. "Now how'd you ladies find out that kind of stuff?"

Viveca rolled her eyes. "We have contacts." They both laughed again. The vibration of their giggles made his tooth shake up and down like a son of a bitch. Really, he had to get rid of them or he'd hurt them.

Darnell's face froze into his killer vampire glare. "You better watch that, hear? If I ever find out you're messin' with those guys, I'll be pissed off. Big time. You don't wanna do that, do you?" Fuck, the fang hurt so much, he was starting to lisp.

Clarissa bit her lip. "We'd never want to piss *you* off, Darnell."

They were laughing at him. Damn, fuck, shit. This could not go on.

"I'm gonna call Wanda. She'll set you straight, set up some other time for you to come back."

He stalked out of the room and, when he was sure they couldn't hear him, howled.

* * * * *

"You're on the refuse-to-treat list of every dental association in central Jersey and eastern Pennsylvania," Wanda Muller, AKA Wanda the Wise, said in her *I'm-a-serious- adult* voice. She loved Darnell like a naughty little brother, but sometimes he could be a major pain. Like now. She could handle negotiations with rival vampire organizations, hospitality for visiting vampires from around the world, the blood supply for all of Jersey, even Darnell's social life. Hell, that was all normal stuff for the chief advisor to any vampire leader. But when he got one of his toothaches...it made her question how anyone could call her *wise*. In her four hundred years, she'd never met another vampire that came close to being as unbearable as Darnell when he got one of his toothaches. And the way he went for sweets, he exacerbated an unfortunate weakness. She'd warned him not to go to that chocolate lovers' convention in Atlantic City. He'd gorged himself on those conventioneers like some out of control rogue vampire. And now he was paying the price. She kept telling him to balance his diet with some strict vegans. But did he ever listen?

He bellowed a stream of obscenities.

"Now mind your tongue," Wanda scolded. "You go making noises like that and I'm out of here."

Darnell glared at her balefully. "Aw, Wanda. All the friggin' dentists you sent me to hurt me. You know I can't deal with pain," he hissed.

The ice bag Wanda gave him to hold against his jaw didn't seem to be helping. "Hold that tighter to your jaw."

"It don't do no good." Darnell flung the ice bag on the floor a little too close to Wanda's toes.

"Now pick that up, Darnell."

"Leave it there."

She folded her arms in front of her and stared at him 'til he bent down and picked it up.

"You want me to get fresh ice in there?"

Darnell shrugged. "Yeah, I guess. But Wanda, you gotta get me a dentist. Tonight."

Wanda tapped her foot. "I told you a hundred times, you can't hurt them just because they hurt you. It's their job. They can't help it."

"Well, I can't either," he grumped.

Wanda shook her head. She'd had a public relations crisis when the last dentist required forty stitches and three pints of blood after treating Darnell… "I'm going to have to pull some major strings to set you up with another dentist. Since that last time, they're all squeamish about treating vampires."

"We pay good."

"Not that good."

"Shit." He began to pace, looking as if he wanted to try to run away from his pain. "I thought vampires weren't supposed to get toothaches." He waved his arms about menacingly. "Bad enough when I had them in my other teeth. But this one hit me right in my friggin' fang I can't even feed, keep up my strength."

Wanda sighed. As an accomplished student of vampire history and science, she'd studied and thoroughly learned all about what was and wasn't supposed to happen to the undead. "Most of us don't ever get cavities. But you were switched over by Bucky Dent, right?"

"Yeah, so, what of it?"

Wanda shrugged. "Like heredity, you know? He gave you his mutant bad teeth. Gave them to all the vamps he turned."

"Sounds like the friggin' curse of the vampires," Darnell bitched.

Wanda's patience was running out. "Just be glad you weren't turned by Nutless Nate."

Darnell cringed and his hands went to his crotch. "You mean it's true about…?"

Wanda nodded.

"Yeah, you're right about that," Darnell said. "Better my teeth than my…"

"Right. Now I'm going to have to call in a very special favor to take care of that tooth. But I won't call anyone 'til you give me your solemn oath. Your solemn blood oath."

"What you want this time, Wanda?" He was pressing the ice bag against his cheek.

"Are you going to act right? You promise me you'll do everything this dentist tells you to—and no nastiness?"

Darnell groaned, but he nodded. "I gotta get better 'fore I meet with Miccio."

"Okay. I'm going to call the best dentist I know. The best dentist in the universe. But brother, you mess this up, and you're on your own. Got it?"

"Oh, yeah," Darnell promised.

Wanda went through her personal address files and found the number she had been waiting for just such an occasion to use.

Chapter Two

Jack T. Nipper, one of the new young vampires recently arrived in Trenton from the boonies of eastern Pennsylvania, drew the short straw and had to drive Darnell to the dentist's office. Wanda bent down so her face filled the driver's window of the stretch Hummer to give Jack very explicit directions. Then she moved over to the back window and gestured Darnell to lower the glass. "Now don't you give Jack a hard time. You know what happens when he gets nervous." Nail biting was a vicious habit for a vampire.

Darnell, holding a fresh ice bag against his aching jaw, nodded slightly. "I just need to get there," he lisped before lapsing into silence.

"And don't you forget what I told you about how to act with the dentist. Her name's LaLilia Guitry. Don't you make me sorry I called her."

Darnell grimaced, his face contorted into a mask of pain. "I'm going to a *chick* dentist?" he croaked.

Wanda raised an eyebrow. "I hope you're not even *thinking* about pulling any sexist bullshit with me."

She could swear Darnell rolled his eyes. But she expected him to get over that macho crap. Time and again, with her strategies, her plans, and her counsel, she'd proved herself the best chief advisor he ever had—not to mention the most loyal. Comments like this one demonstrated she still had a ways to go in getting him to fix his attitude. However, she was just the woman to do it.

"Now, Wanda," he protested. "You know I love women..."

She growled.

"I love women and I respect them," he continued. "But a *chick* dentist? Hell, that goes against nature."

"What in the name of heaven and earth do you mean by that?" Wanda asked, almost more curious to see what nonsense he was going to hand her this time, than offended by his sexism.

"Heh, heh, heh," he chuckled weakly. She could tell he knew he was on thin ice. "Come on, Wanda. You know I only want the babes to see my good side, to know Darnell at his best. I don't want some chick to see me when I'm like this, reduced by agony to some pitiful specimen..."

Okay. So she'd give him points for originality and thinking fast on his feet. But she wasn't about to crack a smile. "She's a topnotch and very professional dentist, Darnell. For once, get it through your thick skull that not every female in the universe wants to get you in the bedroom."

With one hand still clutching the ice bag and the other reaching for his heart, Darnell moaned, "Wanda. You really know how to hurt a guy when he's down."

Wanda curled her lip in disgust. "Get over yourself. And don't you dare hurt LaLilia. Or you'll deal with me, and I'll hurt you far worse than any junky fang." With that she stood up and stomped away from Darnell's limo.

* * * * *

Darnell could swear that Jack T. Nipper must've hit every fuckin' pothole in the road before he finally delivered him to the dentist's office.

"Wait here for me," Darnell barked after he got outta the limo.

He might as well go in and get it over with so he could finally get himself together for his upcoming rumble with Miccio. Not rumble. They were calling it something else. But Darnell and Miccio had history together. Their confrontation was not just about who was gonna run Trenton. It was personal too.

So he'd have to shut up and deal. Wanda the Wise would have his head if he messed up with the dentist. Miccio would have his head if he didn't get his shit together.

Wanda'd told him the chick's name was LaLilia Guitry. Pretty name for a woman doing ugly work. He stepped into the darkened lobby of the building and looked for a directory. He started reading the names of the people in the offices and didn't find no LaLilia Guitry. He was just about to read a second time when a musical voice asked, "Are you Darnell DeLouis?"

Darnell looked about warily for a second. Then, despite his enormous agony, he almost grinned. Must be the dentist's nurse down to greet him, give him a proper escort up to her office. He liked this.

He more than liked the gorgeous fox smiling at him like an angel. Shit, he must be far gone to think an *angel* would be coming over to personally escort him up to the dentist. That's what he got for reading love poems. Here he was now, thinking of foxes as friggin' angels. But he couldn't shake that thought.

Tall and built like a lingerie model, this angel looked a lot like Halle Berry and smelled the way he imagined Halle would, like some prize roses spiced with cinnamon and vanilla. Her skin reminded him of coffee served just right, and she had the biggest, brownest eyes, like two pools of fine chocolate he'd give his left nut to fall into. She wore a filmy, fluffy white gown, like a cloud, that clung in all the right places and covered just enough to, despite his pain, get him hard. And then he caught sight of what he could swear were angel wings coming outta her back—which was when Darnell began to suspect that maybe he'd lost a few marbles from sheer agony.

Shit. Talk about a fantasy. But if this was a hallucination, he wanted more of whatever shit would take him here again.

He shook his head to get it clear.

"Pleased to meet you, Darnell."

She even sounded like Halle. Her voice curled 'round him like a mellow sax. Darnell couldn't help himself. To see if she was real, he pulled on a wing and, by accident, pinched her. He expected her to disappear into thin air. Instead, she furrowed her gorgeous brow and said, "Ow. Why'd you do that?"

She was real. Even with the angel wings. Holy shit, she was *real*. This gorgeous babe was really here with him. Unless he'd died and gone to heaven, done in by a killer cavity.

Only he couldn't be dead because his friggin' jaw hurt too much. A tear rolled down Darnell's cheek. He clawed that sucker away.

Which meant the gorgeous babe next to him wasn't just a delusion. She was here, beside him. Now. "Fuck, uh, shit." Darnell nearly hit himself upside the head. Not the way to talk to an angel. He searched his head. "Look, I'm s-s-sorry." Shit. He never said that word. He put his hand out, wanting to tell her he didn't know what the fuck he was saying or doing. "Never seen nobody like you before. Wanted see if you were real."

She bit her lip and lowered her lids. "You pulled really hard, and that pinched. My wings are firmly attached to me." She rubbed her back, and he wanted to kiss her there and make it all better. He wanted to kiss her everywhere.

But he didn't want to piss her off more. He let his eyes get all big like he used to when he was a kid caught with his hand where it shouldn't be. "Please, Angel. Bad as my fang feels, I'll feel worse if you don't forgive me."

She put her hands over her heart, on one of them perfect breasts, and Darnell's cock damn near wiggled out of his pants. "Well, I guess I'll have to forgive you when you ask so nicely."

She let him off the hook. Darnell smiled with his whole body. "Who are you?"

She laughed, sounding like a fine crystal bell and revealing magnificent white teeth. "Now I must ask you to forgive me," she said, extending a hand. "I'm LaLilia Guitry."

Darnell took her smooth, cool hand in his overheated one and never wanted to let go. Then he swallowed hard. This was the dentist? He shook his head to clear away the cobwebs. He must've heard wrong or something. The toothache was messing with his brains. Could this amazing angel, better than all them slick magazine models, really be the dentist? A hot babe like her couldn't be involved in producing dental pain, could she?

"LaLilia Guitry?" he repeated. "Oh, I thought that was the name of the dentist Wanda got me an appointment with tonight."

LaLilia laughed again. "My dear friend Wanda Muller called and asked me to see you for a very serious problem. I'm happy to be able to accommodate her—and help you." She pressed a button for the elevator, which arrived seconds later.

Darnell's senses were whirling as they rode up. Wanda should've warned him. He felt like some dang idiot, not being prepared for this beauty. Wanda would have his balls on a gold platter if he came on to her friend. Darnell shifted, trying to get his cock into a less compromising position.

A bell dinged and they arrived at the floor with the only office where the lights were on. "Wanda says you have a cavity in your fang. Which one?" LaLilia asked.

Sounded like this dentist didn't have no problem dealing with vampires. LaLilia, some kinda magical creature he couldn't quite figure out, seemed cool about him. Just minutes after meeting her, he was having all kinds of feelings busting out in him. Feelings different from anything since he was a boy, head over heels for Maralise.

* * * * *

LaLilia tried to stay calm as she led Darnell into the office she'd appropriated for tonight. Wanda had warned her that Darnell was a total, shameless womanizer, but why hadn't she also said anything about how magnificent he was? Even with his left cheek swollen and the pain of his cavity distorting his features, he was one tall, dark, hot hunk who had her fantasies standing up and demanding attention. Not to mention other, lower things. She knew about Darnell the warrior from Wanda.

But her heart was shouting loud and clear that she'd just met Darnell the lover.

The lover? She had to get hold of her reeling senses. Most of all, she reminded herself she had a mission beyond healing him. This was not just a simple dental transaction that was about to go down, and Darnell was not the only vampire leader her group was targeting. She had to keep her higher purpose foremost in her mind—even if Darnell brought out instincts that usually resided in much lower regions of her body.

Mind. She had a mind. And Darnell held an important key to what she wanted for the larger community. She'd put so much work and effort into bringing good to the world. Now that she and her companions were finally making some progress, she couldn't let her own feelings and needs get in the way. But something special and deep had clicked for her the moment their eyes met. When she looked at Darnell, LaLilia felt the heat of desire rise and threaten to take over. She could not let herself go there now. Not her. Not LaLilia, who'd never even think of kissing a man 'til she'd known him for one solid month or three dates. But 'til now, she'd never been so intensely attracted to a man she'd just met. *Knees knocking together, eyes crossed, can't breathe* attracted. She had to get in control of herself, immediately.

She took a deep breath, cleared her throat and put on her best professional manner. "Sit back in the chair and I'll take a look at that tooth."

Darnell got into the chair and stretched out stiffly. Talk about stiff. No matter how much he shifted, LaLilia couldn't help seeing his impressive erection tenting out the cream-colored linen slacks of his designer suit. She ran her tongue over her teeth, and imagined she was running her tongue over his cock.

She had to get her mind back on what she was doing. "Are you comfy?" she asked softly.

Darnell shifted in the chair, and she could swear his erection grew even larger. Oh, yeah. Her fingers itched to do a little walking. Instead, she prepared to drape a protective bib around him to protect his beautiful shirt and suit. When she suggested that he take off his jacket, he stood awkwardly. He handed her the jacket, which she put aside neatly. LaLilia bit her lip and struggled to look away from Darnell, whose erection looked ready to take over the world. She helped him back into the chair and said, "Now open your mouth and let me see that fang."

Darnell's eyes grew wide with some emotion—probably fear, but not just that. She patted his cheek to reassure him, and his cock rose up farther. LaLilia suspected things might be getting a tad tight for him down there.

She ran her fingers across his full bottom lip, and electricity shot through her. *You're a professional*, she reminded herself in what had to be her mantra of the night. He opened his mouth wide.

"Oh, yes," she said, touching the fang. "That's some cavity you've got there. I don't understand how you're managing to walk around when it's probably causing you so much pain."

Okay, so she was laying it on a bit thick. But heck, men needed coddling. That was as much part of her job as anything else.

"Are you gonna drill me?" Darnell asked, his words almost impossible to understand.

"I have my own very special methods for filling cavities," she said. "And they don't include shots or drilling. Try to relax."

He moaned incoherently and crossed his legs in a futile attempt to conceal his raging erection.

LaLilia had to rescue him from his pain. She turned his head to her and squatted down so they were eye level with each other. "Now open your mouth as wide as you can," she crooned.

Darnell opened his mouth fractionally wider. She didn't really need him to separate his lips any further, but she did want to get him into the spirit of cooperating with her.

Then LaLilia moved her head directly in front of Darnell and drew closer, ever closer to him. She covered his lips with hers and, extending her tongue, licked his ailing fang with long, slow strokes—once, twice, and a third time.

Darnell started at the first contact of her tongue and his tooth. Then he relaxed into her kiss, and his arms closed around her in a warm embrace that she wished would never end.

Within moments, far too soon, LaLilia knew that she was done, at least as far as healing his cavity went. With the greatest reluctance, she withdrew from Darnell. She'd accomplished the easy part of her task. Now she had to get on to the meat of her mission.

But Darnell was breathing hard. He struggled to hold on to her as she tried to ease herself away from him.

"Baby, tell me you're not going to leave me like this," he said, half sitting up, his erection looking like it would bust his pants open.

Chapter Three

Darnell had experienced many strange things, but none stranger than being treated by this dentist, LaLilia. If he didn't know better, he'd suspect someone'd slipped some crazy weed or drug in his last feed. Or maybe he was on one of them TV reality shows.

Wanda the Wise was always straight with him. She'd set him up with this LaLilia Guitry chick, said she was a for real dentist. But here Darnell had been bracing himself for one of them nasty shots and the drilling and the squirting and all that other shit dentists did.

Not only did LaLilia outfox every fox in town, but this chick bent over him and kissed him. Closest he'd ever been to coming from just a kiss since he became a man. And damn all if his tooth didn't stop hurting! How'd she do that?

Then she began to pull away from him like what she did was nothing, the way she stuck her tongue in his mouth and got up close and intimate with all his teeth, 'specially the bugger that was killing him all night. And now here he was with a hard-on that could shatter concrete. Shoot, she wasn't going nowhere… Not and leave him like this. You'd think a chick who could fix teeth like that would have the friggin' sensitivity or whatever to know what she started.

Hell, the pain of the damn cavity was nothing compared to the blue balls he'd have if she didn't bring herself right on over to where she would do him the most good.

"Hey, baby," he said, clutching on to her like a life preserver. "I like your bedside manner. Let's see some more of it." He shifted uncomfortably. "This ain't a bed, but, hell, we're talkin' *emergency* here."

He thought he saw her bite back a smile, and her face lit up like they were in one of them fancy Bucks County restaurants with the candles and the flowers, instead of a dentist office. If a woman could look good under the ugly lights here, she must be a goddess.

"What is it you want?" LaLilia murmured, sending shivers of desire up and down Darnell's spine. It was like her voice and scent and everything about her was hardwired to his cock.

He groaned. "Oh, baby." He waggled so that she couldn't miss his erection. "I got something here with your name on it."

"Why Darnell, I guess you *are* feeling better," she said, batting her eyelashes at him.

"Oh, yeah," he growled. She was flirting with him. This amazing, classy angel chick was flirting with Darnell DeLouis, who'd come up the hardest way from Trenton's projects. He didn't know what was twitching harder, his heart or his cock. She held his heart, and he didn't know what to do first. All he could think of was to bury his cock so deep in her he'd need a map to find his way out. "The tooth is great. Now there's another part crying out for your loving attention."

"But I'm a dentist," she said coyly. "I'm only trained to take care of teeth."

He grinned now, showing all of his. "Oh, I'll give you all the training you need on taking care of the rest. Why don't you sit your sweet butt down right here on my lap?"

* * * * *

Warning bells and whistles exploded in LaLilia's head. She wanted nothing more than to touch Darnell everywhere, to have him touch her. All her hormones had gone on full alert the moment she locked eyes with him. Needs she'd been suppressing for far too long suddenly clamored for attention.

But getting involved with Darnell, letting romance distract her from her goals now, would derail her mission. She'd made a solemn vow to herself that there'd be no romance and no lovemaking until she could point to a solid success in her peace efforts. And she hadn't even brought up the topic of peace with Darnell, hadn't yet begun to try to convince him not to fight Vinny Miccio. She had her mission, always her mission, to focus on. If any of her companions found out how she'd wanted to spend her private time with the leader of the Trenton Black Guards before they ever spoke of bringing an end to confrontations...

Committed as she was to her ideals, LaLilia could no longer deny her needs. Loving Darnell now was so not what she was supposed to be doing, but her heart urged her to overrule her head. Damn it all, she *wanted* Darnell with every fiber of her being. She'd been too long without a man, and Darnell was just the guy to end her dry spell. Not only was he totally hot, but poetry crackled in the air around him. Like she could just *touch* him and he'd recite Shakespeare's sonnets to her. There had to be a way to have it all. To listen to her heart and fulfill her ideals.

She wanted to kiss Darnell again, this time without any thought of curing his cavity. Seeing and feeling his excitement, her own growing hunger drove her to get satisfaction—fast. She wanted to feel that hard cock deep inside her, touching all her hidden places, pleasuring her 'til she forgot everything but the man and the rhythm and the dance.

* * * * *

Darnell was never one to hold back, but he couldn't believe he'd just made a pass at LaLilia when she still had him in the dentist's chair. Damn, the woman might go ballistic on him and start torturing him with one of the drills. She stepped over to him with a gleam in her eye, and, though he'd face a silver bullet before admitting it, he had a moment's fear. Then, to Darnell's everlasting surprise, relief, and gratitude, LaLilia smiled at him, and his heart did a happy dance. Better than any poetry. He looked down and saw her press a lever with her foot. Next thing he knew, he was lying flat as a tortilla in that chair. His beautiful LaLilia lifted her gown and, putting one long, gorgeous leg over him, straddled him. Through the layers of her gown and his linen pants, her pussy made initial contact with his cock and Darnell nearly flew from the chair.

"Oh, yeah, baby, like that," he said. He closed his eyes for just a moment, but quickly opened them. He didn't want to miss a moment of looking at her. His cock throbbed with desire and joy. He needed to be in her. He wanted to be naked with her, feasting his eyes on her gorgeous body, having full skin-to-skin connection. But the friction between them was so hot, he couldn't bring himself to stop long enough for them to pull their clothes off.

Foreplay. A babe like LaLilia deserved foreplay. Kissing, sucking, all that. But if he didn't get into her soon, he'd come in his pants. And an orgasm like he had building would be a crying shame to shoot off anywhere but deep inside her.

* * * * *

Electric sparks fanned out from where his hands clasped her. He had long fingers, and he moved them on her like a concert star on a grand piano. Now he was thrusting his big, hard cock against her hot, wet pussy in a dry hump that had them both gasping. She stretched out on top of him and fell into his embrace. When she kissed him, he kissed her back, his tongue gaining full entrance to her mouth in long, lingering dances. At the same time, they arched and bucked into each other, their embrace growing tighter by the moment. Every time she moved on top of him, the sensation of his cock against her hungry pussy nearly sent her through the roof.

Darnell broke the kiss and howled, a long, primitive cry of need. "I'm so hungry," he moaned. He licked the sensitive skin of her neck 'til he found the spot to feed on. Ah, yes. She knew he couldn't have fed all night because of his pain, and now her insides clenched with pleasure at the thought of giving him what he so wanted and needed. She wanted to feed him in every way, every dimension. As he sucked the life-giving brew from her, she rubbed her clit against his cock, shuddering with the vibrations flowing through her, a long sustained orgasm. She was ecstatic that she could give him so much at this moment, that with her body and her essence, she could start to show him how deeply he pleasured her. How much she hoped to pleasure him equally. He met her, thrust for thrust as he sucked and licked and ran his tongue over her neck. LaLilia had never felt so connected with another being, and didn't think she could ever feel closer to anyone than she did to Darnell at this moment.

When he'd swallowed the last drop of his breakfast, LaLilia wanted her turn. With a moan of delight, she sank her fangs into him and tasted his essence. Goddess! He was so delicious, her pussy continued to contract with pleasure. Her Darnell was a heady brew of man and leader and lover and more. He writhed with pleasure as she continued to feed, sucking from him and humping him, her body humming with sensuous joy.

With one hunger satisfied, LaLilia was beyond ready to focus on getting naked and getting laid. She moved away from Darnell for just a moment to remove the gown and the tiny silk thong that separated her from her heart's desire. She heard Darnell lower a zipper, sweet music to her ears. She saw him lying in the chair with ten inches of magnificent mahogany manhood standing upright and calling her. He didn't have to call twice.

* * * * *

Man, the pain must've turned him deaf, dumb, and blind How could he not know LaLilia was a vamp 'til she sank her teeth into him? Maybe it was the wings that had distracted and confused him. He'd never met no vampire with no wings before. Her being a vamp-fairy-angel had his head twirling on his shoulders like that kid in that exorcist flick. In all his years loving women, thousands of women, he'd never wanted anyone this much. His stomach clenched with desire. There was nothing in the world he wouldn't do for this woman, nothing he would deny her.

Her pussy wet, hot and tight, LaLilia lowered herself on his cock, and Darnell thought again he'd die from sheer ecstasy. His cock was twitching and throbbing like the sucker had a will of its own. Darnell had never had a problem going 'til a chick was screaming with her climax. But now, with LaLilia, hell, Darnell was ready to come the moment LaLilia opened her legs and slid on down his shaft.

Damn, it was like his first time. She rode him like she was a cowgirl and he was the championship steed she'd waited for all her life. Her luscious thighs pressed against his hips, heating him up everywhere she touched.

"You're one delicious babe," he said. "Where you been hidin' all my life?"

"I'm here now," she panted, doing some circular move with her hips that nearly pushed him over the edge.

"Oh, babe," he said, putting his hand on her amazing ass to try to slow her down for a moment. Being inside her fed his sweet tooth better than any convention of chocolate lovers. But he wanted to make it last, make it memorable for her. So she'd come back to him for more of the sweet stuff. "What you want me to do?"

She did a little jiggle with her pussy. Damn, the woman had muscle control. Must've been a gymnast or something. "You just keep on giving me all that delicious cock," she said, rippling her muscles.

"Any place special you want me to touch you?" he asked hoarsely. Damn, he'd never talked so much while he was screwin' anyone. But somehow with her, he wanted it to be right. Making love, like they said in the poems. For once, he didn't take it for granted that the fox would have a screeching orgasm.

He ran his hands up and down her back, touching her wings over and over. She groaned when he tugged on them.

The wings felt soft and hard at the same time, kind of like a solid feather if such a thing could be. Fluffy but firm. Rubbing her wings hypnotized him, fascinated him, and he wanted to touch her more. From the way she fluttered them and tightened her legs around him, he could tell LaLilia liked the way he stroked her there.

They only freaked him out slightly. Mostly them wings turned him on like everything else about her.

* * * * *

LaLilia's pussy vibrated like a bell around Darnell's cock. A dentist's chair was hardly the most conducive setting for having hot, steamy sex, but none of that mattered to her. For her time with him, LaLilia let go of everything but the sensation of him filling her. The man knew how to hit every hot button she had, from the top of her head to the edges of her wings. She rode him, fulfilling every fantasy, giving herself up to the swirling stars and lights and sensations flooding her. In moments she was climbing to her climax, one that would have her swinging from the dental apparatus attached to the ceiling.

"Yes, yes, yes," she called out, slamming herself ever harder against him, willing his cock deeper into her. And then she burst apart, calling his name, gasping with her relief.

"Oh, baby," Darnell said, his head moving back and forth. And then she felt him empty himself deep inside her, joining her in the very special place that belonged to just the two of them. The place they'd just created together.

Spent, she bent down to nuzzle him, feeling the super-sensitized warmth that only feeding and sex could produce in their kind.

For now, she felt so close to him, closer than anyone else in the whole world. Surely she could say anything to him, tell him all that was in her heart. Someone who could love her like this in a dentist's chair—it was hard to believe that he could bring himself to deny her anything she might ask of him. Or that she could deny him anything, which made her very vulnerable to him.

Their hearts hammered in harmony, breath mingling along with bodily fluids. LaLilia longed to just spend the hours of the night lying here, depleted, on top of Darnell. But the dentist's chair had to be growing uncomfortable for the poor guy, who'd been stuck on the bottom.

And duty called. LaLilia had to extricate herself from him to move on to her real work, what had brought her to use her special skills on Darnell DeLouis tonight.

Their lovemaking was an extra, unanticipated bonus. But, after all, before being a vampire and a dentist with a mission, LaLilia was a woman. Sometimes in taking care of one identity, she neglected the other.

Tonight, she'd fed all three.

Darnell made it impossible to think about being with other men. Surely they'd be able to be together again. Surely he'd hear her mission and agree go along with it.

"Oh, baby," Darnell groaned and shifted. "Uh, great as this is, I've gotta move or I'll have the seam between the seat and the back rest permanently engraved on my butt."

Stifling a chuckle at the image, LaLilia slid off him. She'd gotten so caught up in her own thoughts, she'd pressed him down in the seat far too long. But nothing could ruin the perfection of his glorious butt.

* * * * *

Darnell hated LaLilia moving away from him. He wished he could just stay here with her all night. Now that he was feeling better and could think clearly, he had to plan out exactly what was going to happen in three nights when he met with Miccio. He'd already lost too much time. Not that he considered anything that happened tonight with the lovely LaLilia a waste of time, but he had responsibilities. He couldn't just think about his own pleasure.

Still, it wasn't like he never had no time for himself. He had to see LaLilia again. And next time, it wouldn't be in any friggin' dentist's office.

In moments, LaLilia had herself together, her dress smoothed, and her hair perfect. He wouldn't have thought it possible, but she looked even more beautiful now than before. Darnell's cock began to stir again.

He reluctantly got dressed. He glanced at his watch. Just past one. Maybe he'd take her home, and they could make love on a real bed. Just the thought of being with her, both of them naked, had him fully erect again.

"I want to see you again, baby. Let me take you home."

"I want to see you again, too, Darnell."

He grinned. "So I'll take you home."

She shook her head. "I've got work to do tonight."

He scowled. "I thought you finished your work when you fixed my fang." He bit down on his teeth and smiled. "Great job."

"Thank you. But that's just a bit of what I do."

"Really? What else do you do?" he asked.

"I'm a tooth fairy."

He opened his eyes wide. "No shit?"

"No sh-sh-shit," she said, stumbling a bit over the word.

He'd figured out she was some kind of fairy, but the *tooth* fairy? Come on. Maybe she was playing some game with him. Or maybe she was a little demented, having some kind of dentist fantasy... Nah. He preferred to think she was playing with him. No way could she continue to fool him for long. "What you mean *a* tooth fairy? I always heard about *the* tooth fairy." Darnell figured if he kept her talking he'd be able to get his head around what she was saying.

"I know. A common misunderstanding. But think about all the children all over the world who lose teeth every day."

"Yeah."

"How could one fairy possibly pick all those teeth up?"

"Good point. But what about Santa Claus? He gets all over the world in just one night."

She smiled at him like she knew the biggest fuckin' secret in the world. "I'll never tell."

She had to be playin' him, right? "Come on, babe. You can tell me."

She shook her head. "You can ask me about anything else, and I'll try my best to answer. But not about Santa Claus."

Darnell let it go. He figured this was just part of LaLilia's act, and he kinda dug it. He'd go along for now. "You're right. Never thought much about it, but you're right. I won't kid you," he admitted. "I never believed in the tooth fairy. Hell, when I was a little guy and stuck my baby tooth under my pillow, all I woke up with the next day was my brothers laughin' at me."

"No one left you anything?" Her eyes flashed with what he'd swear was anger.

He held up his hand. "If anyone ever did, my big brothers woulda taken off with it so fast, my fool head woulda spun."

She shook her head. "Sounds like some fairy wasn't doing her job right. Whoever came by should have made sure you got a gift for your tooth."

He felt a spasm of warmth, imagining what it would have been like to have someone like LaLilia come to his family's crummy little apartment and give out anything. Then he drew himself up and shook away the melting sensation. "Whatever. I like the way you tell it. I'm always a sucker for a good story. And lady, you tell great stories."

She looked sad. "It's not just a great story. I'm telling you the truth."

"I believe you," Darnell said because he didn't want her to be sad. He couldn't get his head 'round all she was saying. He'd pulled on her wings again when they made love and knew they were real. Damned if he could figure that one out. Could vamps have wings surgically attached? Maybe he'd get her to tell him all about it some time. "But I never knew a vampire could be a tooth fairy."

"Duh," she said. He didn't like that because he hated feeling dumb. "*All* the tooth fairies are vampires. You know, we work at night."

"Still sounds like Santa Claus." She frowned at him. Somewhere down deep inside himself, he started to suspect maybe she wasn't lying even a little bit. Shit, everybody he knew, except Wanda, lied some. Most people lied lots. But this woman didn't seem like no liar. To cover his confusion, he chuckled. "Makes perfect sense." He put his arms around her and kissed her. Hell, a woman like that could tell him she was anyone she wanted to be. "So my lady dentist vampire, LaLilia, how'd you become a tooth fairy?"

Now she smiled. "Long story, my friend."

"I've got all night for you." He put his arms around her and pulled her down on the chair next to him.

"But I have to get going soon." She nuzzled his neck, and Darnell got hopeful. "I'll just tell you the short version."

"I'm all ears, baby."

She nuzzled him. "When I was a little girl, I wanted to be a dentist. Used to play dentist with all my friends and even tried to fix my dog Pumpkin's teeth."

Darnell chuckled. "That probably made you real unpopular."

She nodded. "Yeah." She shivered. "I was real lucky the dog was old and a gentle one, or he'd have messed me up real bad after I tried to 'fix' his teeth." She shook her head and laughed. "I used to walk around with some pliers and a gleam in my eye. Funny how fast my friends and even, eventually, Pumpkin, would run when they saw me. Pretty soon, I figured out that no one wanted to see me if I was going to hurt them. So I decided I'd grow up to be the world's most painless dentist."

"And that you are," he said, running his hand over his previously aching jaw.

"Thank you." She smiled. "Couldn't learn what I wanted to at dental school. I was working as a dentist, still not doing too well on the painless part, when I became a vampire. Lucky for me, the tooth fairies heard about my dentistry. The head fairy recruited me, and here I am."

She sighed and got up. "Much as I'm enjoying this, I have to leave now." Was Darnell imagining things or did she look sad? No way could he stand to think of LaLilia being sad. Not when he could put his arms 'round her and...

He stood up next to her and put his hands on her shoulders, looked deep into her beautiful eyes. "There's no way I can take you home tonight?" Hell, no chick ever turned him down when he looked her in the eyes like that.

She stood up real tall, but he still held on. "I'm afraid not. Can't disappoint the kiddies."

Darnell wasn't normally one to back off. But LaLilia talking about her work reminded him he had stuff to deal with back at the social hall. "I can dig it. Hell, I got my own duties calling. And I got some deep shit happening in a just a few nights. But tell you what. Gimme your address and phone number. I wanna see you again. Soon."

She nodded. "I want to see you again, too, Darnell."

Darnell wanted to give a whoop. But LaLilia was classy, so he acted calm, like some preppie dude from Princeton. "Great. So where do you call home?"

She shook her head. "Not so fast. I have something I need to talk to you about before we can make any plans together."

Darnell didn't like the sound of that. But he figured he could sweet talk her into doing what he wanted. Besides, what the hell else could she possibly say that was any more unbelievable than her tooth fairy story? "I'm listening, babe."

She took a deep breath. "If you want to see me again, you have to give up any plans for fighting with any other creatures, especially fellow vampires." She swallowed hard. "All the world's tooth fairies are people of peace. And the only people we can ever let into our lives are other people of peace."

That got his attention. "What? People of peace? What you talkin' 'bout, woman?" Darnell moved away from her like she was splashed with skunk spray.

LaLilia seemed to stand even taller than before. "Just what I said. If you want to see me again, you have to commit yourself to bringing peace to the world. Starting with your corner of it, in Trenton."

"You're crazy," he spluttered. He managed not to say the C word when she told him she was a tooth fairy, but he couldn't keep his mouth shut no more. "You don't know what you're talkin' about." Darnell could not believe it. He just met and bedded, well at least chaired, the most fabulous woman in the universe, and she turned out to be a fuckin' loony tune. As if anything on earth could convince him, chief of the Black Guards, the most elite vampires in Trenton, to turn into some friggin' peace nut. Even the best piece he ever had. A nasty suspicion dawned. Was Wanda in cahoots with this LaLilia chick? Wanda was always yapping about peace for all vampires. He always tuned that out. A vampire leader couldn't listen to that sort of propaganda.

But he couldn't so easily dismiss LaLilia, not after what passed between them. And she couldn't have no idea what was at stake. He shivered at the thought of a stake. Felt like she had one in prime position smack over his balls.

"If you won't commit yourself to my cause, you'll never see me again." She locked her lips in a straight line.

A light went on, burning like a killer dose of sunshine. His brain must've been fogged with too much pain before, but now he was thinking just fine, thank you very much. "I get it," Darnell said, his voice low and gravelly. "The Cosa Nostras set you up. They sent you to get me outta the picture." He scowled. "Not their usual style. You should've run the dentist drill through my heart or something. Would've been friendlier and more honest." He looked at her, all his disillusionment full in his eyes. "Hell, maybe they figured out a way to give me that cavity to begin with."

LaLilia folded her arms in front of her, and her wings fluttered in a slight breeze as the air conditioning kicked in and chilled the room. "I'm not from the Cosa Nostras or any other group except the tooth fairies. And we love peace. I told you who I am."

"The tooth fairy," he growled.

"*A* tooth fairy," she countered.

"Hah. And now it's the tooth fairy's job to break up top level vampire meetings?"

She pursed her luscious lips. "It's our job to gather discarded teeth. We love picking up the ones little kids slip under their pillows and leaving them small gifts. But we hate collecting the teeth people lose through violence. We're tired of it, and we're going to make it stop. And, if your top level leader meeting is going to end up in someone losing their teeth or anything else, I want you to pull out."

He laughed his I-can't-believe-the-shit-I-just-heard laugh. "You have no idea what you're saying."

"All I know is I want people to stop beating each other up. It means the world to me, more than anything else."

"More than me?" He looked at her through narrowed eyes.

"I'm totally committed to the cause of peace," she said, her chin jutting out.

Damn, she still looked hotter than any other chick ever. "Well, lady, you sure ain't gonna start that peace shit with me. Now give me your phone number and cut the crap."

A single tear rolled down LaLilia's cheek. "I'll miss you, Darnell." With that she threw some sparkly crap into the air. When Darnell could see again, she was gone. Disappeared. He wiped his eyes hard, but still no LaLilia.

Fuck, shit, damn. Darnell ached now, almost as bad as when his fang hurt. But this pain was different. Well, hell. He didn't need to get involved with no loony like LaLilia Guitry, no matter how great screwing her was.

A woman like that was too demanding, too complex. A real ballbuster. Why couldn't gorgeous women be...simpler?

Imagine thinking she had the right to dictate to him and convert him into being some peace nut like her.

There were a million dames out there. Couldn't get bent outta shape over one. That's how good men ended up fucked. He was better off without her. Except somewhere inside he knew he wasn't.

Darnell's bellow echoed in the empty medical building. He punched the pager to signal Jack T. Nipper to come pick him up. He had to get home and begin coming up with his strategy for his confrontation with Miccio.

He'd meet with Wanda. She was hell on wheels for coming up with strategy even if she did have some weird ideas about peace.

And he was sure she'd know how to get in touch with LaLilia. Pissed as he was right now about LaLilia, his gut told him that he'd see her again. It would have to be on his terms. He couldn't let himself get soft thinking about LaLilia or peace... Shit, he should probably get rid of his poetry calendar. Reading them poems was making him open up to thoughts of peace and not having to fight and all.

He pushed those dangerous thoughts out of his mind. He was chief of the Black Guards, ready to lead his men in any battle, the more dangerous the better.

LaLilia was a woman. He was a man who knew his way around women. He'd see her again, on his terms.

Right?

Chapter Four

Wanda finished checking email and was just about to make a phone call when Darnell stormed in. She heard him snarl at poor Jack about something to do with the limo. She'd have to make sure to talk to the browbeaten chauffeur soon, tell him Darnell's bad temper was not his fault. Maybe she'd give Jack some nasty herbal brew to coat his nails with, keep him from chewing them down past the cuticles. From the way Darnell sounded, Wanda feared that tonight hadn't gone well. Well, she'd find out shortly. Darnell never kept anything from her.

"Why'd you set me up with that nut case?" Darnell bellowed when he came into Wanda's office.

She was not about to take any garbage from him, tonight or any other night, toothache or whatever excuse he had for his bad attitude—and he'd better realize that real fast. "Excuse me? Were you addressing me?" she asked in her serious schoolteacher voice.

He rolled his eyes, which meant he knew he'd better back down. Mentally tapping her foot, Wanda waited him out. She was not a patient woman, but she knew how to fake it.

"What the hell's up with that LaLilia chick, Wanda?"

Not exactly an apology, but she'd take it for now. "What exactly do you mean? Didn't she fix your tooth?" No vibrations of physical pain emanated from him.

"Yeah. But what's with all the tooth fairy shit?"

She shook her head. "That's the real deal, bro. She's a bona fide tooth fairy. Actually she's a leader of the tooth fairy union— someone you don't want to mess with."

"The tooth fairies have a union?" His voice rose in disbelief.

"A pretty tight one," Wanda said. "They usually keep pretty quiet, just go about doing their job and no one notices. But they are organized, and they're serious about doing their job."

"So you say." Darnell looked skeptical. "I repeat. Why the hell did you ever send me to a cuckoo like her?"

"If you'll remember correctly, just a few hours ago, you were hollering from a toothache. Well, the tooth fairies are the best dentists in the universe. A vamp needs to be a master dentist before she can even apply to be a tooth fairy. She did fix your tooth with no pain, right?"

"Right," Darnell admitted. "But then she went into some song and dance about me becoming a peace nut like her and not fightin' nobody no more. Made me think she knew about me and Miccio havin' plans..."

"You're not telling me everything, are you?" Wanda looked hard at him.

"Hey. Some things are privileged."

"Right," she said. Well, she should have suspected that Darnell would get LaLilia into the sack. Wanda was about the only female who could resist Darnell. Thank the goddess. She saw what he did to the women who became his lovers. She put up her hands. "I don't want to know. But trust me on this, bro. Everything she said and did is the truth. And you'd best not cross her or the tooth fairies. Sounds like you got off on the wrong foot with her."

"I wouldn't put it that way exactly." His eyes took on a dreamy cast. "We were *great* together 'til she started makin' unreasonable demands." He scowled. "Say, Wanda. How the hell did she even know about Miccio?"

Wanda's policy of Darnell handling included keeping him informed on a need-to-know basis only. She'd decided he didn't need to know about her conferring with LaLilia before she'd treated him. But now that Darnell asked directly, she couldn't hold back. "I told LaLilia about what your work as chief of the Black Guards involves. And that includes what you're doing right now, such as getting ready to meet in battle with Vinny Miccio."

He frowned. "Why'd you need to tell her that? No dentist asks for that kinda information."

She shrugged. "Because she's not an ordinary dentist. She especially needed to know your medical history and your condition, including any sources of current stress. And let's face it, you're stressing all over Trenton and Lower Bucks about facing off with Miccio."

Darnell beetled his brows together. "Am not."

"Yes, you are, my friend. And I'm with LaLilia on this one. Call it off. The time has come for the Black Guards and the Cosa Nostras to stop fighting and give some of that energy to spreading peace. Would sure make Trenton a better place to live. For everyone."

"Wanda, is that you?" he asked in horror. "Or did some friggin' aliens come down from space and take over your body?"

"Ha ha. They say you're never too old to learn. Well, Darnell, look around you. Trenton's plenty big enough for us and the Cosa Nostras. No reason to butt heads with them or anyone else."

In response, Darnell threw back his handsome head and guffawed, a sound she totally didn't appreciate. Well, they'd see who'd get the last laugh on this one.

* * * * *

After a night spent reviewing Wanda's notes on Miccio and his preferred methods of operation, weapons of choice, and style of fighting, Darnell was more than ready for a day's rest in his king-size, deluxe, top-of-the-line coffin. Now that his tooth didn't hurt, he'd be able to get a deep rest so he'd be fully ready to start getting serious about the confrontation to come. Only two more nights before he and Miccio mixed it up.

Just before dawn, Darnell stretched out his arms and legs on the fine imported black silk and velvet lining the ebony wood coffin. Felt good to be home. He ran his hand over the lining, making sure his love poems calendar was hidden in its spot. He allowed himself only one poem a day, when he arose. But tonight he was tempted to break his rule and read the next day's selection. Then he thought of LaLilia, and the responsible leader in him said he'd best not let himself get too mushy. Though he'd have liked to. He purposely buried the love poems deeper in the lining, but couldn't help wondering how LaLilia's eyes would look if he read a poem to her. He wasn't one to bring many of his foxes to his coffin. Figured a man's home was his castle. Couldn't remember the last time he shared his rest with a lover. His cock stirred. LaLilia was different. He'd invite LaLilia to sleep in his coffin in a heartbeat. And he'd share his poems with her. If he ever saw her again.

LaLilia made him think things he'd never thought about before. Like how he'd seen his brothers get all goofy about their ladies. Buying their ladyloves flowers and chocolates and shit like that when they couldn't afford a decent pair of shoes for their selves. Acting like Romeo all gaga over Juliet, like there was only one woman in the world for them. Darnell would never, repeat that, *never*, let any female get to him like that. A warm feeling spiraled 'round his heart, and he wriggled it away.

Wanda the Wise would know how to get in touch with LaLilia. Damn that Wanda. First she put him contact with LaLilia. Now, after their disagreement, he knew Wanda would sooner chew nails than give him LaLilia's phone number. Damn woman could be so hardheaded. Served him right for having a chick, one he'd never balled and, lord have mercy, would never want to, as his chief advisor. Gave her ideas. An attitude. He'd have to figure out how to get 'round Wanda on this one. Hell, Wanda'd never been able to keep him away from what he wanted for long. All he had to do was think hard on it... Exhausted, he closed his eyes and fell into a deep sleep...

* * * * *

LaLilia liked to think of herself as a woman of ethics. She and her tooth fairy partner, Sofia Frangela, had made a pact to stick to the highest possible standards of behavior—even exceeding the code they'd both sworn to. They'd also agreed to bring peace to Trenton within a strict time limit, before the DeLouis-Miccio confrontation. If LaLilia and Sofia didn't succeed tonight, other tooth fairies would take over this territory. Sofia and she would be reassigned somewhere less challenging—like Wyoming—so they could better develop their skills.

Normally, LaLilia wouldn't tolerate trickery, even for a good cause. But desperate times called for desperate measures. She and Sofia didn't want to be reassigned. More importantly, she wanted to bring peace to Trenton. And now she had the added desire to be with Darnell. Summoning up Tooth Fairy powers, she would send Darnell a dream to start him on the path to peace.

She had to focus all her energy, imagination, and will onto Darnell—who was hardly an easy target for her dream. But she was determined. Once LaLilia began to spin the dream, she turned her thoughts to Darnell and opened his mind to her. She breathed deeply, feeling Darnell lower his barriers and join the dream. Soon, she would transport herself to the dream and live it with him. Part of the magic was living this experience during daylight hours, when both of them rested. For their joint dream, it would be a very special night.

As she mentally sent dream dust to Darnell and showered him with it, LaLilia had a rare moment's hesitation. She wasn't completely sure dream-spiriting Darnell away was the best way to get him to embrace peace. She was still aware enough to know that, on the topic of Darnell, she wasn't seeing clearly at all. But after conferring with Sofia and meditating, she hadn't been able to come up with a better plan. Maybe she shouldn't have been so emphatic the night before when she gave Darnell her ultimatum. Too late to second guess herself on that. She hoped by sharing a very special dream with him, she could get him to listen to reason.

In the mode of her dream self, LaLilia loved watching Darnell at rest. What could be more intimate than sharing this vulnerable moment? If she had wish magic, LaLilia would have asked for future chances to be this intimate with him. It might never happen again. For now it took all her self-control and her dedication to her mission not to jump his bones, forget everything else, and just love him right there in his coffin.

Though not a tooth fairy, Wanda had become one of LaLilia's staunchest allies in the drive for peace. Wanda told her Darnell's schedule was so full, even in his rest he'd probably be obsessed with all he had to do. But to LaLilia's gratification, the moment he saw her, he'd just cleared his mind and turned all his attention to her. Now if only she could convince him so easily to abandon his confrontation with Vinny Miccio.

* * * * *

Next thing Darnell knew, he was covered with that sparkly shit LaLilia blinded him with last night. Only this time, he wasn't blind. He saw clear as if he was in full sunlight, but he couldn't believe his eyes. LaLilia came to him in his coffin. She swirled on down to where he was lying and, her voice all sultry and sweet just the way he liked it, invited him to fly away with her.

Darnell laughed out loud. Deep down inside, no matter what she'd said before, he'd known she'd come to him. He also *knew* he had to get ready for Miccio. But now that he felt back to his old self, he'd be able to beat Miccio's ass in no time. 'Specially knowing he had a hot fox like LaLilia waiting on him for after.

But the real truth was, he couldn't say no to LaLilia. 'Cept when she went into her craziness about him being a peace nut. But he wanted her so much, he'd forgive her. The sound of LaLilia's voice, a whiff of her mysterious scent, and his cock was granite hard. She held his hand, flapping her wings in smooth, rhythmic sweeps as they flew up together 'cross the night. Stars gleamed white and brilliant above them in the ink black sky. Though he was a powerful flyer—even without wings—he almost never left the ground. Now he wondered why. Just 'cause he was so busy, leading the Black Guards... Hell, he was tired of making excuses for not having a life. LaLilia reminded him of a whole other side he'd been neglecting...

* * * * *

LaLilia loved flying over Trenton with Darnell's hand in hers. She knew he could fly on his own, but using her wings made the trip more romantic than just relying on out and out vampiric flight. His hand felt solid, warm, electric. His palm touching hers sent streams of electricity shooting through her. And she loved sneaking peeks at his erection, which seemed to be a permanent feature when he was with her. She admitted to herself that his prominent, persistent love muscle was one of those features that kept her appreciative.

It was so exceptionally clear that even above a place with urban pollution like Trenton, the stars shone a bright, crystal white and the crescent of a new moon glittered with the delicious promise of romance. She flew them higher than they needed to be to bask in the starlight and moonbeams, to take some time to play.

"What's this, we flying via the North Pole?" Darnell protested.

"Just wanted to check out some of my favorite stars with you," LaLilia said.

"Babe, you're my one and only favorite star," he said, drawing her near and closing his full soft lips on hers. LaLilia's heart grew to what felt like twice its normal size when Darnell kissed her as they floated among the stars together.

"Teeth feeling okay?" she asked when they broke apart.

"Baby, everything feels A-okay when I'm with you. Now no more of that dentist talk, hear?"

He cut off her response with another kiss. With surprising gentleness for such a big, energetic guy, his tongue explored her waiting mouth. And then he grew more insistent, asking her to meet his desire and open herself to him. She longed to be his in every possible sense of the word. Before anything more passed between them, she needed to satisfy her basic hunger—and she could feel his own thirst grow. He trailed his kisses down from her lips to her neck, where he sank his fangs deep into her, and, like bolts of lightning shattering the night sky, she came and came while he drank. All the while her pussy clenched and unclenched, pulsing in the rising pleasure she was drowning in. This was Darnell, elegant, masterful Darnell, deep in her arms and her body. Her excitement spurred him on, and he humped his magnificent erection hard against her as he sucked her blood.

Nearly passed out from the force of her orgasm, LaLilia sighed when Darnell regretfully pulled away from her. He buried his face in her breasts for just a moment, and then she had to take her turn. She cupped his chin in her hands and looked him deep in his big, dark eyes. And then she sank her fangs into his neck and savored the flow of his blood into her, her clitoris vibrating with the sheer pleasure of having him fill her senses. As she drank, he pressed himself against her and stroked the back of her head with those long, magical fingers, probing her most sensitive spots. Sated at last for blood, now she wanted him inside her.

"I want you, LaLilia. Here. Now," he growled.

And oh, did she want him. But she wanted to play with him before they got down to the serious business of getting his hard cock into her soft, wet pussy.

"Just like that, Darnell?" she asked teasingly.

"Exactly like that," he growled, taking her hand and rubbing his cock with it.

"Think you can catch me and make it happen?" she asked, pushing away from him and starting to fly high above him.

"In a New York minute." He lunged after her. She knew her wings gave her an extra burst of speed and strength for her flying, and if she wanted to, she could outfly him.

As if she seriously would want to elude him. Her mama didn't raise no dummy.

But a few minutes of hide and seek among the stars and moonshine wouldn't hurt anything. Didn't anticipation make the heart grow fonder and maybe the erection even harder?

On the other hand, there was no sense overdoing a good thing. LaLilia found a soft, friendly cloud and perched on it waiting for Darnell to catch her.

And once he had in her in his arms, it was clear this man was not about to let go. He held her to him, only releasing her long enough to peel away her lavender gown and sandals. He was taking off his own immaculate linen suit when he suddenly asked, "Uh, what about our clothes?"

"What do you mean?" she asked, though she knew.

"What do we do with our clothes?"

"Just put them down here on the cloud. They'll be fine."

For a moment, he looked as if he doubted that she knew what she was talking about. And then he shrugged, did a world record strip, and, following her lead, laid his clothes down on the cloud.

Thankful for the strength of her vampiric vision, LaLilia feasted her eyes on Darnell, who had to be one of the most magnificent specimens ever created. Tall, dark, with muscles in all the right places, his body tapered from broad shoulders to the slender hips of a tango-dancing gigolo. And his cock. Well, no wonder he had the ladies lined up and waiting at the Black Guards' Social Hall.

And, for tonight, he was all hers.

He ran those magnificent hands up and down her body, making LaLilia feel like the most beautiful creature he'd ever seen or touched.

"I want to look at you, baby, but if I don't get inside you soon, I'll bust," he said hoarsely.

Well, she wasn't about to let that happen. LaLilia rolled over onto her back and opened her legs to him. Darnell covered her body with his. His cock lingered for a moment at the opening between her pussy lips, and then he slid right in as she wound her long legs around him.

Goddess, he was one incredible man. He thrust into her, setting her clitoris and her entire passage alive with sheer sensation. LaLilia chewed on her lip so as not to scream out her delight at the way he moved in her. She was able to wedge her hand in the tiny space between them and cup his balls, two delicious, full taut sacs that reminded her of the ripest, sweetest fruit. Before this dream night faded into dawn, she would have to taste his balls, lick the full length of his thick, hot cock. But now she gave herself over to the rhythm of their dance of pleasure.

Darnell ran his tongue over her lips, licking and sucking his way into her mouth. He tasted like every dream she'd ever had come true. For just a moment, thoughts of her mission intruded on the magic they were making together. And then she banished the thoughts and turned her full focus on the way he was loving her — and she was loving him right back.

"Baby, what do you want?" he asked hoarsely.

"Just what you're doing," she whispered back. After the way she'd come when he fed off her, she couldn't believe she had another huge come in her. But now she felt herself beginning to tighten, building toward an orgasm that was going to shoot off the top of her head.

Darnell raised up his hips and thrust into her with such strength that the two of them toppled off the cloud where they'd lain entwined and began to swirl through the sky like a deranged shooting star. As they whirled and flew, LaLilia clung ever tighter to Darnell, opening herself up deep inside. And then she felt herself start to tremble and cry out as she began a climax that would shake the heavens. Darnell was right there with her, thrusting himself into her like he'd never let her go, calling her name out to the sky and stars.

Spent at last, the two of them clung together as they half-flew, half-fell back to their cloud.

She'd have loved to stay there all night, or should she say day, with him. But now that they'd both fed and loved, she really couldn't postpone her duties any longer. Not to mention her mission. Regretfully, she drew away from him and dressed. He quickly followed suit. LaLilia felt a twinge of regret, fearing that she'd never again experience the sort of joy they shared on their cloud. But other needs beckoned now.

* * * * *

"Where're you takin' me now?" Darnell asked, wondering what else this amazing woman had in store for him. Not that whatever she said could possibly be a deal buster. He'd go anywhere for her and with her. 'Cept for that peace shit. But her being with him tonight must mean she gave up on that.

"I want you to come with me while I do my tooth fairy work," she said, her wings moving up and down in smooth arcs.

Darnell swallowed a flash of disappointment. He'd been hoping for something more romantic, more in keeping with the way the two of them had just been together. Hell, he'd been hoping for a bed or a blanket out in the woods over on the Pennsy side of the river. How were they ever gonna top being on that cloud? No sense trying. Shit, he'd even go back to the friggin' dentist's chair to be with her. But she wasn't talking about more loving now. She wanted to take him to do her work. Well, maybe it wasn't exactly romantic, but LaLilia was telling him she wanted him around. He wasn't about to turn down any chance to be with her. They'd start with her work and end up where he wanted to be. Darnell's lips curled up into a big old smile. The night he wasn't man enough to get her into the sack, he'd just curl up and die—again.

The tinkle of her laughter made him wonder if she could read his mind. Not that what he wanted was hidden. Within minutes, he was good to go again with another hard-on. Hell, with an erection like this one, that had her name written on it in big sparkly letters, he'd be in trouble if he had to try to hide his intentions from anyone.

"Where're you workin' tonight?" he asked, hoping she wouldn't be dragging his ass all over creation. What if she was going to take him to another dentist's office and stand by while she took care of a patient? Darnell didn't think he could handle that, especially if she treated the next guy the way she had him…

LaLilia gazed up at him from under long lashes, her eyes like two pools of expensive dark chocolate. "It's a slow night for me."

"What does that mean?"

She grinned. "Later I have other plans for us."

Darnell perked up at her words and the message of her eyes, and his cock did a happy dance. *Glory's coming again soon, and you will too.* "What's a slow night, sugar?"

"You're calling a dentist sugar?" she asked, her voice sounding like she was pissed. But he could see the twinkle in her eyes. She dropped his hand and flew ahead of him, whirling around clouds and moonbeams like she was an Olympic ice skater. He could keep up with her, but he didn't look nearly as good. And there weren't many situations where he'd admit that.

"Did I say sugar? Shoot, you're a million times sweeter than that old stuff," he said, when he was next to her again.

She rolled her eyes. "Lucky I like you, Darnell."

"Shows you got good taste."

"No modesty there," she said, pulling him into one of her fancy maneuvers, taking him in loops and circles and some designs he didn't know the name of. "I've got only two teeth to collect tonight. They're both right here in Trenton. After that, I have all night to be with you."

Oh, he definitely liked the sound of that. Two teeth in Trenton—didn't sound like no big job to get them. And then they could be with each other 'til dawn. "My territory," he said. "Me and my boys can take care of you anywhere in Trenton and the 'burbs." He frowned. "Least wise, we'll be able to once I take care of Miccio."

She didn't respond, just sped up her flight with him across the sky. Before tonight, he'd been outta practice with his flying. He could see with a chick like LaLilia, he'd better keep in top shape in everything.

"Here's my first pick up," she said, drawing him back down to earth. They stopped at a house in Hiltonia, the old west end of the city with big houses, lawns, and gardens. "Six-year old Antwan MacRae lost his first tooth. Snuck a cookie from the cookie jar, and the tooth came out when he took his first bite. Poor kid was so scared, he didn't want to tell his mom."

"It says all that there?" he asked, pointing to PDA she took out of her bag and consulted.

She nodded. "All that and more. You ready to go into the house?"

Darnell considered. "Won't the little guy pee his bed when he sees us?"

LaLilia shook her head. "Thank you for thinking about that. But no, I'll spread some special fairy dust to make sure no one in the house wakes up and sees us."

"Fairy dust?" Darnell echoed, trying not to smirk and losing the battle. Sounded like a bad joke.

"Give me a break," LaLilia said, her lips pursed. "And behave yourself, or I'll send you right back to your coffin."

"I'll be good, I'll be good," Darnell said, forcing himself to keep a straight face. He really didn't want to return home alone right now, so he'd go along with whatever damn nonsense she took so serious. Hell, he'd say close to anything to be with her.

LaLilia opened the window of young Antwan's room and threw in some of that sparkly stuff Darnell remembered from the dentist's office earlier that night. So that shit was fairy dust.

"This casts a spell on all in the house," she whispered to him as they both climbed in.

Antwan was sound asleep on his bright dinosaur sheets — all reds and blues and yellows. The boy's head — looked like someone just gave him a real short haircut for the summer — lay smack-dab in the mouth of a Tyrannosaurus Rex. With one tight little fist, he clutched his dang baby tooth under his pillow.

Looking at the little guy, whose skin gleamed like mahogany in the dark room, Darnell remembered himself so long ago. Like Antwan, he'd been a skinny six-year old with big eyes and even bigger dreams. His family couldn't give him such a nice place to dream those dreams. Couldn't do it for any of them. Hell, when he was six, Darnell was sharing his bed with his three older brothers — Lorenzo, Maurice, and Thomas. He never had no pillow to his own self like Antwan. He and his brothers would elbow each other for room in the bed that was too small, all of them trying to get their fair share of the nothing by nothing blanket. Darnell learned to be tough in that bed, always fighting to get what he needed.

Where were his brothers now? Darnell shook his head. He needed to get back to the present, concentrate on what the fox was doing instead of thinking on some old memories that had nothing to do with his life now.

LaLilia was shaking something else, some white powder stuff around with her hand. Must be another kinda fairy dust. Darnell bit his lip. Still couldn't think about fairy dust without laughing. But the stuff seemed to be working 'cause young Antwan didn't even move an eyelash when LaLilia took the tooth from his hand under the pillow and put a silver dollar in its place. A dollar? He'd have to give her a hard time about that. What the hell good was a dollar these days — even to a six-year old? The chick needed some grounding in reality. Almost as much as she needed the loving he was more than ready, willing, and able to give her again.

And then Darnell remembered back to when he lost his second baby tooth. The next morning his mama'd handed him two pennies—a fortune back then. "These are from the tooth fairy," Mama said. "Don't you tell your brothers you have these pennies. They're just for you." Now Darnell's mama never lied and didn't tolerate lying from no one. She claimed the two precious pennies were from the tooth fairy, so Darnell had believed her. Even though his head told him that money came from her hard work. But now, with LaLilia here, Darnell had to think on that again.

LaLilia looked at him, and Darnell realized she was reading his mind. "I'm glad that tooth fairy found a way to get to you after all," she said. Though he tried to clear his mind, the long-ago memory lingered between them.

And then LaLilia bent over and damned if she didn't begin to feed from the kid. Darnell's eyes near fell outta his head. But she wasn't there very long—more like a good-night kiss than a real feeding. Next thing he knew, she was licking the kid's neck the way he wished she'd use her gorgeous tongue to lick him in several key locations on his body. His balls gave a jump that almost had him moaning out loud.

LaLilia held up a finger to her mouth telling him to keep his mouth shut. Maybe she didn't have all that much faith in her fairy dust after all. She took his hand in hers and led him to another bedroom. *Really nice house*. Two adults, must be young Antwan's parents, were sound asleep. The man, a tall, good-looking guy with skin as dark as Antwan's, was lying spooned against a woman, a tiny, dark beauty with dreadlocks spread out across her pillow.

Darnell, his head full of questions, looked at LaLilia. She opened her luscious lips so her fangs gleamed in the starlight filtering in through the vertical blinds. "I'll feed from the father, you can take the mother."

"We gonna feed off these people?"

"Just a kiss worth. It's a kind of gift."

He looked at her, disbelieving his ears. But when in Rome or Hiltonia and all that shit... The woman's blood was rich and delicious. Darnell wanted to feed way more than a kiss's worth, but LaLilia tapped his head and reminded him of her directions. Sorry to have to cut off so soon, he licked the puncture wound he drank from.

LaLilia took his hand again. They opened a window, climbed out, and closed up behind them like two serious citizens. Then they flew off.

"Uh, LaLilia," he asked, when they were once more high above the rooftops. "Why'd we have to keep quiet if your fairy dust does its job?"

She laughed. "I'm sure it would be okay, but I always figure, why push my luck?"

Like he would have to do with her if he wanted to get her back in the sack. "Next question," he asked. "How come you feed off the people whose houses you go to? It don't exactly, uh, go with my image of the tooth fairy. Not that I had one before I met you," he added.

"I don't know if I can explain it all to you right now in a way you'd understand."

Darnell did not appreciate that. Was she implying he was too dumb to understand?

She read his mind. "Oh, no, Darnell. Not at all. You're a very smart man, though you've got a skeptical nature that makes it hard for you to believe some things. Like the way a little feeding heals people, makes a young boy's mouth all better so he can grow a new tooth. Helps parents deal with the fact that their cute little one is growing up."

"That's it?" he asked, not quite believing.

"There's some mysticism involved that would take me a long time to try to explain."

"Mysticism, shit," he said. He hated whenever Wanda started spouting that stuff, and he wasn't much more open to it coming from LaLilia.

LaLilia kissed him lightly on his lips, and Darnell forgot about being skeptical. He wanted more, but she backed off. "Not yet," she said. "We've got another house to visit first."

Darnell inhaled deeply. "So where we goin' next?"

Another reading of her handheld. "This one's another little boy. Antonio Varella. Lives in a rowhouse in the Chambersburg section."

Darnell backed away. "Chambersburg? You takin' me to the 'Burg?"

"That's where my next child is."

"You gotta be kiddin'."

"No. Why would you think so?"

Darnell rolled his eyes. "The 'Burg is Cosa Nostra territory. You're not safe there, not 'til I beat Miccio's ass and get him and his crew the hell outta Trenton."

"For tooth fairies, there is no such thing as one group's territory or the other's. Tooth fairies go where we are needed. We take a sacred vow."

"Shit," Darnell said. "Don' you worry none. I'll protect you." But LaLilia didn't look worried. What did she know? Well, Darnell was not about to let her get hurt. No matter what protecting her cost him.

Chapter Five

Antonio Varella and his family lived in one of the typical narrow, deep rowhouses that lined the streets of the 'Burg. Darnell had never been inside of one, never expected to be inside one—least not 'til he got Miccio outta the city.

But now that he was here, he looked around, taking in the fine furniture and all the photos of what he guessed were family members crowding the small rooms. Upstairs, the young boy who LaLilia called Antonio was sound asleep on his bright dinosaur sheets—all reds and blues and yellows. The boy's head—looked like someone just gave him a real short haircut for summer—lay smack-dab in the mouth of a Tyrannosaurus Rex. With one tight little fist, he clutched his dang baby tooth under his pillow. Darnell chuckled. This little white boy with a thick head of black hair was in the same position on the same sheets as Antwan MacRae. He looked over at LaLilia. "They're alike, those two boys," he said.

"They are. Just like you and Miccio."

He stiffened—and not just his cock. "I don't wanna hear none of that."

"I know," she said, her voice all soft and quiet. He didn't want to think he was the one bringing that sadness to her eyes, but he had his limits. No way he could do to Miccio what had to be done if he started thinking about the two of them being alike in any way. He had to hold on to the differences he knew separated them.

"LaLilia, you're a special lady. But don't go messin' with junk a sweet thing like you just can't understand," he warned.

"I understand more than you'll admit," she said. "And I think you do, too."

"You think too much," he grumped. Just like Wanda.

After LaLilia collected Antonio's tooth and they both gave the parents the healing kiss, LaLilia told Darnell she was done for the night. And she invited him to her place—to talk.

Darnell accepted. His erection, solid all night, grew even harder. They'd talk all right. For about three seconds. Hell, they'd been talking all night, except when they made love. And he liked talking to her. But a man had a man's nature. And flying over Trenton with a hot fox like LaLilia made a guy have needs.

Now they flew together up Route One and across, over Princeton and west, out to the sticks. Hopewell. So this honey liked being out in the boonies. Darnell loved life in the big city, but he was willing to take a trip out to the rural back roads to be with LaLilia. Hell, even though he was a city guy, through and through, he could manage to find his way around being in the country. Just wasn't his first choice of the kind of place to be. Yet.

LaLilia brought him to a large, neat-looking cottage, white clapboard with black trim. Even a white picket fence and garden. He never knew no vampire with no garden before this. She unlocked the door and he nearly swallowed his teeth. Tooth fairies must make out real good judging by the high-class furniture. She must've had a hundred candles, and she started like she was gonna light every last one of them. But he didn't have no inclination for a tour of the premises right now, and he sure as hell didn't want her to take the time to light all them friggin' candles. Other needs were hollering for more immediate attention.

He took her in his arms and buried his tongue deep in her mouth for the kiss he'd been waiting on for much of the night. His mouth wide open, he tasted her, exploring her tongue and teeth and lips, pushed by a ravenous hunger that suddenly felt like he'd never be able to get enough of her. She tasted like champagne and chocolate and the classy people with big old summer homes down the shore, like Spring Lake and them places.

This woman, LaLilia Guitry, was a mystery to him, like he had to strip off forty or fifty harem veils and he still wouldn't know who the hell she was. Darnell's brain kept buzzing, warning him he'd never know her one hundred percent, no matter how many of them veils he stripped off. But she teased him. She'd bat those eyes at him and open herself up to let him into her, and he could swear he was close to figuring her out. But it was just another veil. Even as his tongue and teeth conquered her lips, he knew he'd never capture her completely. And that made him hungrier than ever.

He pulled her ever closer, and the sweet pressure of her flat, firm belly against his erection nearly had him weeping and howling like some kid in the ninth grade spying on the girls' gym class. Tonight she was wearing some lavender, silky dress that he could tear into pieces without exerting much strength. He ran his hands up and down her back, finding that they fit perfect in the groove between her wings. Those wings fluttered slowly as the two of them deepened their kiss. She gave as good as she got, her tongue insisting on entry into his mouth.

He growled and bellowed like a lion in a cage. He had to get naked with her now. He had to get into her bed. Now. He had to get into her. *Now.*

Not wanting to move away but having to, he broke the kiss and buried his head in the sweet spot under her neck where he was dying to feed. All his hungers breaking free now. "Where's the bed?" he asked hoarsely.

She looked at him from under lowered lids. "Follow me."

* * * * *

LaLilia loved being a tooth fairy, collecting the teeth she and her fellow fairies used to create mosaics spelling out messages of peace and love on remote mountain tops around the world. Messages for the universe. And usually she was content to go about her gathering alone, fulfilling children's dreams and bringing her healing touch to the little ones and their families. But now that Darnell was with her, she began to realize what a lonely pursuit hers was. She loved meeting the children tonight with Darnell at her side. She even loved answering his questions and dealing with his skepticism.

Most of all, she loved loving him. She'd never expected that this big rough warrior with his elegant wardrobe and dapper way about him would begin to capture her heart while she tried to convert him from his basic belligerence. She wasn't at all convinced that she'd succeed in getting him to cancel his battle with Vinny Miccio. But if she didn't, she knew she couldn't continue to be with him—not even in an enchanted dream like this. And she wanted to share more of his life story, to learn about his family and the experiences that brought him to where he was now. Most of all, she wanted the two of them to have a future together.

Which left her the rest of this dream night to get him to embrace peaceful relations with his enemies. If she didn't manage to get him to commit to at least listening to peace before this night was over, she'd be banished—er, transferred—to Wyoming 'til she could prove herself up to a challenge like Trenton. For a moment, she wondered how her partner, Sofia, was faring in her own mission. Both of them faced the same exile if they failed.

How long had it been since she'd brought a man back to her home in Hopewell, her private refuge, in any state—awake or dreaming? Did Darnell know how special he was to her? The dream was flying by, and she had so much to show him. LaLilia fought back a shudder of desperation. She had to get Darnell to build on his insight of how alike the two boys they'd visited were, to show that they didn't have to grow up to be enemies. But right now, talk was not needed. She'd start with taking him into her beautiful round bed and loving him to pieces.

"Can I take off your clothes?" he asked.

LaLilia shivered with delight and nodded. Darnell's big hands on her moved slowly and confidently, his fingers communicating reverence as he carefully took off her gown, fumbling a bit as he pulled the cloth over her wings. She closed her eyes and savored the sensations.

When he'd removed her silk panties and tossed them aside, LaLilia opened her eyes and smiled. "How about you?" she asked.

He held his arms out wide. "Want me to take them off or you wanna do the job?" How could she resist an offer like that? She took a deep breath, hoping to find a balance between her need to love him and the sensuous delight of taking his beautiful garments off in a leisurely fashion.

Impatience won that round.

They stretched out in the bed.

"Is it okay being on your back, what with them wings and all?" he asked, his voice soft and respectful. LaLilia loved how fascinated he was with her wings.

"What's it like, lying on them?" he asked.

"It's just fine. They're very soft to lie on, like clouds," she murmured.

His eyes lit up at the mention of the word *clouds*. "I want you all comfortable 'cause I'm about to kiss you all over."

That sounded like the best offer she'd had in ages. She stretched out on her white satin sheets. He took her hands in his and spread her arms out wide, holding her down as he began his kissing expedition at the top of her head. His lips and tongue touched her face, followed by little nibbles that resonated in the pit of her stomach and soon had her wondering how long she could hold out before she directed those lips and that tongue to a more strategic spot.

Darnell's cock was so hard, LaLilia couldn't help wondering how the hell he was able to keep his attention focused on his kisses. When he reached her mouth, LaLilia kissed him back, tasting the sweet peppermint of his breath.

"Oh, baby," he said, moving down now from her mouth to her chin and then her neck. Her pulse sped up, and she wanted him to feed off her now. "Just a little snack," he said, licking her neck before he plunged his fangs into her.

Goddess. She couldn't help herself. She needed to have his hard cock inside her as he drank from her, or she'd wither away into a pile of dusty powder. As he fed, she maneuvered her hungry pussy so that she was right at the tip of his cock. A few wiggles, a little directing with her legs wound around his butt, and he was poised where she wanted him. One good thrust, and he was deep inside her.

Having him in both places was like an orgasm in stereo, and LaLilia's senses began to run riot. She was floating through outer space, with his teeth and his cock stirring her deepest, most private, most secret places.

Darnell broke his feed to howl to the moon and stars, and LaLilia knew he, too, was in a whole new place, different than ever before. He clamped his fangs against hers, and vampire energy flowed between them as his cock and her pussy danced together in a dizzying crescendo of ecstasy.

LaLilia heard herself making noises she'd never known herself capable of, glad now that no beings lived anywhere close to her abode. She was shrieking out his name, begging Darnell to take her higher and harder and faster.

"Oh, yes, baby," he panted, his hips pistoning as he danced his cock in and out of her. She clamped her legs around him, wanting to hold on forever. To make it last, only she couldn't. With a piercing scream, she came and came and came. Darnell, now huge in her, exploded with a grunt and a roar. And then they collapsed together.

* * * * *

Darnell loved the ladies. Always had, always would. Now, as the leader of the Black Guards, in addition to all his other duties, he had a *reputation* to uphold. A reputation as a lady pleaser. That was *ladies*, plural. He owed it to many ladies to maintain and expand the reputation of the Black Guards. Hell, any guy they took in had to know his way around a lady. But as the chief of them, well, he had to show exemplary endurance and powers. Otherwise, they'd be looking elsewhere for their leadership. And rightly so.

But this LaLilia, well... She was something else. Smart, beautiful, gentle. Hell, though he'd never admit it, he even liked her ornery, stubborn ways. How would he ever be able to get into being with anyone else after her? She was fuckin' ruinin' him for any other ladies. And that was damn bad news—for all of them. But good news for him, 'cause she had to be the best lady in the world, shit in the whole friggin' solar system and beyond. Hell, Darnell couldn't let himself think 'bout nothing else tonight but being with her. He'd worry 'bout tomorrow *tomorrow*.

He chuckled to himself. Hadn't gotten real far with his plan to kiss her all over. But damn, her neck was so delicious, he couldn't resist a little snack. And then she'd pulled him into her. Ladies' choice on that one. She looked like an angel, but damn...nothing angelic about the way she screwed.

Now he was on his back, and she was kissing him, starting with his eyebrows and his eyes. As her lips flickered over him, her wings fluttered. Darnell's cock stirred. He'd have thought them wings would turn him off, instead they turned him on like a friggin' house on fire. The wings reminded him of the poem he'd read a few nights ago. Before he knew what he was doing, he started reciting the damn poem. LaLilia stopped and looked at him.

When he finished, she said, "That's beautiful. Did you write it?"

Shit, he couldn't believe he'd let loose with a poem like that. The woman got to his brain. Damage control time. "Hell, no. That was just somethin' I heard... Musta been on the radio."

She kissed him sweetly on the lips. "You don't need to be ashamed about knowing a poem. I love poetry."

He was about to deny everything when he saw her reading his eyes, his mind. He couldn't hide nothing from her. Before he knew it, he was tellin' her all about Maralise and his calendar.

"Thank you," she said. "I feel very close to you now."

Oh, baby. Close didn't begin to express how he felt about being with her. She continued kissing him, and then she took a nibble when she got to his neck. His cock was instant marble, huge and hard and aching like he hadn't just come.

He was getting into her sucking his blood—and next thing he knew, she had her head down covering his dick and eating that sucker like he was a gallon of rocky road ice cream and she'd been on a diet for two years.

LaLilia was all over him with her magic mouth, chewing and licking and sucking on his dick while she played with his balls, then switching and getting her mouth where her fingers'd just been. Darnell's eyes rolled in his head, and he lost all sense of anything but the feel of her mouth on him. It was like his cock and balls just grew a million extra nerves, and she was hitting on every one of them. He looked down at the top of her head, her hair shiny in the candlelight, bobbing up and down as her wings fluttered in slow rhythm.

And then she found some little vein in his balls, and damn all if she didn't start to feed off him right there. Darnell was seeing stars and moons and planets, nearly levitating off the fuckin' bed. He screamed out her name as he began to come, and she fastened them two gorgeous lips 'round his dick and swallowed down a chaser for her blood cocktail.

After he came and came, his cock still throbbing in aftershock, she laid her head down on him and licked him some more, like a purring cat getting into the cream. Damn, he never wanted to leave this bed. Didn't know if he could walk just yet.

"Thank you, baby," he murmured when he could talk again.

She lifted up, looked him straight in the eye, and licked his cum off her lips like it was hundred dollar a bottle champagne.

Darnell put his arms out to hold her to him. Oh yeah, this was one chick he did not want to let go of—ever.

* * * * *

Finding about Darnell's poetry sealed LaLilia's fate. She wanted to be with him in every way known to fairy and vampire—and maybe invent a few more. Now that he'd let her find out so much, she knew Darnell was really getting into their being together, at least as much as she was. Things were going better than she might ever have imagined. Maybe now she'd succeed in her mission, and then she could make some room in her life for a man... But she was getting ahead of herself. First things first, she reminded herself.

A short time later, Darnell nudged LaLilia awake. She propped herself on one elbow and looked at him. He had a real interesting gleam in his eye.

"What are you thinking, Darnell?"

He smiled impishly. "Is it okay if I ask you anything? You won't get freaked or nothin'?"

"I promise."

He appeared to be thinking. "Uh, you think you could run them wings over my cock?" he asked at last, sounding almost shy.

LaLilia looked at him in surprise, and then with delight. None of her other lovers had ever asked her to do this. Now that she thought about it, she wondered why. Though her wings weren't her most sensitive part, she started to get a kick out of imagining herself fluttering them over his shaft.

"Wow—let's do it, Darnell. Get on your back."

He did as she asked. His erection rose huge and magnificent from the dark tangle of his pubic hair. LaLilia licked her lips. She'd have liked to run lots more than her wings over his erection. But that was a great place to start.

Logistics. She started off lying down on top of him with her wings over his cock. The contact was too static, far too tight for her to move her wings at all. From the sound of Darnell's groan, though, he seemed to find this position pretty stimulating.

But they could do better.

"Maybe get on your side," she said, lifting herself off him. He moaned again, this time sounding almost as bad as when he'd had his cavity. When they were both on their sides, he grabbed her from behind and pulled her to him—again too tight for wing movement. Then it hit her. The perfect position. She turned around so that they were head to foot. If she leaned away a bit from his cock, she could flutter her wings over it.

"Oh yeah, baby," he whispered. And then she began to move her wings. She could feel the downy soft feathers slowly tickle Darnell's cock, which throbbed with each tiny movement. As her wings moved slowly, one on each side of his cock, Darnell began to lick the sensitive backs of her knees. LaLilia quivered at the contact, as a whole new sensation raced up and down her legs.

LaLilia grew more excited, and she could feel her wings begin to flutter faster as Darnell nibbled first at one leg then the other, thrusting his hips into her wings in perfect harmony with his tiny kisses. And then he encircled her, pulled her closer against him, stopping her when her butt made contact with his face. He buried his mouth in the crack of her ass, and LaLilia inhaled hard. His tongue made lazy circles around and in the rosebud of her anus, sending shooting stars of pleasure out along her nerves.

LaLilia wanted more, so much more. Darnell carefully slid a finger into her well-lubricated hole, and LaLilia whimpered with new need. She wanted his cock there, and she lost all thought of where her wings were. Now she was grinding herself back against the two fingers he had put in her, but she wanted more. "Darnell," she sighed.

He seemed to want what she did. He turned himself around so his cock was where his tongue and fingers had been. Both of them now groaning with need, he slowly filled her ass with his cock, and LaLilia shrieked with the sensation.

Darnell held her tight and began to thrust. LaLilia ground herself against him, taking in every last inch of the way he moved in her. And then she gave herself up to being with him here, now. She cried out his name as she came, and he answered her with his own huge, hot release.

After this loving, she wanted them to be able to rest before she got down to business, but they couldn't take the time. Their dream night was going by quickly, too quickly. Soon, she'd have to make her move. Get him agree to her mission before they both had to climb out of their coffins for the real night to come. Her deadline.

Darnell seemed to be aware of time fleeing, but not that they were in a dream. "I want to see you again, baby," he said. "How about tomorrow night?"

"I'd love that," LaLilia said, her voice sounding low and sultry to her ears.

He sighed. "I won't be able to spend as much time with you tomorrow as I did tonight. The night after next, I gotta finish some important business hanging over my head. But after that, I can have lotsa time to spend with you." He ran his finger down her nose, tracing her lips.

He looked so eager, almost sweet—which was not a word many people would use to describe Darnell DeLouis—that LaLilia hated to burst his bubble. But the moment for reality had arrived loud and clear—and she couldn't let it slip by. "I know about your business with Miccio," she said, her voice still low and calm.

Darnell propped himself up on his elbow and looked at her inquiringly. He narrowed his eyes. "How much do you know?" he asked, suddenly looking less sweet. "What I'm referring to is from some top secret negotiations I been having with…"

"The Cosa Nostra vampires. The ones you accused me of working for the other night. It's all about you meeting with Vinny Miccio and fighting it out for control of the Trenton territory."

Darnell sat fully up now, his eyes now shooting fire. "Wanda really told you everything," he growled.

Oh, no. This was not going the way she wanted and needed. "It's not Wanda's fault," she said.

He furrowed his handsome brow. "Then where did you get all your information?" he asked.

She sighed. "Lots of interested parties know what's going down with you and Vinny Miccio later this week."

"Damn," he spat out, jumping out of bed and prowling back and forth across her room.

"Don't be angry with me," LaLilia said.

His expression softened for a second. "I could never be pissed at you, lovely lady. Just the situation, and the fact that there's such a big leak. Probably that fuckin' Mooch. One of his men probably opened up his mouth. Well, I'll make him pay for that, too."

"No," LaLilia whispered.

"No?" he asked. "What do you mean no?"

"I don't want you to make Vinny Miccio pay for anything. I don't want there to be a battle between you. Any more than I would want one between the two little boys I collected teeth from tonight."

He shook his head. "They have nothing to do with what's going on."

"You're wrong. You and Vinny Miccio are older versions of those two little boys, who have everything in common. In fact, I think they're both more grown-up than the two of you."

"What?" he bellowed. "What do you mean?"

"You don't see them sucking others into meaningless battles."

"The Black Guards' fight with the Cosa Nostras is not meaningless. It's a matter of life or death."

"No, it's just two men who think they're cowboys and Trenton is some ranch that's too small for the cattle."

"Lady, you are so wrong. We ain't talkin' about kids playin' cowboy and Indian here."

"That's exactly what we're talking about." LaLilia held her stance though her voice wobbled a bit. "I want you to cancel your confrontation with Vinny and negotiate with him instead. With words, not force. This is one important example of what I meant the other day. A chance for peace."

Darnell snorted derisively.

"Trenton's more than big enough for both of your groups and more." LaLilia was practically begging, her voice quivering.

"Are you one of *their* chicks?" he asked incredulously. "Is that what's goin' on here?"

"No. I'm just who I've told you I am."

"Right," he said, stretching the word across several syllables. "You're the friggin' Tooth Fairy. And some peace nut."

"People who want peace are not nuts." She straightened with all the dignity she could muster considering she was standing there as naked as the day she was born. "I'm *a* Tooth Fairy. There are many of us. There's no *the* Tooth Fairy."

"There's no nothin'," he hissed. "Just a set-up. Well, lady whoever the hell you are, nobody tells Darnell DeLouis to back down from a battle he's taking on. No fuckin' way I'm ever gonna cancel out on my obligation to my people. I'm meeting with Miccio in two days, and nothing no one can ever say will change that. Now forget that and tell me when and where I can see you tomorrow night."

LaLilia tried to ignore the ache rising from her solar plexus. She longed to see him in the coming night and many more for real, not in a dream. But she couldn't back down now. "No way I'll see you tonight or tomorrow or ever again anywhere, not even in a dream, if you don't promise you'll cancel the showdown with Vinny. And make a commitment to peace."

"What do you mean dream?"

"This is all a dream, Darnell. I thought a dream was the only way I could show you all about peace and…"

He shook his head and quickly began to throw on his clothes. "Shoulda known you was too high falutin' for a simple guy from Trenton," he muttered. He glared at her. "Lady, it's been real. Now it's time for me to say *hasta la vista*. Don't call me, I'll call you. All that. Only I won't."

And with those words, their shared dream shattered.

LaLilia fell fully into reality and gave in to tears. She'd failed at her mission, and she'd lost Darnell. Great job all around, she chided herself. But the real night would soon arrive, so she couldn't even linger over her regrets in private. She'd have to face the night and tell the other tooth fairies what a failure she'd turned out to be. And she'd have to prepare for her relocation to Wyoming, which would come soon.

Maybe someone else could get to Darnell, convince him to change his path. And LaLilia'd have to be a real grown-up and not devolve into a ball of jealous resentment when another woman took her place by Darnell.

It was going to be a long night. With many more of them to come.

Chapter Six

Darnell woke up angry enough to bite off heads. Anyone's. Which was all to the good when it came to strategizing for his upcoming battle with Miccio. But didn't bode well for the two honeys waiting to entertain him soon as he'd left the coffin, cleaned up, and read a poem that woulda had him in tears if he was the cryin' sort.

Tonight he had twins, Tonya and Sonya Burnett, waiting on him when he emerged. Identical twins. Usually he enjoyed novelties like the two of them. They mighta been identical, but they each had different tastes. And Darnell knew they each tasted different, too. But tonight not even the Burnett twins could take his mind off that crazy fairy, LaLilia Guitry. He was gonna give Wanda hell for getting him involved with a mind-blowing ballbuster like that. Wanda should've known better.

"Ladies, sorry to waste your time," Darnell grumped at them. "But tonight I gotta make war not love. Go see Wanda, tell her to book you after my upcoming meeting for a deluxe night with me. And tonight go wine and dine anywhere you want, on me."

The two six-foot dolls batted their eyelashes and tried to change Darnell's mind. Hmm, he thought. He had to be one strong dude, turning down twelve feet of gorgeous fox. It was hard work, but he took his responsibilities seriously and couldn't give in to distractions like twin foxes.

Of course, he had to admit to himself, it wasn't hard, if he was talking about his cock. Not even Tonya and Sonya could move him the way that friggin' LaLilia did. He had a sneaky suspicion that LaLilia would ruin him for other women. He sent the twins off dissatisfied, which went against his usual code of behavior. If he continued like this, there'd be trouble. But he couldn't think about all that now. Instead, he took a fast feed from the companions who hung around, waiting to be fed off of, then hollered for Wanda.

"What do you want?" Wanda hollered right back.

"I need you here, now, to talk about tomorrow night," he bellowed. Damn that Wanda. Though she was an excellent advisor and knew every friggin' thing there was to know about central Jersey and Pennsy, she could be the biggest mother fuckin' pain in the butt he ever had the stinking bad luck to meet.

She was always trying to change him, trying to get him to do things different than the way he'd been doing them for years. His philosophy was, if it ain't broke, don't fix it. But Wanda was never one to leave things be. She always had to look at things different, try seven ways to do a thing 'til she found the one she liked best.

Well this time, hooking him up with LaLilia Guitry, Wanda went too fuckin' far. 'Specially when she told her top secret information about delicate upcoming upper level leaders' meetings. Darnell shook his head. Okay, so LaLilia said Wanda wasn't the only one who blabbed, that she had the information from other places. And pissed as he was at LaLilia, he couldn't believe she'd lie to him. Of all the things he couldn't tolerate, lying was the worst. But she'd lied when she pretended she wanted to be with him, hadn't she? Lied like a fucking world-class, Olympic-level liar. When all the time she had a friggin' hidden agenda.

"Wanda," he hollered out again. Where could that maddening woman be?

* * * * *

LaLilia was glad she had a busy night coming up, her last one before leaving for her reassignment in Wyoming. She had to collect teeth from twenty children, which would be something of a record for her. And she'd be flying all over Mercer County, up into Somerset County, down into Burlington. She even had one tooth she'd have to go over to New Hope in Bucks County for. At least she'd have the chance for a last visit to places that had become dear to her.

New Hope. Maybe she'd start her circuit there. Usually she had no trouble holding on to new hopes and old ones. Everyone considered her one of the most optimistic of the tooth fairies. But this time, she had to struggle to hold on to the merest wisp of her positive energy. She felt so bad about the way things had gone wrong between Darnell and her. For many reasons. And a little voice inside her wondered if she'd ever again be with him.

She soared along, following the Delaware to New Hope on the Pennsylvania side, and tried to concentrate on her work for the night. Letting her concentration slip caused all her problems. If she hadn't let herself lose sight of her mission, she'd never have gotten so involved with Darnell. Maybe by becoming his lover she'd destroyed any chance of getting him to abandon his battle with Vinny Miccio.

Even so, LaLilia couldn't bring herself to regret her time with Darnell. And if she had to do everything over again, she admitted to herself that she'd once again surrender to his charms.

LaLilia checked her schedule. She was due to pick up a baby tooth from a little girl who'd struggled to stay awake long enough to see her come. Poor munchkin. LaLilia wished she could have told her that children had to be asleep before the fairies could come to them. This rule was number one in their handbook.

LaLilia swooped down and performed her usual ritual on the little redhead who slept so fiercely, and on her parents. Another tooth for the mosaic of peace. At least she could contribute that to the cause so dear to her heart. She'd failed in her mission, but she came away from New Hope with the hope that her partner in this had fared better. Perhaps all was not lost. Perhaps they'd somehow succeed in bringing peace to Darnell and to Vinny. And perhaps one day LaLilia could be with

Darnell again, at a time when he learned to love peace as much as he loved her.

Right now, she couldn't believe that he loved either. She swallowed back her tears and threw herself fully into the night's work.

* * * * *

Darnell sat back in his exclusive, black leather, top of the line desk chair and put his cowboy-booted feet up on his desk. "You been studying them notes you made 'bout the way Miccio fights?" he barked at Wanda. "So what'd you come up with? What's he gonna throw at me?"

Wanda pursed her lips. "I do not appreciate talking to the soles of your boots, even if they are fancy."

Darnell scowled, but he knew better than to mess with Wanda when she was in one of her moods, which she sure as hell looked like she was in tonight. If he didn't know better, he'd swear she was on the rag. For the first time all night, he almost smiled at the thought. If Wanda read his mind now, she'd probably stake 'n' bake him faster than some fuckin' vampire hunter. Wanda was real particular on what she called respect. So under Wanda's glare, Darnell put his feet on the floor and sat up.

"You still insisting on going through with the nonsense two nights from now?" Wanda asked.

"What do you mean?" he asked, for the first time suspecting that Wanda might not be with him one hundred percent.

She looked at him now. "Isn't it time that you and Vinny Miccio grew up and stopped acting like two stupid boys fighting over a corner of the schoolyard?"

Darnell glared at her. If he didn't know better, he'd start to think that some Mafia types kidnapped his Wanda and replaced her with an alien that looked right but talked shit. "Wanda, what's got into you? You been drinkin' funny blood?" When she didn't answer, he continued to think of other, scarier possibilities. "Vinny and his boys ain't got to you now, have they? Bribed you with some of their dirty money?"

Wanda jumped like someone stuck a silver bullet up her ass. "I do not have to sit here and take your insults," she growled.

Darnell rose and pointed for Wanda to sit. "Didn't mean no insult by that. Come on, Wanda, sit back down."

She sat but looked to him like she'd jump up and run away if he so much as blinked at her funny. "I've been thinking, Darnell. You know I have your best interest at heart. Yours and the Black Guards."

Yeah, Darnell knew Wanda wanted what she thought was best for him and his men. Trouble was, she sometimes got some weird ideas in her head. And then the light went on. "You been talking more to that loony fairy, LaLilia Guitry, ain't you?" He leaned forward across his desk.

Wanda recoiled like he'd hit her. "You being disrespectful about the dentist who saved your fool ass the other night when all you could do was moan and groan and complain?"

So much happened since LaLilia fixed his fuckin' fang, that whole part of what went down between them clear skipped his mind. "You know she's after me to just give up, tell Miccio he and his Cosa Nostras can do whatever the mother fuckin' hell they want to in Trenton?"

Wanda nodded. "I didn't talk to her specifically about this, but I know tooth fairies want peace. It's part of what they do."

"You knew that and you sent me to her?" His voice got loud.

Wanda rolled her eyes. "If you use your head, you'll remember that just last night, you were begging me to get you a dentist who could help you and not hurt you. I did—and now all you do is heap abuse on both of us." She stood up. "I really don't have to listen to this."

He jumped up. "Yeah, you do. You're my advisor. You're supposed to advise me, which means you have to listen to me."

Wanda mumbled something under her breath. "I have my limits."

"Sit back down," he growled. When she did, he began to pace. "Come on, Wanda. You're the most brilliant strategizer in Trenton. Help me plan for my battle with Miccio so the good guys can win."

"My best advice to you is to forget the battle you have planned. Go, talk to Vinny. Divide up Trenton. Better yet, share the city. There's enough here to be fair to everyone. Let me help you come up with that kind of plan."

He shook his head vehemently. "Not what I want. So let's go to plan B. You know, where I knock his head off. Then the Cosa Nostras leave Trenton and the Black Guards take full control of the city."

"Don't want to," Wanda said, jutting out her full lower lip.

Fuckin' shit. This was all he needed tonight. Here he was strung out over LaLilia and now Wanda was turning weird on him. That's what he got for lettin' a woman, any woman, get to be too important to him. Turnin' into some pussy whipped wuss. Darnell felt his blood heat up. No way was Wanda going to get away with dictatin' the terms of their relationship. After all, he was the guy in charge here. He'd been letting Wanda get away with murder. No more.

"I don't give a flyin' fuck what you want," he hissed. "You're my advisor. That means you give me the advice I want, not what you want. Got that, Wanda? And you don't like my terms, I better find me a new advisor. Shouldn't be hard." He knew there were lotsa people around who'd wanna be his advisor. Of course none of them came close to being in Wanda's class. Too bad she knew that.

"Now you listen to me, Darnell D. DeLouis," she hissed. "If it was just you I had to worry about, I'd be outta here so fast, your fool head would spin on your shoulders. But I care about the Black Guards, I care about our community. I even care about you, you big idiot. So against my wishes, I'm going to give you the advice you think you want for tomorrow night. But if you go against my best advice, which I'll also give you, this is the last time I ever advise you about anything. Got that?"

"Got that," he said. "Now tell me what I wanna know."

She started to talk and soon gave him some brilliant ideas for exactly how to deal with the Mooch. "You've got to go for his weak spots," Wanda reminded him. "Remember that he really wants to be a pastry chef, like he used to be, for Neighbors' Bakery. Got transformed when he tried to mooch too much flour from another bakery before dawn."

"Yeah, so how do I use that?" Darnell asked.

"When he tries to get near you, tell him you ate his cannolis and they messed up your stomach. Gave your cousin *agita*, a major attack of nerves, in the bowels."

"Bad cannolis? You want me to accuse a guy of giving my cousin *agita* of the bowels?"

"Tell him his cannolis had the guy running from both ends."

"Geez, Wanda, you're a hard woman." Darnell rolled his eyes. "He's gonna come at me with chains, knives, semiautomatic weapons, probably even a chain saw. And what am I gonna do? Hell, I'll stand there and insult his cannolis. That'll get him."

Wanda gritted her teeth at him.

"Like how the hell is that gonna work? *Bad* cannolis. I want to know what weapons I'm gonna have, and how best to use them. Like do I stab him first or shoot him?"

"Listen hard, Darnell. You know I never steer you wrong, right?"

"Yeah, whatever." He shrugged, but watched her carefully.

"You ever heard of the Achilles' heel?" Wanda asked.

"What's that? Some shoe store in the mall?"

She put her skinny lips together. "No, Darnell. It's from a myth, an old story. A guy who's strong who has a weak spot. Everyone has one."

"I don't."

"Like your teeth."

Darnell didn't wanna go there. "Go on."

"Well, Miccio was always proud of his pastries, especially his cannolis. He won awards for them, was always bragging on them. Not only him, but his whole family. It's what they grew famous for. When someone criticizes his cannolis, it's like they're saying his mama wears combat boots and his daddy's not his daddy. Get it?"

"Yeah, and…"

"And then he loses his head and starts getting wild. Like a bull with one of those red capes. You start talking bad about his cannolis, and he's going to lose it. Which will give you a chance to win, if you can keep your head."

Despite himself, Darnell had to admire Wanda for her sheer hardheadedness. Of course, he wouldn't admit none of that to her. The damn woman had too high an opinion of herself as it was. And he sure wouldn't let her get away without giving him a better plan of action. Wanda knew exactly which weapons Darnell should be ready to use when. She wasn't happy talking about weapons, but that was too bad. After all, Darnell wanted to win this battle.

So she gave him a winning battle plan. But then she also told him this was the last time she'd be his advisor. She was gonna sign on with the peace people and go live with them. Darnell thought she was joking, but she swore she meant every word. He couldn't believe that all the people he cared about were turning into peace nuts. Made it awful hard for him to keep pushing thoughts of peace away.

Once she was gone, Darnell found himself with too much time to think. Shit. Even though Wanda said she was through with him, he knew he could find a way to coax her back to being his top advisor. Give her a raise, another title, something. No woman was ever able to resist him once he turned the charm on. Except LaLilia. He didn't want to go there. The long hours of the nights and days he'd be alone stretched before him like a desert. He had to devote tonight and tomorrow to getting himself ready for Miccio. Nothing could distract him. Not even an aching cock and a broken heart.

Once he finished off Miccio, then he'd think about getting himself a special lady. Not that he liked to give up all the chicks he was used to, but deep down somewhere, Darnell admitted to himself that LaLilia was better than a hundred babes. Maybe a thousand. Maybe a million. He punched the air, hard.

Fuck, he couldn't let himself think she was so special. Like the only one he'd ever want. There had to be another lady out there for him, someone who'd make LaLilia look like a reject. Maybe he'd get him another tooth fairy. LaLilia said she wasn't the only one.

Mother fuckin' shit. Wasn't nobody nowhere could ever compare to his LaLilia. But he'd have to pretend.

He got himself one of those pads of paper Wanda used for making lists and began to write a poem. For LaLilia. He made sure to burn it before dawn.

Chapter Seven

Darnell could not believe it. The night of his big showdown with Vinny Miccio, and he woke up in the worst possible agony. Pain so bad he never felt nothing like it. Not since… Not since the other night, when he had the killer cavity in his left fang. For a second he thought LaLilia and Wanda were getting some sick form of revenge on him and made his tooth bad again.

But this pain was in his right fang. Darnell crawled out of his coffin. He barely had the strength to read his nightly poem. Shit, shit, shit. What the fuck was he gonna do? No way he could turn to LaLilia again. She'd only try to blackmail him, refuse to fix him up 'til he gave her what she wanted.

LaLilia. Thoughts of her had his cock stirring, giving him a moment of rest from the constant pain of his friggin' fang. But then the pain in his heart and the pain in his fang united in one big ball of agony, and Darnell howled.

What the fuck was he gonna do? He clamped his hand against his fang and began to pace in his room. Tonight to prepare for his battle, he'd postponed screwing the babes 'til after he mopped up the floor with Miccio's head. The plan was for him and Miccio to meet in the boxing ring in a gym in neutral territory, down by the Capitol building. Lucky his men had transported his weapons there the night before and hidden them. Darnell didn't think he'd be able to lift them. Maybe by some miracle he'd have some strength by the time he got to the gym.

Before that, he was supposed to feed off one of the guys who hung out at the hall. But with the cocksuckin' pain in his fang, he couldn't even think about feeding. Shit. With him like this, Miccio would win. And then what would happen to the

Black Guards? He couldn't stand the thought of letting his men down.

Wanda. Wanda would know what to do. He bellowed her name—and heard nothing in response. Oh, fuck. Shit. He forgot she'd left. Just when he really needed her.

No matter how much pain he was in, he had to go to the gym. And he couldn't let Miccio know what bad shape he was in. Darnell had to pull his shit together. Now or never. After all, he was a leader. And a leader had to be like one of them super hero types. Not just give in to any head crushing, killing, murdering, bitching agony that would cripple an ordinary creature.

Even if he had to crawl there, he'd show up at the gym. And even if he had no chance at all against Miccio, he'd go down fighting.

After Darnell managed to get dressed in his killer black silk suit, looking good in spite of his pain, he braced himself for the trip to the gym.

He was almost at the door when he heard a familiar voice. "You called?"

Darnell's heart lurched. Wanda. He almost smiled. He knew she wouldn't be able to stay away from him. But he couldn't admit his weakness. He just had to act strong and get her to get help—fast.

Darnell resisted the impulse to gloat over Wanda's being there.

"What is it?" she asked, looking at him with concern in her eyes despite the icy tone of her voice.

Act cool, he reminded himself. "My fuckin' tooth," he said, his voice breaking on the last word.

"Your tooth? Not the one LaLilia fixed?"

"No, the other fang," he said, his voice now a slobbery mess.

Wanda shook her head. "You can't possibly expect to fight with Vinny Miccio tonight. I'll call his people and tell them we can't be there."

With his last iota of strength, Darnell batted Wanda's cell phone outta her hand and slammed that sucker onto the floor. Friggin' piece of shit broke. He'd have to buy her a new one, but it was worth it to keep her from fuckin' everything up so bad nobody could fix it.

"Why'd you do that?"

"You want me to *forfeit* to Miccio?" Darnell asked, not knowing what was worse—Wanda's craziness or his fuckin' fang.

Wanda's face puckered like she just drank a pint of tainted blood. "Forfeit? You think we're playing some kid game here?"

"No, dammit straight to hell. I know how serious it is. That's why I ain't just gonna hand Miccio a victory without a fight."

Wanda rolled her eyes. "Men," she grumped. "Well, if I can't talk you out of this insanity, I'd better help you. Do you want me to try to contact LaLilia? See if she can fix your cavity before we leave?"

With all his heart, Darnell wanted this. But his head told him no way. He knew LaLilia's demands, what she'd expect in exchange for helping him even in an emergency. And there was no way he'd give up his responsibilities as a leader of his men, not even for her. Even to let her fix his pain. Even if he wanted to. Boy, did he want to. But he couldn't. He felt like no battle he could ever have with Miccio would be as tough as the one inside him. But he couldn't give up, not now. "No way. Gimme one of them ice packs. I'll make do."

Muttering to herself and shaking her head, Wanda went off and got a cooler full of ice packs. "I think you're the one who's nuts. Let's go, or we'll be late."

Trying not to feel like he was heading for his doom, Darnell followed Wanda out to the limo they'd be riding in to the gym. Jack T. Nipper smiled nervously at them.

* * * * *

LaLilia hated failure, and she wasn't too fond of her new home in Wyoming. Her only comfort was that Sofia was right there with her.

Even with all she had on her mind, LaLilia wasn't able to forget that about Darnell and his upcoming battle. At this very moment, carefully calibrated with the time difference in mind, she knew Darnell was on his way to his meeting with Vinny Miccio for a blowout battle. Nothing she'd been able to do made an iota of difference to those plans. All the way out in Wyoming, she had to admit to herself that she'd been waiting for a summons from Wanda the Wise, or even better, from Darnell himself to say that the battle was off. That would be enough to end her exile. But nothing had come, and she had to assume that, this time, no news was bad news.

She looked at her assignments for the night, which were dismayingly light. Just when she wanted to keep herself busy. But there weren't that many people in Wyoming, let alone children losing their teeth. Well, she might as well get started.

The first child of the night reminded her of the boys she'd dream visited with Darnell. Double darn it all. In their shared dream she'd been sure he'd *get it.* Once he saw how alike the two little boys in the different parts of the city were, he'd have to realize more united them than divided them. She'd been sure he'd be able to relate that to himself and Vinny Miccio. Especially when she made an explicit point of their sameness. Especially after he remembered his own experience as a little boy with a tooth fairy. But her efforts ended up ineffective, insubstantial as a dream, because nothing Darnell had done since indicated any softening of his attitude.

Triple darn. She had to stop thinking about her life in terms of Darnell's place in it. From now on she had to devote herself to other ways of bringing about peace between her fellow creatures.

LaLilia struggled to bring her full focus to her work for the night. After all, even if she had made thousands of pick-ups, each tooth loss was unique for the families involved. She owed it to them and to her reputation as a tooth fairy to deliver her best in every visit.

Despite these internal conversations, LaLilia knew she was waiting for something… Some indication, some summons, that she and Darnell were not as over as she feared they were.

* * * * *

The gym where Darnell was due to meet with Miccio may have been neutral territory according to the official party line, but Darnell balled up his fists and got ready to fight the minute he arrived there. Felt like he had to defend himself and everything that was important to him. And he wasn't being some supersensitive wuss from feeling the worst agony ever known on the face of the earth. No, there was something else going down. If he didn't know better, he'd swear he was entering some sorta ambush, a trap worse than sunlight he should've kept away from.

Wanda the Wise, looking like she was tryin' to suck down a bad batch of blood, was coming with him. Not that he'd ever be a man to hide behind some female's skirts. But Darnell had to admit he was glad Wanda took back what she said and agreed to come. She made it clear that tonight was really the last time she'd be his advisor. He'd deal with changing her mind again later. Assuming there'd be a later.

The room was dark, and the smell of sweaty bodies hit him like an assault weapon. What the fuck was up with the lights off? Didn't these suckers pay their electric bill? "Turn on the fuckin' lights or I don't go another step!" Darnell demanded. Only problem was, between his tooth and the ice pack he was cradling against his cheek, sounded more like he was saying, "Toofle down step," or some shit like that.

"Jus' a minute," a voice called out from a corner, so the message musta gone through. Didn't sound like Miccio. Darnell heard some mumbling and grumbling, then the lights came on. He instantly dropped the friggin' ice pack, and the sucker landed with a thud on his right foot. Fuck, shit, damn. Now not only his tooth was killing him, but his fuckin' big toe stung like a son of a bitch.

But he couldn't let Miccio see him like that. Darnell called on all his strength of will, all his history of being the leader of his pack, the strong man. He needed to face his enemy down now.

And then his ears pricked up as he caught the sound of the most pitiful moan he ever heard. Shit. Fuck. He couldn't stand it. Despite all his intentions, he made that sissy noise. Worse than shittin' his pants. Now that mother fucker Miccio would know he was a friggin' wreck. Miccio would beat his ass, and all the Black Guards would have to hustle their shit outta Trenton. Might have to head down to Bordentown or some other two-bit town. This was the worst night of his life.

Then he heard the moan again, only louder and more pathetic sounding. Wait a fuckin' moment. He didn't make that sound. Someone else was groaning like a stuck pig.

Darnell looked all around him. Vinny Miccio was sitting on a stool in the corner of the boxing ring. Miccio was a tall skinny guy with a lot of black hair and dark eyes, like a pirate. His skin was what they called olive, but tonight it looked more like pea green. Dressed in a crummy T-shirt and cheap jeans, like he was going to baseball practice or some shit instead of a high-level meeting.

Holy shit! Darnell could not credit his eyes. But he was seeing what he was seeing. Miccio was holding a goddamn mother fuckin' ice pack to his jaw. Vinny the Mooch Miccio looked like he had a toothache 'least as bad as Darnell's. Darnell stifled the urge to moan and laugh at the same time. First thing he did was bend over and pick up the ice bag, put it back exactly where it belonged—'cause his tooth hurt a hell of a lot worse than his toe.

Vinny, with the aid of his tiny *consigliore*, rose on wobbly legs to face Darnell. Hell, if the *consigliore* didn't have his arm around Vinny like he was a Boy Scout helping a little old lady cross the road, the head of the Cosa Nostra vampires would probably land flat on his bony ass.

Darnell, trying not let on that he was in trouble himself, looked on over at Vinny and asked, "You ready for us to meet in combat?" He glared at Vinny with what he hoped was his killer vampire stare.

Miccio looked like he wanted to spit nails. But he couldn't keep that tough look on his ugly mug. In fact, the mother fucker couldn't hardly talk. "Mr. Miccio has an unfortunate situation," the *consigliore*, sounding like he had marbles stuck in his trap, said.

Wanda the Wise stepped forward. After all, if Miccio's advisor was going to do the talking for him, then the protocol required his equal from the other side to answer.

"What is Mr. Miccio's situation?" Wanda asked, her voice dripping icicles, the way she was expert at. Darnell almost smiled. Maybe, just maybe, they weren't all dead meat quite yet.

The consigliore conferred briefly with Miccio, who held the ice pack with one hand and was waving the other one 'round like he was chasing flies off a dead dog. The consigliore nodded, then looked back over at Wanda. "Mr. Miccio has a very serious medical condition. A massive ache in his right fang."

Darnell almost yelped, but he bit back his response. The fucker had the same pain as him in the same place. For a moment of weakness, Darnell almost felt sorry for the mother fucker. He bit down hard on that feeling.

Fuck. He could not let his mind go there. Miccio was shit outta luck. That meant Darnell and the Black Guards just *won*. After all, he was ready to fight. If Miccio wasn't, tough shit on him and the Cosa Nostras. Darnell wouldn't be sorry to see the last of their asses boogeying the hell outta Trenton.

'Cept before he could claim victory, there went Wanda shooting off her big mouth. "Mr. DeLouis finds himself in the identical situation," she said, still cool as an ice pop right from the truck. Shit, fuck, of all the mother fuckin' stupid bonehead crap to say. What'd she hafta go and open her big trap? Who asked her? He nudged Wanda, hard. She hissed at him, and he backed off. Wanda could be very scary.

"Wanda," he said softly from a distance, his voice as filled with menace as he could make it.

She looked at him like she was asking why he was bothering her.

"Shut up," he said so that she could hear him and they couldn't.

She put her hands on her hips. "I certainly will not shut up. This has gone far enough. Now you and Vinny Miccio both have toothaches. We need to do something about that."

Darnell furrowed his brows together. "What you mean, do something? We don't need to do nothing 'cept declare victory. Sounds like Miccio here ain't in fit shape to do battle with me. Which means I win by, whatchamacallit? By the fault. Yeah, that's it."

"You mean by default?" Wanda asked.

"Yeah, right. Default."

The *consigliore* was shaking his head and looked like he was gonna jump up and down and holler. Miccio, who looked like he was totally out of it, sat with the ice pack still clenched against his cheek. "You can't win by default."

"Right," Wanda agreed. Darnell wished now he'd let her go when she quit two nights before. Big fuckin' help she was being.

"Wanda, you're killing me over here," he hissed.

"No," she said loud and clear, "it's your tooth that's killing you. Not me. And what I propose is that we take care of your toothaches first—yours and Vinny Miccio's. After that, we can come to a reasonable agreement."

"What?" Darnell cried out. Not only did his fuckin' tooth rattle every pain cell in his whole friggin' body, now Wanda was burying him without benefit of a coffin.

The *consigliore* was conferring with Miccio. He raised his little bald head several moments later. "Mr. Miccio agrees with this plan." No surprise there.

But Darnell wasn't ready to give up, not yet. "No way!" he called out. With his tooth feeling even worse, his words came out sounding like a moan. Shit. They were all ignoring him now. He couldn' believe it. Wanda patted him on the shoulder and said he'd feel better soon. Must be hallucinating. She never touched him. He tried growling at her that he was pissed as hell, but she ignored him.

"Mr. DeLouis had this very same problem just a few nights ago," Wanda said. "We found the perfect dentist. I'm sure she'd help out."

Darnell's eyes grew huge. Of all the mother fuckin' bad luck... And then it hit him. Wanda was proposing that LaLilia come and do her special dentist tricks on Vinny Miccio. Oh, he couldn't let that happen. The thought of LaLilia's tongue going into Miccio's mouth, her fangs feeding from him. Too fuckin' much. Darnell roared his disapproval. The three of them just looked at him like he was a cockroach crossing the wall.

No way he'd let LaLilia get anywhere near Miccio. He didn't care what he had to do. Hell, he wouldn't mind taking Miccio apart, piece by piece. But the *consigliore* was talking now. He said, "Oh, we have a special dentist who took care of Mr. Miccio recently when he had a similar problem... She told us she'd come to take care of him any time, anywhere. We'll call her now."

Wanda nodded. "And we'll call ours. Shouldn't take long for the two of them to get these two back to their normal selves." She glanced with what almost looked like affection from Darnell to Miccio. What was going on with that crazy fool?

Well, once he got his tooth fixed and his head on straight, he'd be ready to destroy Miccio. And no one could ever accuse them of not fighting fair. After all, Miccio was going to get fixed too.

And he'd get to see LaLilia. A bonus he hadn't counted on. Despite his pain and the situation, Darnell felt his cock begin to twitch in anticipation.

* * * * *

All the way out in the wilds of Wyoming, LaLilia got the call she'd almost convinced herself would not come. Despite herself, her heart began to hammer at the thought of seeing Darnell again. And, of course, she felt bad that his other fang was hurting him. She hated to think of him in pain of any kind. Well, maybe a little part of her smiled because she knew this particular pain would be easy to fix. But she knew the bigger pain, for both of them, was much more of a challenge.

Her cell phone rang again. This time it was Sofia Frangela, her tooth fairy partner in the current initiative and in exile. "I just got the call," Sofia said in her sparkly voice. "Need to fix Vinny Miccio's right fang."

"What a coincidence," LaLilia said. "I also have to fix Darnell DeLouis's."

Sofia giggled. "I understand they're both at a gym in downtown Trenton," she said. "Let's fly there together. We'll be in Trenton in no time."

"Would love to," LaLilia said. "That will give us a chance to plan our strategy."

LaLilia prepared carefully for being with Darnell once again. Though they'd parted so harshly, she'd missed him. The way things ended between them, she couldn't even go to him in dreams any longer. Now she realized she had a second—and probably last—chance to make things work out between them. This time, she hoped and prayed, nothing would go wrong.

LaLilia was wearing her most beautiful gown—gold chiffon and sequins and beads swirling from head to toe. "Wow, you look great!" Sofia, who looked pretty gorgeous herself, exclaimed.

LaLilia wondered if Sofia had grown close to Vinny Miccio the way she had with Darnell. Romancing the battlers was not part of their script as peace bringers and peace keepers—but tooth fairies were famous for their independence of spirit and action. Still, LaLilia couldn't help questioning whether her lovemaking with Darnell had made matters worse. With a pang she realized the prospect of never seeing him again, never being with him again left an ache in heart almost as bad as the one she felt when she witnessed fighting and discord.

But, no matter what, she was committed to playing her part in ending the warfare between Darnell's group and Vinny Miccio's. It was one small but essential step to bringing peace to the world. If she had to sacrifice her romance with Darnell to accomplish this aim, so be it. She shivered at the thought, knowing in her heart she wasn't nearly as firm as she was in her mind.

"The strategy is that we fix their teeth only if they agree not to fight," Sofia said.

"You think they'll go along with that?" LaLilia knew Darnell was one stubborn man. Even if Wanda hadn't told her this, she'd been able to see this about three seconds after meeting him.

Sofia raised a well-shaped black eyebrow. "We have to strategize here. Make it look like whatever happens is their idea, not ours."

LaLilia thought this over. Sofia was craftier than she'd ever expected. She liked that in a colleague. "So how do we do that?"

"How well did you get to know Darnell when you fixed his first fang?" Sofia asked.

A smile played around LaLilia's lips as she remembered the deep sensual intimacy between them.

Sofia's eyes sparkled. "I thought so," she said in a low, sultry voice. LaLilia had a flash of regret at being so transparent, and then she began to suspect that Sofia might judge her negatively for letting her feelings take over the situation.

"Me too," Sofia admitted before LaLilia's emotions sunk any lower. "I couldn't resist the big galoot. Those big brown eyes and thick black hair, those great hands. But most of all, when he gets romantic he reads me his pastry recipes." Sofia sighed. "But now I can't be with him unless he gives up his warrior chief status, and that breaks my heart."

"So we're in the same boat," LaLilia said.

"So to speak, my friend." Sofia linked arms with her as they flew toward the gym. "Well, sister, what do you say we put our heads together and come up with a brilliant plan? I figure we have, oh, thirty or so minutes before we get to the gym."

Trying not to get too excited about the stirring of hope, LaLilia nodded. She was positive, between the two of them, they'd come up with something totally brilliant.

* * * * *

Now that both combatants 'fessed up to having aching fangs, the gym sounded like a fuckin' hospital ward. Darnell, who was sure he was suffering from way stronger pain than that wuss Miccio, made sure to bellow louder than him—careful all the time to hold the ice bag tightly to his poor face. Outta the corner of his eye, he saw Miccio thrashing around the floor like his mother fuckin' ass was on fire, actin' pathetic. Wanda the Wise and Miccio's *consigliore* stood in a corner of the ring, whispering some shit back and forth. Darnell didn't like that, but he figured he couldn't do nothing much about it at this moment.

And then whoosh, like a stream of light and fresh air, two balls of energy flew into the gym. Darnell paused in his wiggling and whooping to see what the hell this was. And then his fool heart nearly stopped when he saw LaLilia arrive. Woman couldn't let him suffer. In spite of all the shit she said about him not wiping the floor up with Miccio, he was happy to see her. LaLilia arriving almost made his tooth stop hurting. Almost.

LaLilia was wearing some gold swirly gown that made her look like the goddess of the sun or some such stuff. Damn, she looked like some piece of candy from heaven.

Next to LaLilia stood another babe, a white woman with black hair, red lips, and all her curves filling out a pink gown — and wings. Darnell sensed that Miccio forgot about his friggin' fang ache when he got a peek at the other chick. Must've been another of them tooth fairies.

For about a million reasons, he was glad to see LaLilia. Not least was that the woman knew how to take care of his tooth. He almost smiled, thinking he was about to get kissed — and get his fang fixed.

But LaLilia was in no rush to come over to him. Instead, she and the other fairy went over to talk with Wanda and the *consigliore*. What was this shit? He didn't need her here to *talk* to them. He needed her next to him, her tongue doing magic and then the rest of her... Using the last bit of his fading strength, Darnell propped himself up on his elbows and glared at the people yakking in the corner.

They all seemed bent on ignoring him and Miccio. Even that wuss shut his yap and was sitting up looking the same place Darnell was. What the fuck? Darnell looked over at the wuss, who was looking back at him through bitty-slitty eyes.

"What kinda shit you pullin' here?" Miccio asked, his words hard to understand as they came out through tightly clenched teeth.

"What you mean I'm pullin' shit?" Darnell protested. "You the guys with the rep for pullin' shit. Wouldn't surprise me if..."

"Shut up, the both of you," Wanda and the *consigliore* commanded simultaneously. Darnell, so shocked that Wanda would talk to him like that in front of his enemy, did shut up. Darnell would have to give Wanda a talking to later. Then he remembered she already left him and was only here as a favor, so maybe there wouldn't be no later. Miccio, looking as surprised as Darnell, also shut up.

"As you can see," the *consigliore* said, talking so soft Darnell had to sit up and listen carefully to catch his words, "help has arrived. The two dentists who fixed your other fangs. They're willing to help you out now, but only on one condition."

Darnell knew what condition LaLilia made for being with him. Now she was also playing that game about taking care of his aching tooth. He did not like this one little bit. And he refused to let her blackmail him or whatever the hell she was doing. Yeah, she was the most beautiful, wonderful lady he'd ever done anything with. Yeah, she made every other babe in the universe look like dog meat. But that didn't mean he could just give up and do what she fuckin' ordered. He'd start doing like that and there'd be no living with the woman—or any of them.

He had to show her who was boss.

To give him time to think, he asked, "I need to hear what condition that is." Damn, Miccio asked the same fuckin' question at the same time. Darnell did not like to think the two of them were alike in any way, shape, or form other than being male vampires in Trenton. Male vampires in Trenton with aching right fangs. Other than that, nothing in common. Except being the leaders of their groups, which meant they were supposed to fight it out tonight. Of course being head of the mother fuckin' Cosa Nostras no way, no how compared to being head of the Black Guards...

Okay, so a bunch of things in common. Didn't mean a mother fuckin' thing.

The two fairies looked at each other. The white one smiled and bent her head a little to LaLilia. Darnell couldn't help noticing that Miccio couldn't take his fool eyes off the white one. He'd better the hell keep his eyes and everything else off LaLilia, or Darnell would beat his sorry ass. Which Darnell was supposed to be doing anyway.

LaLilia, looking gorgeous but drop-dead serious, said, "The condition is that you, Darnell, and you, Vinny, call off the battle between you. Make peace. Resolve that Trenton is big enough for both of you and your groups. Do that and my friend Sofia and I will be happy to treat you."

Darnell snorted, a noise that he hoped sounded like a laugh but suspected was more of a groan. He folded his arms in front of him and twisted his face into fierce warrior mode. "No. Fuckin'. Way."

Miccio said the same thing, minus the "fuckin'" but added some other word Darnell didn't quite catch.

They both turned to each other with hatred in their eyes and nodded once. Then they instantly looked away.

Darnell did not appreciate the look of sadness in LaLilia's eyes. And Wanda, who he caught out of the corner of his eye, looked like she was fixing to spit fire.

Sofia shrugged and ran her tongue over her very full, very dark red lips. "Then, LaLilia, I guess we have no choice. Let's just go back to our work for the night."

LaLilia nodded slowly. Darnell heard Miccio growl softly, like he wanted to get his pecker into Sofia worse than he needed to get his tooth fixed. Darnell, whose own cock was at full alert, found one more thing he had in common with Miccio. Except, of course, he wanted to bury his cock deep into LaLilia.

Darnell looked to Wanda the Wise for a little help here. But she refused to meet his eyes. So he knew it was up to him, again, to save the day. To come up with a way for him and Miccio to get their teeth fixed without caving to the two fairies. He racked his brain. And then he came up with the answer. "I've got it," he howled.

Chapter Eight

All eyes were on Darnell. If he wasn't in such agony, he'd string this out longer. But he needed to get patched up, now. It was so quiet in the gym, like they were all holding their breaths.

Darnell came as close as he could to a smile. Then addressing LaLilia and the other chick, Sofia, he said, his voice soft and reasonable, "Ain't you two ladies dentists?"

The two of them looked at each other, like they weren't so sure where Darnell was heading. He liked that. "Yes, part of being a tooth fairy is being a dentist."

He nodded, happy with the way the conversation was going. "Correct me if I'm wrong about this, ladies." He was never wrong about nothing and wished these here folks would realize that. Well, he was about to blow them away with his intelligence. Despite his killer pain. "Don't dentists have to swear somethin', some famous oath?" He paused to let his words sink in. "You know, that you gotta help any poor sucker who comes to you feelin' like shit?"

Now both of them looked like he got them. Yeah. He was going to get what he wanted without having to give in to their *conditions*. Hell, he was also saving Miccio's ass. Miccio would owe him.

Darnell tried to read the expression on Wanda's face, but her features showed nothing. Damn, he was sure she had to be impressed with how smart he was. She just didn't want him to know. Playing hard to get.

Well, he was never one to brag much on his victories. Hell, at this point, he just wanted his tooth fixed so he could beat Miccio's ass. After that, he'd see to getting LaLilia into his life on his terms.

LaLilia, her beautiful brown eyes wide with sadness, said, "You're right, Darnell."

He nearly jumped up and down like some fool clown when he heard those words. Wished he could make a tape of them. Play it for Wanda the Wise and all them other hard-headed women he had the misfortune to get stuck with.

"We can never turn down a patient in need," LaLilia continued. "Even though you and Mr. Miccio refuse to meet our reasonable requests. So, we will indeed have to try our best to cure you."

Hallelujah. Darnell struggled to keep from smirking. "Just lead me to wherever you need me to be so you can fix me with your magic," he said, holding his hand out to LaLilia.

She wrinkled her beautiful brow and looked at his hand like it was a lump of dog shit from the sidewalk. "You misunderstand," she said, sounding all hoity-toity like some society bitch down from Princeton.

"What you mean, I *misunderstand*?" he asked, suddenly feeling less cool and sweating his ass off to sound tough.

LaLilia's lips went into a smile so dazzling he needed sunglasses. "I'm going to heal Mr. Miccio," she said, holding out her hand to that worm. "Sofia is going to take care of you." The other fairy stepped forward.

Shit. Fuck. Mother fuckin' women's brains. Darnell's poor head whirled at LaLilia's foul plan. Normally, he'd be okay with that chick Sofia sticking her tongue in his mouth. But not when he could have LaLilia. And the thought of LaLilia sticking her tongue into Miccio's mouth... Well, he swore on his gravestone he'd sooner let the guy stake him in the heart than let that happen.

Miccio made a grab for Sofia's arm. Looked like he wasn't none too cool with the fairies' plan neither.

Sofia hissed and arm-wrestled herself away from Miccio so fast the guy's fool head was probably spinning. Darnell, who'd been about to make a grab for LaLilia, was glad for once to come in second in a race. Let the other guy look the fool.

Wings fluttering, the two fairies zoomed back away from the men. Wanda the Wise and the *consigliore* jumped up, rushing between them and their bosses. Wanda, her voice cold as a bottle of milk left on a stoop in January, said, "The ladies agreed to help you out. But as you rejected their condition, they have come up with the only way they can possibly heal you and stay true to what they care about."

Darnell rolled his eyes. If he didn't get his friggin' tooth fixed soon, he'd go on some mad outta control rampage. Would serve them all right, too. But instead, using the last reserves of his self-control, he said, "Miccio and I dislike the plan them ladies came up with." He did not appreciate having to talk for Miccio. But it would be worse if Miccio tried to talk for him. "There's gotta be another way for them two dentists to take care of him and me."

Sofia and LaLilia looked at each other and shrugged. They had a fast whispered conference with Wanda and the *consigliore*, who nodded his head. Then the *consigliore* spoke. "The ladies said they'll listen to any idea you have as to how they can treat you and maintain their principles of bringing peace to Trenton and the world. But they can only stay here one more hour before they need to return to their duties. So, the two of you talk. If you can come up with a plan that's acceptable to them, they'll heal you."

Shit. He needed to talk to Miccio if he wanted a shot at having LaLilia take care of him. Fortunately, Miccio didn't look no happier with the prospect than he did. Like they had any choice. Them two fairies had him and Miccio by the short and curlies.

"I don't know about you," Miccio said, moving closer so the two of them could talk just between them. "But if I don't get this fuckin' fang fixed soon, I'm gonna put a fuckin' stake through my own fuckin' heart."

"Yeah," Darnell found himself sympathizing, "them fang cavities are a bitch." A terrible thought smacked Darnell right between the eyes. It wasn't normal for vampires to get cavities. Darnell remembered what Wanda told him about that. "Uh, Miccio, who turned you?"

He made a face. "Bucky Dent."

Darnell couldn't believe it. This nearly made the two of them *brothers*. And explained why they had such mother fuckin' crappy teeth. "Shit. Me too. The fucker had bad teeth."

Miccio made a face like he just swallowed some of that refuse blood the hospital dumped. "Figures. Well, man, what're we gonna do here?"

"Ain't no way I can let LaLilia take care of you," Darnell growled, baring his fangs and nearly croaking when the air hit.

"Ditto for me and Sofia," Miccio moaned. "So what're we gonna do?"

"Miccio, I hate to say it. But I think we gotta give in to them."

The other man nodded. "I think you're right." He scowled. "But I could always kill you later."

Darnell wanted nothing more than to get a shot at this arrogant bastard — his brother. But he couldn't lie, not to LaLilia. "Hey, man. Once I give my word, I stick to it."

"No shit?" Miccio asked, his eyes looking almost like he had some respect for Darnell somewhere in the middle of all his pain and bad ass attitude. "Like some fuckin' Boy Scout."

So much for fooling himself that Miccio would show any respect. "No, Miccio. Like a man," Darnell said.

Miccio didn't answer.

'Hey, man. I need to get my tooth fixed. LaLilia's gonna take care of me. That means I ain't gonna fight with you. Got it?"

This time Miccio nodded. "Yeah, man. Let's go get fixed."

They broke away from their powwow and told the others they were ready to deal.

"No fighting?" LaLilia asked.

"Right," Darnell groaned. Now that he knew she was gonna take care of him, he couldn't wait another minute.

"Not now, not ever?" Sofia asked. "I need to hear it from you, Vincenzo Alberto Giovanni Miccio."

"Yeah, yeah, whatever," Miccio spat out.

Darnell rolled his eyes but, when he caught LaLilia glaring at him, said nothing. Vincenzo Alberto Giovanni. Jeez.

"And you'll live together in peace and harmony, Darnell Dexter DeLouis? Trenton can be home for the Black Guards and the Cosa Nostras?" LaLilia asked.

Darnell wouldn'ta believed she could be so hard. Exposing his middle name like that. Wanda musta told her. But he had nothing left to deal with. "Yeah, yeah."

"We want you both to shake hands now and feed off each other," both fairies said at the same time.

Too much. "Fuck that," Darnell said. Miccio howled. "That would hurt!"

Sofia turned to LaLilia. "I'm willing to postpone the peace ceremony 'til after we heal these two. How about you?"

LaLilia nodded. Then she held out her hand to Darnell, and his knees nearly collapsed like he was some old lady needing a walker.

In a moment she flew him to some dentist's office. He didn't know where the hell they were. He didn't care. She laid him out, and then she was on him, her sweet tongue caressing his throbbing tooth.

Like the snap of fingers, he was good to go again. Darnell collapsed with the sheer relief of the pain halting in its tracks. Now he was fit to face Miccio.

Except he'd made a promise to LaLilia. And he really couldn't break his word. Of course, this probably meant he was finished as chief of the Black Guards. But she was worth it. Now that his tooth was all better, it was time to start paying attention to the other parts demanding some loving care. Like his huge erect cock.

* * * * *

Had it been too easy? LaLilia wondered why she didn't feel more satisfaction when Darnell and Vinny caved and agreed to what Sofia and she demanded. After all, they'd both averted a battle that would have ended in one of the vampires being damaged and one of the groups banished from Trenton. But this didn't feel like the full-hearted embrace of peace she and Sofia needed the men to commit to in order to cancel their exile in Wyoming and return to Trenton.

Darnell reached for her, and LaLilia wanted nothing more than to feed on him and love him, sealing their reunion in the best possible way. But were they really back together? Or was Darnell just taking advantage of the situation to have a little fun and games with her before he reverted to his old way of being?

Didn't matter. Delicious as his erection looked and felt, moist as her panties were with her desire for him, she had to steer Darnell back to the boxing ring to formalize the peace between him and Vinny.

Mustering all her strength, she simply stood up and said, "Sorry. No can do."

Darnell, who evidently had his strength back, sat up. "What do you mean? Why not? Don't you want me, baby?"

With all her heart and every nerve ending in her, but she couldn't let him know. She needed to be strong, couldn't waver when she was so close to making a huge step forward in the peace process. "We have to meet back with Vinny and Sofia so we can finalize the agreement between you two."

Darnell scowled. "We said we ain't gonna fight. Ain't that enough?"

"It's a start. But we want something more formal from you two. The sacred exchange of blood and the binding oath."

Shit. "You really gonna make me feed off that mother fucker?" Darnell's voice rose.

"You know that's our way," LaLilia said.

Darnell folded his arms in front of him. "Can you give me back my toothache?" he grumped.

Despite herself, LaLilia laughed. "Come on, Darnell. It's not that bad. You've been through the worst already. Time to try out the fang, make sure I did a good job healing it."

"I'd rather try it on you," he said, his voice husky.

"First things first," she said. She held out her hand to him. "Come on. Time's flying by."

* * * * *

Miccio didn't look no happier to be in the ring getting ready to feed off him than Darnell felt. Darnell'd never before gone through nothing like this to get a woman. But then he'd never before met a woman like LaLilia.

Wings fluttering, the two fairies stood outside the ring and watched. Now Wanda and the *consigliore* took over. First they administered the oath. He and Miccio had to put their fingers on their fangs and repeat the words after the two of them. "I swear and promise," they said, "on my gravestone, that I will uphold peace between the Black Guards and the Cosa Nostras. I will do everything in my power now and always to make sure that Trenton is a good and safe home for the vampires of both groups and their friends."

Darnell wanted to fuckin' puke when he choked out the words. He knew what he said had to be what he did from now on. And then, even worse, he had to feed off Miccio. Feeling sicker than after he drank from a guy with salmonella food poisoning, Darnell sank his fangs into the other man's neck and sucked his blood. But strange thing. As he drank, Darnell started feeling peculiar. Hard to put into words. It was like he *understood* Miccio, and he even could almost like the guy. Like they really had way more in common than he thought before. By the time he licked the puncture wound on Vinny's neck, he practically felt like hugging the guy.

He held back from that. But he'd tell LaLilia about that later. And then Vinny began to feed off him. Man, the whole fuckin' thing was so good, Darnell was practically crying like some sob sister watching a love story. He couldn't believe it. Part of his brain was saying this wasn't possible. The other part was asking if Vinny was feeling the same thing he was.

And then Vinny licked his wound. And just like that, the two men were slapping each other on the back like the best two buds in the world. Darnell knew no way he'd ever be able to fight Vinny again. And peace between them somehow, strangely, felt a hell of a lot better than war.

He got it. He couldn't wait to tell LaLilia. Right after they made love. But when at last he turned away from Vinny so he could go to LaLilia, she was gone. Sofia was gone too. Vinny and him looked at each other. Now that they were friends at peace, why did their women go off and leave them?

"Let's go after them," Vinny growled.

"Yeah, man." Darnell looked to Wanda. "Where'd they go?"

"They both congratulate you and say they're proud and happy. But they had to return to their new home and finish the work they have there."

Darnell turned to his new friend Miccio and said, "That's bullshit."

"I'm with you, man. Let's go after them."

"Wanda, where'd you say they were?" Darnell asked.

"Wyoming."

"Where the hell is that?" Miccio asked.

"We'll find it," Darnell said.

Chapter Nine

Leaving Darnell was the hardest thing LaLilia had ever done in her life. At least Sofia was as miserable as she was. Misery loved company and all that. Sad, depressed, and feeling many emotions that went against the job performance code for tooth fairies, the two women decided that they'd better keep each other company as they made their way back to Wyoming that night.

"Did we really have to leave them?" LaLilia asked Sofia for the hundredth time. "They did do what we wanted."

"Yes," Sofia said. "But only under duress. Are they really going to spread peace, or will they begin to fight again? They may not fight each other, but that doesn't mean they won't have other battles. We've seen that happen before."

LaLilia sighed. "I suppose you're right. But Sofia, I have to tell you. I miss Darnell. He got to me, made things seem magic in ways that no one else ever has…"

"I know just what you mean…" Sofia sighed.

Subdued and occasionally stifling a sob, the two fairies flew back to their new home and their nightly collection.

* * * * *

Darnell and Vinny learned a lot about each other as they flew to Wyoming. They also made plans for how they'd change Trenton once they returned with their women.

"I'm tired of those bars on the windows of the Black Guards Social Hall," Darnell admitted. "I like them window boxes with flowers much better."

"Yeah," Vinny said. "Adds class. And talk about class, what do you think about havin' a festival in Trenton every year?"

"What kinda festival?" Darnell asked.

"Garlic and chocolate," Vinny said.

"I like that. But man, how we gonna get the fairies to come back with us? I can't believe they ran out like that."

"I got a plan," Vinny said. "Fairies are, you know, romantic. We gotta sweep them off their feet."

"I thought I done that already," Darnell said.

Vinny punched his arm. "With the ladies, you gotta keep doing it again and again."

"Is that right?"

"Yeah. Now with Sofia, I'm gonna get over to her and whisper the most tender, sweet, romantic words I know. She won't be able to resist."

"Oh yeah? Like what?"

"Like I'm gonna tell her my top secret recipe for cannolis." Vinny laughed. "She'll follow me anywhere after that. Whatcha gonna say to LaLilia?"

"Gonna tell her one of my poems," Darnell admitted to Vinny. Jeez, it was neat havin' a friend he could talk to. Even admit he wrote poetry. His heart was beating like a fuckin' hammer. LaLilia had to love his poem. She had to.

* * * * *

Right before dawn, when LaLilia and Sofia arrived at their coffins after a long night's work, the two men were waiting for them. Without saying a word, LaLilia and Sofia went off with their men.

LaLilia's head began to swim. Seeing Darnell here now was like having all her dreams come true. But dawn was rapidly approaching, and they'd have to take their rest.

He drew her into his arms and tenderly kissed her.

He carried her to her coffin, gently laid her inside, and whispered these words:

From the highest mountains,
From the deepest sea.
I want to shout
That I love my fairy.

Be with me now,
Be with me always.
Love me tonight,
Don't send me away.

You've brought me love,
And the peace is swell.
So say you'll stay with
Your Darnell.

LaLilia's eyes misted. She pulled him into her extra deep, wide coffin and closed the lid. They kissed, tenderly at first. After that, they both wiggled out of their clothes—and forgot about gentleness. Goddess, she needed him too much to let there be anything gentle. Their lips locked in a ferocious kiss, both of them starving for the taste and the feel of the other.

Darnell's tongue probed into her mouth as if he'd suck her into him. And then he broke the kiss to feed, and she was lost. She came, shrieking his name, the moment he bit into her tender neck with his now healthy fangs. And she came again when she bit into him and drank of his essence. She could already tell that he was a changed man, not the one she'd made love to before. And all the changes were for the good.

He licked her puncture wound, and then his tongue was everywhere on her body, along with his teeth, his lips, his fingers. She couldn't get enough of him. And then he tongued her clit, and LaLilia went into raptures. Every flick of his tongue on her sent ripples of pleasure radiating up and out and over, consuming her body in a crescendo of need.

She managed to take his huge, gorgeous erection into her hand, and it was like she'd never let go. He moaned, now from pleasure instead of the pain he'd been in before. "Oh, baby," he groaned.

She opened her legs wide and arched her hips up. She wanted to get his cock into her mouth, but that had to wait. Now she needed him to come into her, to move his cock everywhere inside her. She didn't have to ask twice.

Darnell rolled over onto his back. LaLilia straddled his hips and slid on down his pole, and she went into spasms of ecstasy. Everything that man did, every way he moved, started a new wave of pleasure. He clutched her ass with his strong hands, massaging her there as he filled her pussy completely. His cock was like a work of art, long and thick, as gorgeous to feel as it was to look at.

LaLilia rotated her ass, and Darnell's cock jumped in her. "LaLilia, I can't hold out much longer," he whispered.

"Come in me, baby," she said. "I want to feel you come deep inside me." She thrust her pussy forward, taking him in further with every word.

He groaned. Now he was playing with her ass, fingering her, starting a new fire wherever he touched.

He moved harder, stronger, faster, thrusting into her front and back. LaLilia was flying high, flying, flying, and then she shattered into a million pieces. And came back together better than ever.

"Oh baby," Darnell screamed out. And then he came, shooting what felt like a gallon of cum into her. Then, their hearts hammering, they fell together—sweaty and slick from their sex.

They lay together in silence for a bit. LaLilia didn't have the words she needed now, and she could sense Darnell didn't either.

And then he said, "Don't leave me again, LaLilia. I want you with me. Come back to Trenton tonight with me. And Vinny and Sofia."

LaLilia's heart soared. But what if she was wrong? What if he hadn't changed? Was she still giving her heart and body to a committed warrior? "I know you and Vinny are good together right now. But what about the groups you lead? The Black Guards and the Cosa Nostras?"

"We're going to be partners in making Trenton a better place to live."

LaLilia leaned back against her pillows. Then she propped herself up on her elbows. "You ain't shittin' me, are you, Darnell?"

He raised his eyebrows and laughed. "Never thought I'd hear the *tooth fairy* use a word like that," he said.

LaLilia grew warm with embarrassment. "Answer the damn question."

Now Darnell sat up. "I'm a man of my word, LaLilia. And I give you my word, I'm a man of peace now. And I wish I'd heard how good peace is a long time ago. Woulda saved a lotta wear 'n' tear. But I figure better late than never."

"Oh, goddess. Darnell, I think I love you."

"I know I love you, baby. Now come here. Gonna make up for lost time."

Things were going too fast. "Hold on, Darnell. I need to make a brief phone call." She reached for her cell.

"Say hello to Vinny and Sofia for me," he said.

She just looked at him. How had he known? Sofia, sounding dreamy, reported that Vinny had changed as much as Darnell.

"It's a miracle," LaLilia said.

"Two miracles," Sofia said. "Talk to you later." And she hung up.

LaLilia returned to Darnell, who was waiting for her with a huge smile and an enormous erection. "It's got your name on it, baby. Come on here."

"I believe you," LaLilia said. "And I'm here for good."

Darnell took her in his arms and began to show his appreciation as only he could.

They even managed to get some rest that day. And that night the tooth fairies and their men flew back to Trenton.

Epilogue

With the intervention of the two Tooth Fairies and the heads of the rival vampire gangs, a new era of peace and prosperity began to flourish in Trenton. Vinny the Mooch Miccio opened a new bakery and became the most honored pastry chef on the East Coast, known especially for his cannolis. Darnell DeLouis operated a much-praised high-end men's fashion emporium, known for its late-night hours. He even got Vinny to upgrade his wardrobe. Darnell also gained fame as a poet whose verses turned up in songs and love letters. He saved the best ones for LaLilia's eyes only. LaLilia Guitry and Sofia Frangela were in frequent demand as lecturers on Peaceful Dentistry. The two couples met often and loved to go on vacation together, always scheduled so that they never missed Trenton's annual garlic and chocolate festival.

Trenton rose on the Vampires' Central Register of desirable cities to visit and live in. Not quite at the same level as New Orleans, but definitely up from the basement position of previous years...

Wanda the Wise chewed her lip as she thought what to write next.

"Wanda, get your butt in here," a voice bellowed.

Wanda rolled her eyes. *Some* things never changed.

About the author:

Exploring the erotic side of romance keeps Mardi Ballou chained to her computer—and inspires some amazing research. Mardi's a Jersey girl, now living in Northern California with her hero husband—the love of her life—who's also her tech maven and first reader. Her days and nights are filled with books to read and write, chocolate, and the pursuit of romantic dreams. A Scorpio by birth and temperament, Mardi believes in living life with Passion, Intensity, and Lots of Laughs (this last from her moon in Sagittarius). Published in different genres under different names, Mardi is thrilled to be part of the Ellora's Cave Team Romantica.

Mardi welcomes mail from readers. You can write to her c/o Ellora's Cave Publishing at 1337 Commerce Drive, #13, Stow, Ohio 44224.

Also by Mardi Ballou:

Frannie 'n' the Private Dick

Delilah Devlin

Trademarks Acknowledgement

The author acknowledges the trademarked status and trademark owners of the following wordmarks mentioned in this work of fiction:

Sardi's: Sardi's Restaurant Services, Inc.

Pop Rocks: Zeta Espacial S.A. Corporation

Lifetime Movie Network: Lifetime Entertainment Services Cable LT Holdings, Inc., Disney/ABC International Television, Inc., Hearst LT Inc. and Hearst Holdings, Inc. and Hearst/ABC Video Services

New York Knicks: Madison Square Garden, L.P

Benihana Grill: Benihana National Corp.

K-Y: Johnson & Johnson Corporation

Chapter One

Francesca Valentine had died and gone to Hell.

No other explanation made sense. She swam back to awareness through a molasses-thick void to find herself suddenly spat out from a dark womb into a cold, hollow space. Blind, and so still she knew she didn't breathe—her mind turned over like a sluggish engine before revving into high gear.

Quickly, she assessed what she knew. She lay on a hard surface, covered with a scratchy square of thin fabric, unable to move a muscle. A low whine, like that of an air conditioner, came from the opposite side of the space. Harsh light shone from above, warming her face, but hurting her closed eyes. So, she probably wasn't blind after all. But she was definitely dead. Stone-cold. Her chest wasn't moving in and out, but she didn't feel starved for air.

She knew who she was and what had killed her, but hadn't a clue what new fix she'd landed herself in. From nearby came the scrape of footsteps and a tentative humming, then...

"Bee-ooot-ee-foll Dreeeeamer, wake unto me..."

She was in Hell all right. A demented spirit hovered over her, emitting an off key warbling that set Frannie's teeth on edge. By the rusty sound of the grating voice, her tormentor must be an ancient female, and the she-devil was trying to remove the skin from her face in slow, abrasive circles with...*apricot-scented facial scrub*? Frannie'd had a chemical peel the week before. The last thing she needed was a dime-store product applied to her professionally maintained skin.

God must be punishing her for the sin of vanity—for all the hours she'd spent being teased, plucked, painted, and waxed. Each moment endured to make her the perfect trophy for Vinnie to parade around his "business associates" for them to kiss, pinch, and swat.

Now she wished she'd gone to Mass more often, or hadn't lusted after the young Irish priest, or hadn't snuck out her bedroom window to canoodle with Vinnie. Especially that.

Her mother had predicted just such a fate when Frannie got engaged to Vinnie Ricchione, and had even sworn to wear black to the wedding.

But Mama had described the fire-and-brimstone version of the ultimate southerly location in vivid detail. Obviously God hadn't designed Hell as a one-size-fits-all sins destination.

"Star-liiiight and dooo-drops are waiting for thee…"

She could almost see her mama now, shaking her finger at Zia Grazia. "What did I tell that girl? Vinnie's no good."

Zia Grazia would nod her gray head and masticate on her slipping dentures, too deaf to care about Donatella Valentine's latest tirade.

But that wouldn't stop Mama. She'd scoot closer to shout into her aunt's ear. "Do you think a daughter listens to her mother? Now look at me. No daughter. No grandbabies. I told her Vinnie'd come to a bad end — and her along with him!"

Well, Mama had only been half-right.

Paralyzed, forced to submit to a facial flaying and the demon's ear-shattering trills, Frannie's penance had a certain poetic justice.

She was dead because of Vinnie.

While her death hadn't been precisely his fault, she'd never have followed him if he'd been the faithful sort of fiancé.

He'd said he was meeting the boys. "Don't wait up, hon. We got shipments comin' in." But Frannie had known better. One time too many, he'd come home smelling of cheap whiskey and even cheaper perfume. This time, Frannie would catch the cheating bastard in the act.

That night, she'd teetered on three-inch boot heels on a wooden crate behind his shipping company office, peering into a darkened room. She'd almost decided Vinnie had slipped the noose when she heard a commotion coming from beneath the window where Vinnie's desk sat. At first, she hadn't understood what she heard, then the sounds had grown louder—punctuated by groans, bumps, and slurps too large and energetic to be two mice doing the bunny-hump.

Irate, she'd screeched and toppled off the crate. But falling into the trash bin wasn't what killed her.

"Sounds of the ruuude world heard in the daaaaay..."

She'd crawled backward out of the dumpster, glad the only things clinging to her hair were bits of packing peanuts, when she heard a door slam and footsteps entering the alley. She brushed herself off, picked up her purse from beside the overturned crate, and stalked toward the street.

"Hon, what the hell are you doin'?" Vinnie shuffled toward her, tucking his shirt into his pants. "Now, baby, I can explain—"

She raised her chin, held out her hand, and stomped right past him, proud she kept her chin from wobbling. *The bastard's not gonna make me cry.*

"Frannie—honey, wait!"

She quickened her pace and turned the corner onto the sidewalk. As luck would have it, a taxi was driving straight toward her. She started to run, waving frantically at the car, but it didn't slow. She stepped into the street, but her foot tilted on the edge of a gutter and her ankle turned. The heel of her boot snapped, and Frannie threw out her arms as she stumbled into the path of the taxi.

But the taxi hadn't killed her either.

The cab screeched to a halt, and the driver flung open his door. "Lady, you okay?" He was a big, burly guy—Irish, she'd have guessed, by the look of his dark brows and square, rugged jaw if his faintly accented speech hadn't already given him away.

"Please!" She held out her hand in his direction.

"Francesca! Honey, don't move," Vinnie shouted.

She didn't have to force a tear into her eye. Her ankle throbbed. She stared at the driver and gave him what Vinnie called her "diamonds-or-flowers" look—the one guaranteed to make a man do her bidding.

The Irishman straightened his shoulders and pushed back his shirtsleeves, revealing thick wrists and muscled forearms. "Is this man botherin' you, ma'am?"

She nodded and let her chin wobble.

The driver bent down and swept her easily to her feet. Frannie let herself lean against his broad chest just long enough to test the depth of his indrawn breath. She could tell a lot about a man's attraction from a telltale gasp, and she needed this man's attraction to flare long enough for Vinnie to notice.

The driver's chest expanded, and the arms that held her tightened fractionally.

"I'm not a man—I'm her husband," Vinnie shouted. "Get your hands off her!"

"You're not a husband until we share joint checking and a last name!" she shouted back. The driver hesitated, and she clutched his sleeve. "Please, help me! I swear he's not my husband."

"Near enough!" Vinnie said.

Looking up at her rescuer from beneath her lashes, she added softly, "I have to get away."

His gaze locked with hers for a moment before swinging to pin Vinnie to the spot. "Looks like your lady doesn't want anythin' to do with you at the moment." The driver gently pushed her behind him. "Ma'am, you go ahead and get inside."

As she limped toward the cab, Frannie looked over her shoulder.

Vinnie's face was a mottled red. "Now look here—"

"I think you'd better back off." The burly Irishman clenched his fists.

Vinnie peered around the mountain-sized man at Frannie as she ducked into the back seat of the taxi. "Frannie, you come back here. We gotta talk. What you seen wasn't nothin', I swear! It wasn't even me!"

Frannie pulled the door shut and waited for the driver to back his way to the taxi.

Vinnie stood in the middle of the street, his shoulders drooping. She almost felt sorry for him, until the door to the company office swung open. Raeline Curtis, Vinnie's secretary, hurried down the street, tugging at the seat of her tight skirt.

Frizzy, over-bleached blonde hair, broad hips and *cheap shoes*—Vinnie'd cheated on her with Raeline? Confused, Frannie peered through the back window as the taxi drove away, Vinnie's swarthy, slender face and slumped shoulders growing smaller in the distance. He'd wait at home—and be truly, miserably sorry for the pain he'd caused her. And she'd probably forgive him—after her pride had been soothed with lots of groveling and gifts.

But tonight, she needed to make the snake sweat.

"Where can I take you, ma'am?"

"To another life?" she muttered. Louder, she said, "Drop me at *Lizards 'n' Suds*."

"You sure about that? That joint's kinda rough for a lady like you."

"A lady like me?" *I live in sin with a man whose "business associates" send Christmas cards from the federal penitentiary.* Frannie sniffed. "Thanks for your help back there, but I'll be just fine."

He shrugged his massive shoulders. "Whatever you want. It's your dime."

What she'd wanted was something she'd never have now.

"Lull'd by the mooon-light have all passed awaaaay…"

That's me all right – all passed away. A tear trickled down the side of her cheek.

"Well, that's one for the books," the quavering, aged voice said. "Wouldn't think you'd have any juice left."

Something soft and spongy swept away the tear, and then the sponge was back with the familiar smell of makeup. A cheap musty foundation, if Frannie's nose was any judge. This place was Hell all right.

"Such a shame. You were a pretty little thing. And that man of yours is cryin' buckets over you."

As well he should! The lying, cheating bastard! She hoped he was very, very sorry, that his privates shriveled to a nub, and that he'd be haunted by her beautiful face for the rest of his life.

Then maybe he'd feel a tenth of the hurt she'd felt as she'd tried to drown her sorrow at *Lizards 'n' Suds.* The first beer tasted sour, and the bubbles made her burp. She looked around to make sure no one noticed, but the music was so loud she quickly lost her inhibitions and burped again. The second beer was much sweeter, but her tummy pressed against the waist of her skirt and everything felt tighter.

Especially her engagement ring.

She'd glared at the shiny solitaire and tried to tug it off her finger, but couldn't get it past the first knuckle. After a stealthy glance over her shoulder, she dunked her hand into her icy-cold beer. Perhaps the chill would make her skin contract.

"You know, most people drink their beers."

Frannie blinked and glanced to her right.

The taxi driver slid onto the stool beside her.

She glared. "Are you following me?"

He grinned. "I was due a break. Decided I'd hang around and see if you needed a ride home."

His smile was killer—white teeth, full lips framed by dimpled cheeks. She hadn't noted much about his appearance before—just his immense size. But even in the subdued light shining from behind the bar, she could see he was a very handsome man—if you were into black-haired paddies with blue eyes. His hair was on the long side and scraped back into a ponytail. The dark-blue shadow on his jaw added to his rangy, masculine appeal.

She realized she'd been staring. "I don't need a ride—in your car, that is." Oh, God, she'd just said that out loud.

His lips curled at the corners, but he looked at the bartender and raised a finger. A cold brew was deposited in front of him, and he took a long draw before setting it down. "Is there a good reason your hand's in your glass?"

"Oh!" She pulled out her hand and dried it with a napkin. "I was just trying to get this off." She tugged the ring again, but it still didn't budge.

"Let me try." His large hand enclosed hers, and he pulled it toward his face.

Frannie's heart fluttered, and then heat swept across her cheeks. Was he going to kiss her hand?

Instead, he opened his mouth and swallowed her finger.

She was so surprised she yelped and tried to draw back her hand.

His grasp tightened. Then his gaze never left hers as his teeth closed gently around the ring and slid it slowly off her finger.

Sure she was well on the way to melting into a puddle at his feet, Frannie sighed with relief when he released her tingling fingers.

The diamond sparkled brightly between his white teeth as he grinned. He plucked it from his mouth and dipped it in his own beer before handing it back.

Frannie clasped her hands firmly in her lap. "I don't want it," she said, her voice flat.

"You're just angry. You'll want it later." He slid it over the tip of his pinkie finger. "I'll keep it for you—for now. What's your name?"

Frannie jumped. "Why do you want to know?"

"Just in case I lose you in this crowd—I'd like to know who to return the ring to."

Frannie watched his expression closely for a clue to his true intent. The explanation sounded reasonable enough, but Frannie knew every guy had an ulterior motive for every good deed—and it usually had something to do with sex.

He held up both hands. "Honest. I'm not askin' for a date—I don't go for almost-married ladies." He wiggled the finger with the ring. "This doesn't look like a knockoff. When you're over bein' mad, you'll want it back."

Frannie sighed and stuck out her hand. "Francesca Valentine."

His much larger hand swallowed hers, but he gave her the gentlest squeeze and let her go. "Niall Keegan."

Frannie felt a reluctant smile tug at her lips. "I knew you were Irish."

He lifted one dark, perfectly shaped eyebrow and grinned deliciously. "Must have been my stunning good looks."

That she couldn't deny, but she'd be the last woman to feed *another* man's ego. "You've a trace of a brogue in your voice," she said, imitating his accent.

"Me mother would be mortified, she would," he said, exaggerating the lilt. "She sent us all to school to learn to speak like Americans."

Frannie tilted her head. "Why? I think your accent's lovely."

"She didn't want us taken for every other Irisher straight off the boat."

"That's kind of an archaic sentiment in this day and age. Who in this city isn't right off the boat? In your profession, especially—I don't know when the last time was I caught a cab with someone who could actually speak English."

Niall shrugged. "Well, it was a long time ago. Things were a little harder in her day."

"She sounds like Zia Grazia." At his quizzical expression, she added, "My mama's aunt. Now, she was straight off the boat from Italy. Literally." She started to raise her glass again and then remembered the places her hands had been tonight. She wrinkled her nose and set it down.

"Would you be wantin' another beer?"

Frannie sighed. The man wasn't going to leave her alone to wallow in her misery. "I suppose so. But I'll buy my own. This isn't a date."

He waved at the bartender. "Another beer for the lady."

Frannie pulled out a ten and quickly laid it on the counter, then gave him a warning glare.

Niall stared at the bill. "Don't go getting' nervous now. I'll let you pay."

"I'm not...nervous, that is. It's just—"

"I know. This isn't a date."

The bartender replaced her beer, and an awkward silence fell between them.

"So, you want to talk about what happened back there?" Niall asked quietly.

Frannie didn't have to guess what he was talking about. She supposed it was pretty obvious what had happened at the shipping office, what with Vinnie half-dressed and Raeline slinking away. But admitting to this man that her fiancé had cheated on her was too galling. She stared at her glass, at her lacquered fingertips—anywhere, but into his knowing eyes. "Nothing happened."

"All right. I can take a hint." He leaned close and his voice dropped. "But I'm a good listener. You'd be surprised the things I hear."

Her mind went momentarily blank as she breathed in the spicy scent of his aftershave. "Oh yeah. I suppose taxi drivers hear plenty."

"See plenty, too."

She glanced up to see a wicked gleam shining in his eyes. And that was all it took. One wicked gleam and she relaxed — and forgot about the louse waiting at home. The man sitting beside her was too tempting, too large to ignore. His warm, deep-timbered voice and navy eyes seduced her into letting down her guard. At least, that was the excuse she gave herself for gifting him with a smile.

His eyelids dipped and his gaze fell to her lips. Then he drew a deep breath and glanced away. "He's a bloody damn fool," he gritted out.

The roughness in his voice had Frannie squirming on her barstool, recognizing his awareness, feeling excitement pricking the tips of her nipples and an unexpected curl of warmth settle in her belly. She felt almost giddy with this sudden sensual dawning. She hadn't known this feeling since her earliest days with Vinnie. And she couldn't recall it ever being this intense or urgent.

Never one to question an impulse, Frannie leaned toward Niall. "Would you mind kissing me?"

He drew back his head sharply and stared into her eyes. "I'm not goin' to be your revenge, sweetheart."

"It's not revenge...not really." Her cheeks flooded with heat. "It's just I haven't been with anyone but Vinnie for years, and I was...curious. I mean, what if I died tonight? I might never know the difference."

"The difference between what?"

Frannie shrugged, feeling embarrassed and a little foolish. Perhaps she'd misread his interest. Before she lost her nerve, she blurted, "Between lust and love."

His nostrils flared. "Sweetheart, there are kisses...and there are kisses. The kind I'd give you wouldn't answer your question."

She looked at him from beneath her lashes. Her "look" had worked before. "Try me?"

Some dark emotion flickered in his eyes, and he leaned close. He was so large and his expression almost angry that she felt a moment's alarm. But Frannie closed her eyes tight and tilted her head.

His breath brushed her lips a moment before his lips briefly touched hers.

She blinked and opened her eyes, giving him a frustrated frown. "I've given Zia Grazia kisses more passionate than that."

One dark brow quirked upward. "Oh, you were lookin' for passion?"

"Well, you could have shown a little enthusiasm," she muttered. She was a fool—a selfish, self-centered little fool. Just because Vinnie and Papa had told her there wasn't a more beautiful girl in the whole wide world didn't make it so. The Irishman probably thought she was an idiot. "This was a bad idea. I'm sorry." She bent to reach for her purse on the ledge at her feet.

His hand closed over her arm. "I just needed for you to spell it out, sweetheart."

Frannie shot him a startled glance, and her body tightened with desire at the flare of heat she saw in his eyes.

"Ah, you're a temptation, Francesca Valentine. But if you're wantin' to experiment, it may as well be with me."

She licked her lips in anticipation of another, deeper kiss.

He shook his head. "Not here. Not sittin' at a bar. I'll want to touch you."

Oh, she wanted that too! But only enough to ascertain whether her attractions were universal. Seeing the woman Vinnie had chosen, and was willing to risk her affections over, had dented Frannie's confidence. If she could tempt a handsome man like Niall, she'd know her appeal wasn't withering on the vine.

Not that she'd stand for anything too intimate—she was almost a married lady after all. A kiss with a little caressing wasn't *really* breaking her vow. Besides, Vinnie had earned a little tit for his tat with Raeline. "Where then?"

Niall searched her face, shaking his head. "You're a reckless girl."

"Then you'll just have to make sure you keep me safe."

"I'll kiss you outside...on the way back to my cab. Then I'll take you home to that man of yours."

Francesca let him help her from her stool with a light touch of his hand on her arm and leaned down to pick up her purse. Niall led the way out of the club and into the street.

Outside, the sky was cloudy, starless, and a mist reflected light in rainbow-hued halos around the streetlamps. His taxi stood alone near the corner of the street. Niall tugged her hand, pulling her toward it.

Frannie's heart pounded fast and furious, and a trembling excitement tightened her stomach, making her slightly queasy. Funny, she didn't remember lust making her sick to her stomach.

Just as they neared the cab, Niall pulled her within the shelter of a shop doorway. Into the shadows. Then his hands slid between the lapels of her leather jacket and parted it to smooth over her breasts and around to her back.

Shock and delight made her body quiver. It was too much, too fast. *I have to stop this now.*

"Give me your mouth."

Frannie decided that was just about the sexiest thing a man had ever said to her, or maybe it was just his tone—deep, resonant, wickedly masculine.

The extent of Vinnie's romantic vocabulary was, "Why ain't ya in bed already?"

She leaned toward Niall, yearning for his caress. His face was hidden in shadows, his body loomed, large and blatantly male. Frannie reached to slide her hands across his chest. The broad expanse was so hard she couldn't resist squeezing the muscle she found there. At the ripples that rolled beneath her palms, her heart hammered faster.

His hands settled on her bottom. Before she had a chance to so much as give a startled squeal, he dragged her up on her toes. As Niall's head descended, Frannie's breath left in a rush.

Now this was a kiss! What Niall's mouth did to hers couldn't be described with such a short, innocent word. His lips molded hers, drew hers into his mouth where he sucked and bit first the upper then her lower lip.

Frannie gasped, and his tongue forged into her mouth, gliding along hers, tangling with it, until they surged together in rhythm with the movement of his hips as he pressed his long, hot erection into her soft belly.

Frannie's hands clutched his shoulders, her nails raking upward, digging into his scalp to keep his mouth clamped right where it was.

His thigh pressed between hers, and Frannie's heart galloped like a spooked mare. But she opened her legs and strained upward, rubbing the top of her mons against his cock. Damp lust gushed from her body to soak her panties. His hands tightened on her ass, holding her still with a bruising grip, and she rose higher to meet his shallow thrusts. *Ohmygod! Ohmygod!*

Niall groaned into her mouth.

Frannie began to shake, feeling near to explosion—and her with every stitch of clothing still intact!

Vinnie had cheated her of more than just his fidelity. *Vinnie!*

Frannie tore her mouth from Niall's and stared at his hard, strained face, horrified.

If Niall lowered his pants, she'd be tempted to let him take her here and now. With a Herculean effort, Frannie shoved at his chest. "Let me go!"

Niall closed his eyes for a long moment, and then lowered her until her uneven heels met the ground.

Still shaking, Frannie backed away and wrapped her arms around her stomach.

"I'll take you home now," he said, his voice hoarse.

"No!" Good lord. Vinnie would take one look at her face and know something had happened. What had she been thinking? One little kiss did not erase three years of waiting for Vinnie to set a date. "I'll catch another cab."

"Don't be ridiculous. Mine's right here."

She backed away, afraid he'd touch her with one little pinkie and reignite the fire banked in her loins. "No! I can take care of myself." She took another step backward.

Niall's eyes widened. "Frannie, stop!"

She whirled and stepped out—and off the curb. A loud honk and a bright light were all she knew before she found herself flying through the air.

Only it wasn't the bus that hit her—it was the Irish freight train behind her that knocked her to ground.

"Get off me!" she gasped, trying to suck air back into her lungs. Why was he sitting on her chest?

No, he was at her side, his forehead creased with concern. He lifted her in his arms and carried her back to the sidewalk.

Still she couldn't seem to catch her breath, and from there her memories grew fragmented. She had the impression she'd slept for a time. She moaned and shook her head.

"Don't move, sweetheart. I'm so sorry, love," Niall said, his voice laced with regret. "You'll only hurt for a moment." Although his face was inches above hers, Niall's voice sounded like it came from the bottom of a deep well.

"Don't hurt," she muttered. "Tired. Cold. Can't...breathe."

"Hold on, sweetheart." He gently tilted her head to the side.

Frannie felt the heat of Niall's amazing lips clamp on the side of her neck, followed by a pricking pain. Then her world narrowed as darkness closed around her.

No, the Q59 bus to Flushing hadn't killed her.

Niall Keegan had.

Chapter Two

"List while I woooo thee with soft melodeee..."

Frannie winced, inwardly of course, at the wobbly high note. If only she could get the old bat to shut up.

What an odd purgatory she'd landed in. Frannie wondered what she'd done so wrong to earn her fate, and whether God would clue her in how long she had to suffer here. *Surely, not an eternity.* She hadn't been a bad girl—maybe just a little lazy. Maybe a lot dependent upon the men in her life. First, her father, then Vinnie. But she'd gone to Mass with her mother every week and endured confession occasionally to be absolved of her sins. Just how much time in purgatory had she earned?

"Gone are the caaares of life's busy throoong..."

So slowly she almost didn't note it, the rigidity that had held her body paralyzed eased, and she knew with a certainty she found puzzling that the sun was setting.

Then a sweet aroma like, yet tantalizingly different from the most succulent steak she'd ever eaten at Sardi's, assaulted her senses. Her mouth filled with saliva. Was this a new nuance to her torture? Not only must she suffer the demon's ministrations, but now there was the smell of dinner to forever torment her.

"Bee-ooot-ee-foll Dreeeeamer, awake unto me..."

The singing halted, and the she-devil made a clucking sound. "Who'd have thought a young thing like you would have a weak ticker. And your eyelashes are a little on the skimpy side," the creaking voice said.

Skimpy! Frannie bristled.

"Let's find something to fix that...something that'll open your face right up."

Mentally, Frannie blanched. Was her face about to be split open? Would she be awake to feel the pain?

There was a rustling, and the sound of drawers opening and closing. "These lashes should do. Now where's that superglue?"

Lashes? Superglue? Was the she-devil going to superglue false eyelashes to her lids? *That tears it!*

Frannie simmered. Every atom of her being concentrated on putting a stop to her punishment. This was too much to accept! She'd have said a hundred thousand Hail Marys on her knees on a cold, stone floor rather than face her current fate. *Someone* was going to hear her complaint.

The demon shuffled toward her accompanied by the pungent smell of adhesive.

Just as the scent hovered over her face, Frannie's eyes obeyed her command and opened. She found herself staring up at a wrinkled old woman with blue hair, thick blue eye shadow, and a large mole with an inch-long hair growing from it.

The old woman squealed and drew back, clasping a hand to her chest. "Lord, have mercy!" She took a deep breath and chuckled nervously. "I'll just have to superglue your lids together, too, otherwise you'll frighten your family to death."

Once more, the tube of superglue descended toward Frannie's face. She concentrated again, sending every ounce of anger to her hand. Her fingers trembled for a moment, and then her hand shot up and grabbed the old woman's wrist.

This time the woman shrieked, and her eyes rolled back as she sank toward the floor.

Frannie let go of the woman's arm, wincing at the loud thud as she hit the floor. Then she tested the rest of her limbs, one by one. They all appeared to be in good working order, if a little weak. She pushed off the table to a sitting position, and the fabric covering her slithered to the floor, leaving her naked. Frannie inhaled, drawing cool air deep into her lungs, and then she ran her hands over her arms and legs. She didn't appear to be any worse for wear despite having been hit by a bus. Oh yeah, not a bus—a damn freight train!

Holding her breath, she smoothed her fingertips over her face. Again, she discovered no sign of injury. Had she really suffered a heart attack? She felt perfectly fine.

If she didn't know better, she'd think she hadn't died at all!

Then her hands went to her belly, and she discovered a ridge of bumps trailing from below her breasts to her lower abdomen. Alarmed, she looked down to find a row of stitches made of a thread like thin fishing line. It closed an incision that was only a pale pink scar and seemed to fade before her eyes.

She tugged the thread, but it was deeply embedded. She gave up for now and jumped from the table. Her legs wobbled and she crumpled, falling in a heap on top of the old woman.

The woman didn't stir, but Frannie hadn't frightened her to death. She could hear the old woman's steady heartbeat although her ear wasn't pressed directly to her chest. Frannie didn't think about that odd fact for long. She sniffed the woman's neck, drawing in the warring scents of formaldehyde and cloves—and that luscious steak *tartare* aroma. Her tummy burbled loudly.

Frannie scrambled to her knees and gripped the edge of the metal table to haul herself to her feet. Then she had her first good look around the room. It was outfitted like a doctor's office—mint green walls, stainless steel tables, and a large sink with multiple gooseneck faucets and odd-looking nozzles attached to long, rolled-up hoses. The strong smell of bleach and formaldehyde permeated the air.

But the major differences between this room and any doctor's office she'd ever seen were the lack of silver stirrups—and the open, rosewood coffin sitting on a gurney near the door.

Good Lord, she was in a funeral parlor. This wasn't Hell—she was being prepared for her own funeral!

Frannie decided she'd better find some clothes before she went looking for the dummies running the funeral home to tell them they'd made a terrible mistake.

As luck would have it, a black dress hung from a hanger on a coat rack. She plucked at the silky fabric and immediately recognized her own dress. The one she'd worn to her papa's funeral. A plastic grocery bag hung from the rack as well. Inside were thigh-high hose, white panties and a bra, and black pumps. Her mother had provided the clothing. The dress and the conservative underwear hadn't made the move to Vinnie's apartment.

She dressed quickly, feeling hungrier by the minute—almost nauseous from a lack of food. How many days had she been here? Weren't they supposed to embalm her? She remembered the rough stitches on her stomach and felt more confused.

But hunger was uppermost on her mind.

Rustling sounded from the floor behind her, and she glanced back to see the old woman struggling to rise from the floor. Frannie hurried over and offered her hand.

The old woman's eyes grew wide as saucers, and she drew back. "Z-z-zombie!" Another strangling screech erupted from her throat.

"Calm down, there's nothing to be afraid of. There's been a mistake—"

The woman's eyes rolled back again, and she slumped back to the floor.

Frannie sighed. She couldn't leave her there—she was elderly and the room was chilly. Frannie chewed the edge of her lip, and her gaze drifted to the rosewood coffin with its creamy, satin interior...

* * * * *

Niall Keegan waited in an anteroom of the funeral home hidden behind a thick velvet curtain as mourners gathered in the parlor. Dusk had fallen an hour ago, and he'd hurried here to continue his vigil.

However, he had taken the precaution of feeding just before entering the building—on a haughty doorman at a hotel he'd passed, and then a woman walking her ferociously growling Pekinese.

His appetite had been off since the night he drank from the fragrantly delicious vessel that was Francesca Valentine. But he'd forced himself to feed anyway. Tonight, he'd need his strength.

Guilt and anticipation made his stomach roil. It wasn't every day a man took a mate. Not that he'd given the idea much thought before that night outside the *Lizards 'n' Suds* as he'd held her slender, fragile body while her life slipped away. But Frannie's pale face and large, brown eyes had pleaded with him to end her pain. She lay dying because of him.

He hadn't any choice. *If* he had, he might have gone for someone a little less flashy—less obviously high-maintenance. Someone less self-absorbed. But he couldn't regret the package. He could lose himself for months, maybe years, exploring her sweetly curved body.

But first things first, he had to rescue her from her coffin before the burial in the morning. He knew firsthand how traumatic waking inside a closed pine box could be.

He wiped his sweaty palms on his blue jeans and peeked from behind the curtain.

The voices of those gathered to pay their respects to the nearly departed Francesca were muffled. Most stood in awkward little circles, their expressions appropriately sad. The women blubbered into handkerchiefs, no doubt kept in scented drawers for just such an occasion. Many of the men wore expensive suits with heavy golden jewelry. Friends of the fiancé.

His gaze narrowed on the fiancé who sat in a folding chair, his back shaking with his deep sobs. The blonde woman, his secretary Raeline Curtis, sat beside him patting his shoulder.

Watching the couple with avid interest was Grazia D'Amato, leaning heavily on her cane.

Donatella Valentine stood next to the closed casket, arguing with the funeral home director. From the set of her chin and ramrod-straight back, she wasn't complimenting him on the spray of gardenias that decorated the top of the gleaming casket. "I specifically requested the casket be opened tonight." Her imperious voice rose above the sound of Vinnie weeping.

The tall, gaunt director tugged at the collar of his dress shirt, his cheeks growing red. "That won't be possible tonight. She's not prepared. My cosmetician isn't anywhere to be found."

"But I want to see my baby one last time—" Donatella's jaw tightened and her lips trembled.

Niall almost felt sorry for the woman. Her machinations had set this chain of events into action. She had to feel a world of guilt settling on her shoulders over her daughter's fate. He'd never collect his fee from her now.

Then Niall noted a movement from a doorway opposite his hiding place. A slender woman in a knee-length black dress paused at the entrance. Despite the dark glasses and the frightful bun she'd forced her brunette hair into, he knew in an instant he was staring at Frannie.

He held back a groan. How the hell would he get to her before she caused a scene? Likely, she didn't fully understand what had happened. And there were "rules" she shouldn't break—like not revealing herself to a crowd of people who knew her when she lived!

Just as he reached for the curtain and yanked it back, a commotion sounded behind Donatella and the director. All eyes turned in their direction, expressions filling with horror and dismay as thumps and a muffled caterwauling emanated from the casket.

Niall blew out a deep breath, immediately guessing what had happened to the missing cosmetician. While everyone else's attention was turned to the drama at the head of the parlor, he skirted the crowd until he reached Frannie. Her attention was also on the elderly woman being assisted from the coffin by burly henchmen.

Hands on her hips, Donatella glowered at the director. "You've lost my daughter!"

The director stuttered a response, which was quickly lost in the excited chatter from the mourners.

The old woman wept hysterically, muttering about naked people rising from the dead. As the women crowded around her to soothe her, her gaze fell on Frannie. "She's over there! The zombie's loose! Run!" the old woman screamed.

Niall didn't waste a second. He grabbed Frannie's hand and pulled her behind him, racing for the exit, the sound of Grazia D'Amato's laughter cackling in the distance.

"Wait a darn minute!" Frannie screeched. "They've made a mistake."

"No time to explain," he shouted over his shoulder. The thunder of feet pounding behind them spurred him faster. He pushed the bar on an emergency exit and lunged into the darkness, dragging Frannie with him.

He didn't slow down until he turned the corner. Reaching his taxi, he flung open the passenger seat door and shoved her roughly inside, then trotted around to slide behind the wheel.

"You're insane!" Frannie pushed back the hair falling into her face and grabbed the door handle.

He pulled back her arm. "Not now, sweetheart." He turned the key in the ignition and hit the gas just as a group of tough-looking, well-dressed men barreled around the corner.

"He's kidnapping me!" Frannie screamed, pounding on the window.

In the midst of the crowd stood Vinnie, his mouth gaping open. As they pulled away, Niall was very gratified to see the *capo* slip to the pavement in a dead faint.

Frannie rounded on Niall as he steered the taxi deftly among the cars crowding the busy street. "What the hell do you think you're doing? Are you insane?"

"I must be," he muttered.

"Stop this cab this instant! I have to go back." He hit the brakes, and Frannie braced herself against the dash in front of her.

"Sorry, love. There's no going back." He spun the steering wheel and forced the lumbering taxi to dart into the oncoming lane of traffic, before pulling past two cars and sliding neatly to the right in front of them, just missing a head-on collision with a delivery truck.

Frannie grabbed her seatbelt and buckled herself in.

"We have to get a few miles between us and your friends first," he said calmly.

Frannie tore the sunglasses from her face and tossed them. They bounced off his head and clattered to the floorboard. "This is all your doing!"

"Guilty." His cheerful tone rankled.

"Was this some sort of plot? I bet you set this whole thing up. Did you drug me to make everyone think I was dead?"

"You are dead, love."

She snorted. "I'm in a speeding taxi with a crazy man. *I'm every bit as alive as you!*" she shouted.

"True," he said, then laughed.

The bastard had the nerve to laugh at her! "So are you doing this for ransom?"

"No, I told you. You're dead."

"Everyone *thinks* I'm dead—or did! Now they'll be looking for you." She shuddered—they wouldn't be nice about it when they did catch up to him. Why that bothered her considering her current predicament was a mystery. "You can't hide from those people," she said, her tone imploring him to understand.

"I won't have to. They know what we are."

"What? Fugitives? Maybe you. I'm a victim—and Vinnie Ricchione's fiancée. They will most certainly look for me. Do you even know who you're messing with?"

"Honey, after they scrape him off the sidewalk, Carmen Gambuti will set your fiancé straight."

"I knew it! You do know who they are. You're working for a rival family."

"Nope. Wrong again. But I have done some work for Carmen a time or two."

Frannie settled back against her seat. How had she ever thought this man was someone she could manipulate? He was crazy! Certifiably so. Carmen would grind his handsome carcass into mincemeat without losing a minute of sleep.

They raced past brightly lit shops and restaurants. Past a deli that made the most amazing Reubens, an Indian restaurant whose Tambouri chicken was so tender the meat melted in her mouth. "I'm hungry." Her stomach knotted, and she thought she might puke if she didn't eat soon.

"I know you are. I'll be takin' care of that."

"I'm hungry now!" Distressed, she opened her seatbelt—it cut into her tummy. Hunger boiled like acid inside her now.

"Almost there, baby."

"You're passing everything." Familiar gleaming, golden arches conjured pictures of hamburgers, dripping with juicy grease and blood… "Stop there!"

"I know what you're wantin'—and I promise you that's not it."

"Hurry!" she sobbed.

Niall turned down a dark street and hit a garage door opener clipped to the visor in front of him, and a metal door rose. He drove inside and cut the engine.

As the door slid closed behind them, Frannie fumbled for the door handle and nearly fell out onto the concrete, but Niall was already there to help her. Crying softly, Frannie gripped his shoulders. "Help me!"

"Baby, hold on." He lifted her easily into his arms and headed toward a door.

Frannie pressed her hot face into the curve of his neck as he shouldered his way through the door and down a passage that led past a glass-fronted office, then beyond it to an apartment door.

He smelled unbelievably delicious—of musk and spicy aftershave. Rubbing her nose along his skin, she noted the pulse of his blood, racing just beneath the surface. She gave his neck a little lick, so small she hoped he didn't notice. She had to know how he tasted.

Fumbling to reach the keys in his pocket, he laughed—a short, strangled sound. "Hold that thought." He shifted her, and the deadbolt clicked. The door swung open, and he lurched toward a sofa, dropping her onto it.

Frannie yelped and came to her knees in the middle of the overstuffed navy cushions. She knew she should bolt for the open door, but her heart pounded loudly, the sound was almost as distracting as the warm, lusty scent of the man.

He kicked the door closed and turned toward her, pulling his shirt from his jeans, yanking open the buttons until his chest was bare.

Intellectually, she knew she should scream bloody murder. However, her physical need for him was too strong. It coiled like a snake, wrapping around and around itself, deep inside her belly, constricting around her core.

He raised his hand and pointed to a vein that pulsed just to the side of the strong column of his throat. "Bite me here."

She didn't ask what he meant. A picture filled her mind of long teeth sinking into flesh, of blood washing down her throat. Frannie mewled and reached out her arms as Niall sank to his knees before her.

Her lips closed over his flesh, and she didn't have another coherent thought. She bit deeply, and blood gushed into her mouth—hot, coppery, salty blood.

But it wasn't enough—he wasn't close enough. She crawled over him, parting her legs to straddle him, rubbing her clothed breasts along his chest as she drank.

He groaned and his hands grabbed her ass, pulling her groin flush with his.

Her nipples beaded instantly. He still wasn't close enough. She pushed the shirt off his shoulders and glided her hands over his naked back, kneading the muscles there like bread dough, trying to shape him, to draw all of him inside her—now!

"Trust me?" he asked, his voice strained.

"Mmmm." She gripped his shoulders, but couldn't stop drinking long enough to even nod.

Her dress parted down the back with a loud renting sound, then her bra followed with a snap.

Cool air hit her back and Frannie shuddered, knowing soon his hands would follow.

Clumsily, he pulled away the fabric bunched between them until she was naked, save for her panties and her thigh-high hose. The hard points of her breasts nestled into the fur on his chest, and she sighed.

He tugged the clasp that held up her hair until it sprang open, and raked his fingers through her hair. Next, he tore away her white panties, then he reached between them and opened his pants.

As quickly as his sex was freed, she centered her hot pussy over him and sank down, taking him deep into her body—his cock piercing her tender flesh as surely as her teeth penetrated his neck.

She needed no encouragement to move on him—up and down, up and down—until the moist heat building in her cunt rivaled, and then surpassed, her hunger. Withdrawing her teeth, she rubbed her tongue on the little holes on his neck—a kiss of gratitude, and then she let her head fall back as wave after wave of release washed over her.

And still it wasn't enough. She fell back on the carpet, bringing him with her, and wrapped her legs around his waist. "More!"

He groaned and rose over her, supported on his arms. His face was flushed; his eyes glittered brightly. "Fuck me! I knew you'd be like this." He pulled partway out, until only the head of his penis remained inside her dewy warmth, then slammed back inside.

Frannie screamed and tilted her hips to take him deeper, savoring each glide and jerk of his hips as he tunneled inside her pussy. Sweet Mary, how he filled her!

His cock crowded her vagina, stretching her, reaching so deep he pounded against her womb. Then that glorious feeling, the one that felt like Pop Rocks bursting on her tongue, exploded in her core, radiating through her legs and belly like falling stars streaking though a nighttime sky.

When it passed, Frannie found herself staring up at Niall. Their bodies were still fused together, but his gaze held a wariness that brought her to her full senses with a sickening crash.

Ohmygod! I sucked blood from his neck and fucked him like a cat in yowling-loud heat!

Me — almost a married lady!

Chapter Three

Niall's gut twisted when the tears leaked from her eyes and ran in fat rivulets into her hair. He'd taken advantage of her first hunger—used it to try to bind her to him with sex. Bloody brilliant sex, but nonetheless what he'd done was wrong.

Fuck! "Now Frannie, don't cry," he said softly.

"B-but I acted like an a-animal!" Her sobs were shallow, like a child's—and noisy.

Niall sighed and lowered his body onto hers to free his hands. He wiped away the tears with his thumbs while he thought about what he could say to lessen her shame. She was new to this life—new to the intensity of the hunger that rode a vampire's body.

"I sucked your blood!" she wailed.

He couldn't help the little smile that stretched his lips. "Will you think about what you just said?"

Her tears stopped, but the frown that creased her brow was adorable. "I don't want to. It's too weird."

"Haven't you figured it out yet, sweetheart?"

"No! I don't understand." She sniffed. "But it's all your fault. You make me crazy. First, I'm kissing you when I'm engaged to another man, then I'm being hit by a bus—"

"You weren't hit by the bus—"

"—then I'm waking up in a funeral parlor with a blue-haired woman trying to superglue my eyelids together. Then I'm—" She hiccoughed. "—s-sucking your blood!"

"It's a natural thing for us, love. Not the almost gettin' hit by a bus—but the blood and sex. It's as natural as breathin'." As natural as his awakening arousal pressing deeper inside her hot, tight channel.

She didn't appear to notice. "But I wasn't! Breathing, that is." She shook her head, confusion in her eyes. "When I first woke up, I wasn't breathing—but the sun set..." Her gaze met his directly. "I don't understand."

There wasn't really any other way to say it. "You're a vampire," he said, and braced himself for a storm of denial and wailing.

Her face crumpled, and the tears started again. "I kno-ow," she sobbed softly.

That wasn't what he'd expected. "You know?"

"Of course, I do." Her doe-like eyes tugged at his heart. "Not that I ever dreamed vampires really existed, but I know I died. Yet I'm still here." She sniffed again, and wiped away the tears on the side of her face against his hands.

He smoothed back her hair. He'd never petted another person in his life, but he wanted to soothe this woman's hurt and fear. "Is it really so bad?"

"Of course it is! My hairdresser doesn't do nights!"

Niall bit the inside of his lip to keep from laughing. "We'll find another."

Her eyes grew large. "Ohmygod! I'll never see myself again."

"What are you talking about?"

"Mirrors!"

The way her mind leapt from one disaster to another left him a little winded, but greatly amused. "Why would that be so bad?"

Her glower looked every bit as deadly as Carmen Gambuti's. "I'll have to live the rest of my life in disguise. Like I did tonight."

"It didn't work."

"What?"

"The disguise." He shook his head. It was beginning to hurt. "What disguise?"

She smacked his shoulder. "The glasses and the bun. I couldn't find a mirror, but I knew after looking at the old woman I couldn't go anywhere with a face she'd made, so I washed it all off."

"Well, the mirror thing is a myth. We have substance, therefore we reflect light."

"Thank God!" Frannie took a deep breath. "So, what now?"

Niall rocked his hips. "You have to ask?"

She sniffed, and then her face turned bright red.

Niall adjusted his position, leaning his torso away from her while he waited for her to respond, which pushed his cock an inch deeper inside her body.

Frannie tilted her head to the side and gave him a look from beneath her dark lashes that was both shy and coy at the same time. "Are we going to do this a lot?"

Damn, but this woman would make a corpse hard! Already her cunt was ripening, growing damp with excitement.

"It's a vampire thing, love. We need it like we do blood."

She walked her fingers along the top of his shoulder. "So, you're not a twice a week man?"

Although, he dreaded the thought of a new spate of tears, he had to lay to rest one particular ghost. "Was Vinnie?"

Frannie's expression grew thoughtful. "I can't go back, can I?"

"No. You can't. We're night owls, you and I. Would you really be willing to live half a life with him? Would he settle?"

Her eyes widened. "Am I immortal?"

Apparently, Vinnie was a far less intriguing subject than her new vampire "powers". Niall sighed and resigned himself to the fact that Frannie wasn't going to get down to business until her curiosity was satisfied. "Near enough—if you follow a few rules."

She stared down her belly and traced the long row of stitches. "I was embalmed, wasn't I?" Her mouth twisted with a look of utter disgust.

Niall blew out a gust of air and clenched his fists with frustration. "I hate to tell you this, but you've got one of those on top of your head, too."

Frannie's eyes rounded, and her fingers searched her scalp. "Does this mean I don't have a brain?"

He couldn't resist. "Something's changed?"

The acid of her frown could have stripped paint.

He trailed a finger up the line of stitches to his true destination, pausing to cup her breast. His thumb rasped over the distended nub and it stiffened. "Just for a day or two. We regenerate while we rest. I swear you have a full complement of organs now." He tweaked the nipple.

"That's disgusting," she said, but pushed her breast hard against his hand. "You're going to be awfully busy with tweezers later, mister."

He waggled his eyebrows. "It's the price I'll pay."

She lay back abruptly. "Will I age?"

"Barely." Niall dropped his hand to the floor and gave an exaggerated sigh. "Are we going to talk all night?"

She shrugged, and her mouth formed a pout. "Maybe. It's not everyday a girl wakes up dead. I have a million questions."

"We've years to find answers for them all." He grabbed her hip and squeezed.

"All right," she huffed. "But then you're pulling these stitches." She wrinkled her nose. "They itch."

"So do I." He dropped his voice to a growl. "Want to guess where?"

She gave him a flirty look from under her eyebrows. "Just one itsy-bitsy question more?"

He groaned. "Is it important?"

She nodded, her expression telling him the answer was very important to her.

"Okay, what?"

"Can I give up my seaweed masks?"

A bark of laughter surprised him. He leaned closer and kissed the tip of her nose. "In a hundred years you'll be as lovely as you are now."

A smile trembled on her lips. "Is it the blood or the frequent sex that keeps us young?"

He gave her a wicked smile. "I'm thinkin' we'll never find out."

She flashed him a flirty look. "Well, just in case..." She slid her feet over his buttocks and pressed. "Can't take any chances, can we?"

Finally! Niall leaned down and kissed her soft, plump lips, ready for a slower exploration this time.

Frannie wasn't having any of it. Her hands went straight for his buttocks, and she dug her nails into his skin. "I don't want ordinary — give me the starbursts."

Niall chuckled and rolled with her, until she sprawled on top of him. Frannie wriggled from his tight embrace and sat up, driving his cock deeper inside.

"Oh, my!"

"You did say you wanted starbursts." Lifting his head, he sucked a rosy-tipped nipple into his mouth.

Frannie clutched the hair at the back of his head, moaning. He guessed her nipples were especially sensitive. His teeth closed around a hardened bud, and he tugged.

"Ooh! Do that again." Frannie's hips undulated, her inner muscles constricting around his cock, giving him a sexy squeeze that had him delving deeper to seek her honey.

He released her nipple and nuzzled between her cleavage, drinking in the sweet, floral scent of her skin. Frannie's breasts were a tasty treat — small, but firm and round, and set high on her chest. Her softer-than-velvet nipples were large, cherry-colored disks. When aroused, like now, the tips beaded like the little rock candies he'd savored in his mouth as a child.

Niall rolled his tongue around the treat and chewed gently, then he licked his way across her chest to capture the other nipple, earning him another appreciative roll of her hips.

Frannie tucked her knees close to his body and levered her hips to rise and fall, seeming to delight in the long, slow glides that alternately buried and exposed his cock.

Niall released her nipple. She was killing him slowly. Her thighs quivered, her breaths grew labored, but she didn't quicken her pace. And sweet Jesus! She was beautiful. Slenderness and wiry strength, creamy-white skin with cherry lips and nipples, hair the color of night that drifted like a silky cloud around her shoulders and played peekaboo with her lovely breasts.

Niall grasped her buttocks, curving his palms around her soft bottom to force her to move faster. Frannie resisted, so he lifted one hand and smacked a fleshy cheek.

Frannie gasped, but her pace picked up. That worked so well, Niall smacked the other cheek, and her thighs widened, shortening her strokes. She closed her eyes and bobbed faster, ending each glide with a grind that rubbed her passion-slick clitoris against the curly hair at the base of his cock.

The friction between her juicy cunt and his shaft was building—but not fast enough. He slid a fingertip along the crease dividing her buttocks.

"No!" Frannie's eyes shot open, and her movements grew jerky.

Niall ignored her plea and glided his finger downward until he reached her little nether mouth. He circled it, pressed against it—scraped it with his fingernail.

Frannie cried out. She leaned forward and gripped his shoulders. Her expression was taut, her cheeks flushed—her dark eyes wild. Her hips slammed down and jerked up, faster and faster. Her breaths grew jagged, ending on gusting sobs.

Deciding now was the time to introduce her to the best part of vampire sex, Niall leaned up and licked his way along her collarbone, until he reached her throat. At the same time he pressed the finger stroking her anus inside her hot little hole, he sank his teeth into her neck.

As he drew her blood into his mouth, Frannie came apart. She groaned, not a feminine little mewl—this was a full-throated, I'm-gonna-die groan. She rode him like a jockey on a thoroughbred racehorse, bent low over the saddle, pumping up and down, the strokes shorter still, faster. Sweat moistened her skin, trickled down her neck. And her cunt—

It caressed him end to root with writhing contractions that milked his cock, encouraging him to give up his cum. Niall mouthed her neck as he sucked, and fucked her ass with his finger until he felt the shuddering climax that broke over her, tightening her pussy around his sex.

Frannie screamed, and finally, Niall gave himself to the release that tightened his thighs, balls, and cock to stone as cum gushed up into her body in an endless, scorching stream.

A groan wrenched from his throat, and he withdrew his teeth, lapping at her neck to close the punctures as the waning pulses emptied the last of his cum inside her body.

"I take it you didn't get a mouthful of formaldehyde?" Frannie asked, gasping for breath.

Niall snorted and pulled out his finger. Then gliding his hands over her back, he gave her a bone-crushing hug. "No. You were delicious." He kissed her neck and let his head fall back to the floor, dragging air into his starved lungs.

Frannie grinned down at him. "I was fantastic, wasn't I?"

"The best I ever had, baby." He clasped the back of her head and brought her down until he could bless her lips with a kiss. "What do you think of vampire sex now?"

A deep rosy blush colored her cheeks. "I'm not sure. The sucking part was incredible. The other was...a little embarrassing."

Niall waggled his eyebrows. "You loved that part. Just wait until I give it to you, full-on in the ass, sweetheart."

"Augh! The things you say." Her cheeks flamed scarlet. "I don't think that would work."

He couldn't help teasing her a bit more. "Why not?"

Her gaze dropped to his chest. "You're too big," she said in a little voice.

He pretended he didn't note her embarrassment. "I'll fit. You'll see," he said cheerfully.

A frown creased her brow, and she opened her mouth wide over a very loud yawn—too loud to be real. "Lord, I'm tired."

Frannie's passionate nature pleased him. Her modesty, despite the fact their bodies were still joined, amused the hell out of him. He let her change the subject. "Are you hungry?"

Her gaze lit with enthusiasm. "Mmm-hmm."

"I've snacks in the fridge. What's your pleasure?"

"It's odd." She wrinkled her nose—an endearing expression to him now. "Chocolate used to be my idea of a heavenly snack—but I'm dreaming of chopped liver and steak."

"You have new appetites. Lusty appetites." His smile stretched his mouth.

"I'll say I do," she muttered.

"Let's eat. Then if you're really good—I'll show you how much your ass will love a little fuckin'."

Frannie jerked upright, which did interesting things to his cock still lodged inside her body. "Don't say that!"

"Why not?" he asked, trying to keep his attention on the conversation instead of his renewing vigor.

"Because you're embarrassing me."

Niall pushed back her hair from her face. "What if I told you," he said, dropping his voice to a rumble, "that you can ask me anything—any nasty thing you want—and I'll give it to you?"

"I'd say...this is a little overwhelming." Her eyes grew alarmingly moist. "And I'm not sure I'm ready."

"Then tell me to go slow, and I will," he said softly. "When you're ready for darker adventures, just say so."

Frannie gifted him with a shy smile. "Sounds like a deal."

He smacked her bottom and moved her off his body. "Time to eat."

* * * * *

Frannie stood naked in the kitchen, sure her blush painted every bit of her skin. She'd never flaunted her body like this before a man. Of course, Vinnie had been her one and only, and he preferred a little modesty.

Not so, Niall. The man bent to retrieve a packet of liver from the bottom of the fridge, not the least disturbed that he gave her a delicious glimpse of his balls between his legs, and the long dangling cock that fascinated her endlessly.

She felt a little proud that she'd taken all that length inside her body. Her breasts tingled, and she knew if he looked at her now, he would see her growing arousal.

He straightened and cast her a devilish glance over his shoulder. The man knew exactly what he was doing to her! "The question now, is whether you want it raw or slightly cooked."

Raw! The way he'd drawled the world conjured visions of hot, sweaty sex. Frannie dropped her gaze to the packet of meat in his hand, glad to have an excuse to look away from the slight smile curving his lips. Lips that had sucked her nipples until she'd been ready to scream. "Cooked!" Even to her own ears her voice sounded hoarse.

His mouth stretched to a full-fledged grin. "Seared on the outside, juicy on the inside, hmm?"

Her nipples beaded instantly, and Frannie fought the urge to cover them with her hands.

Niall chuckled and turned up the flame on the stove, and then retrieved a frying pan and oil from beneath the counter. He quickly had the liver frying in the pan.

Frannie inhaled the smell of the sizzling meat, and her stomach growled. "I think it's done."

He raised one eyebrow. "It's barely cooked."

He was right. The meat was a pale gray and blood oozed from inside. Frannie licked her lips. "I know, but I'm craving a little—"

"Juice?"

"Mmm-hmm." She could hardly wait for it to cool to slip a bite into her mouth.

With tongs, he piled the bite-sized chunks on a plate and set it on the counter between them, pulling out stools for them to sit on. Armed with forks, they attacked the plate. It was the oddest snack Frannie had ever enjoyed, but she ate every morsel.

When they'd finished, she pushed away the plate. "So what happens now?"

"Is that your way of asking for sex?"

Frannie rolled her eyes. "No. I mean, what am I going to do now? I can't go home."

Niall covered her hand with his and squeezed. "I made you. You're my responsibility. I'll take care of you."

Frannie sat frozen, a twinge of pain twisted inside her chest. She pulled her hand from beneath his. "But that's part of the problem. My problem." She turned on the stool to face him, trying her best not to notice the impressive erection that rose from his lap.

In fact, everything about the man was pretty impressive. His chest was broad, lightly furred, and heavily muscled. His waist tapered to narrow hips. The picture of his equally impressive, heavily muscled ass as he'd bent down in front of the refrigerator would inspire wet fantasies forever.

But she needed to stand her ground on this issue. "I've always been taken care of. If I'd been more independent, I wouldn't have hooked up with a guy who cheated on me—and then stayed with him."

Niall drew a deep breath and his expression grew serious. "I won't ever cheat on you, Frannie. I promise you that."

His dark blue eyes stared straight into hers, and she believed him.

"I can make you happy. I'll show you how to go about this life."

Fighting the ripening desire that pooled between her thighs, Frannie shook her head. "No." She wanted more. If she couldn't have a hearts-and-roses kind of love, she wouldn't settle for a relationship that was so one-sided. Sex couldn't be the only thing she gave him. "I know I need someplace to stay—until I get on my feet. But I need a job and to learn to take care of myself."

A frown lent a darker kind of beauty to his face. His jaw hardened.

A little thrill of alarm pricked the back of her neck.

"Why are you doing this?" he asked. "Don't you like the company?"

"Of course I do. That's not the point. I hardly know you, but you're talking about eternity." *And you aren't talking about even the possibility of love.*

"Are you holding a grudge against me for turnin' you?"

"Of course not. That wasn't your fault—my dying. What you did to save me was—well, I thank you for that. I understand now."

He snorted, and his expression grew darker.

Frannie suspected this was the man who dared to stand up to the Gambuti crime family. Oddly, that hint of danger made her all the hotter. She cleared her throat. "What am I supposed to do while you're out making a living for us both?"

"Whatever it was you did before," he said with an irritated wave of his hand. "I have money. I've had several lifetimes to accumulate a bit. I work because I'm accustomed to workin'."

Frannie lifted her chin. "I don't want to do the things I did before. I was getting bored, anyway." She tamped down a twinge of regret. "I mean, I thought eventually I'd have kids, and they'd fill my life." She aimed a glare straight at him. "But that's not going to happen now, is it?"

"No, it's not. Are you holdin' that against me?"

She gave it a little thought, knowing her pause would give him a moment to stew. But the truth was, she hadn't been all that keen on having kids. "I guess not, but a girl likes to have options—you just removed one."

His eyes narrowed, and his hands fisted on his naked thighs. "Then what would you like to do, sweetheart?" he asked, his voice deadly even.

Frannie swallowed, wondering if maybe she'd pushed him too far. What would he do if he really got mad? "Maybe you could teach me to drive, and I could get my own taxi."

One side of his mouth quirked up in a semblance of a smile—but it didn't quite reach his eyes. It was a mean smile. "You want to be a taxi driver, like me?

Her heart stuttered, then began to beat a slow, thrumming tattoo. Moisture seeped from her pussy to wet the leather stool beneath her bottom. Did he know how hot she was getting? Sure her nipples couldn't bead any tighter or poke out at him any farther, Frannie dared one more prick. She lifted her chin. "Yeah. I want my own cab."

That wicked grin spread across his mouth. "Sweetheart, there's somethin' I forgot to tell you."

Frannie shivered at the powerful aura of amused masculinity that emanated from the man ranging on the stool across from her.

He looked deceptively lazy—like a lion sitting on his haunches just before pouncing on its next meal.

"Look, I know driving taxis at night's a little dangerous," she said nervously, "but I've got like super-powers, right?"

"You'd still be vulnerable, but that's not what I'm talking about."

"Then what is it? You don't want me to make my own living? Don't you want me to be my own person?"

"No, love. I'm not a taxi driver."

Chapter Four

"You're not a taxi driver?"

Niall slipped off his stool, which put his body—his very naked, flagrantly aroused body—inches from Frannie. If she bent over just a few measly inches, she could take his cock into her mouth.

By the heavy-lidded look he gave her, he was thinking the same thing, too. "No, I'm not." He lifted her face with his fingers, and stroked her lower lip with his thumb.

She puckered her lips and kissed his thumb. "Not what?" She sighed.

"A taxi driver."

She swayed toward him, drawn by the heat in his gaze. "Then what are you?"

"You mean, besides the man who's goin' to fuck you into a coma?"

Her mouth gaped and she swayed closer. "You can do that?" She straightened and cleared her throat. "Yeah, I mean besides that." She didn't bother trying to deny she didn't want to explore the coma part.

He lifted her hand where she'd clenched it on her thigh and brought it to his erection. "You know, you were right. You don't really know me." His hand guided hers along his lengthening shaft.

Frannie gripped it hard, as excited by the harsh baritone his voice had slipped into, as she was by the heated steel beneath her hand. She moved on her seat, rubbing her swollen pussy on the surface, smelling her own growing arousal. "Tell me what you are," she said, her own voice made husky by the desire tightening every muscle in her body.

How did he do it? How could a look, a growling inflection, and a hard shaft have her ready to crawl all over him? She'd never gone for the primitive type. But here she was, ready to go down on a man she hardly knew just to please him. She licked her lips in anticipation.

Niall lifted his free hand and speared his fingers through her hair, urging her closer. "I'm a dick."

"Yeah you are," she breathed. She stuck out her tongue and aimed the point at the tiny eye on the crest of his burgeoning cock.

His sex pulsed, and his fingers gripped her hair hard. He pulled her closer.

Frannie didn't give him what he wanted. Instead, she nuzzled his cock, smoothing her cheek along the satiny skin stretched taut over the tempered steel of his rod. She rubbed her chin, her nose, her closed lips along his length, drawing the musky scent of him deep into her lungs.

She'd never given cocks much thought before, but Niall's was a thing of beauty. Ruddy when engorged, like now, with a tracery of blue veins, it rose from his groin strong and proud like the rest of his body.

Niall pulled her hair just hard enough to sting, and Frannie gave a husky laugh. But she was just as ready. She opened her mouth and swallowed the fat, blunt head of his cock, taking him deep inside until he butted the back of her throat. Then she drew back, suctioning hard, before gliding back down to meet their joined hands wrapped around the base of his penis.

She spread her fingers on his shaft, and his slid between. Together they fisted around his sex, working in opposition to her suctioning mouth.

His body trembled and his hips pumped forward and back, his harsh breaths interspersed with deepening moans.

Frannie glanced up at his face and found his hot gaze watching her every movement. In that moment, she felt powerful. She had the vampire at her mercy. She reached between his legs and cupped the heavy sac that held the essence of his manhood and squeezed.

"You're a witch, Francesca." Niall groaned. "Do you even know how powerful this thing is between us?"

Oh, she did. But she wouldn't let him use it to bind her to him. Never again, would she be a man's plaything. She gently scraped her teeth along his shaft.

Niall let loose a blistering curse that made her laugh, but she kept up the torture, tonguing his length, sucking so hard she was sure she could bring up his cum, twisting their intertwined fingers on his cock until he shuddered so hard she felt it to her teeth.

Then suddenly, Niall tugged her hair, pulling her mouth away. With a move so fast she was left gasping, he flipped her onto her stomach over the stool and plunged his cock into her pussy, gliding like a knife through butter deep into her moist core.

The legs of the stool rattled on the floor with his powerful thrusts. Frannie gripped the counter above her head to steady herself, and then pushed back to meet his hips.

The hard, relentless pounding produced a wetness from her pussy that drenched her cunt and thighs, and added a percussive consonance to the sounds of their joining—a sharp slapping sound that excited her all the more. Frannie spread her legs as wide as the stool would allow to feel the full force of his pounding on her tender flesh.

Just as she was sure she'd never experienced a more wonderful fuck, Niall's large hands parted her buttocks. The shock and anticipation of what he'd do next left her completely breathless

When the first thick digit pressed inside her ass, she thought she'd die from delight. When the second joined it, she screamed with pain and the most intense pleasure she'd ever known. When the fingers shoved in and out, matching the rhythm of his thrusting cock, Frannie knew she wasn't long for this world.

The orgasm that rocked her body pushed her higher than she'd ever flown, exploding like rockets inside her head. She heard an ear-piercing scream and sank into darkness.

Niall Keegan had killed her again.

* * * * *

Niall whistled as he listened to the messages on his answering machine. He was feeling pretty pleased with himself. He'd left Frannie snoring peacefully in his bed. She hadn't opened her eyes once since the orgasm to end all orgasms.

Now, she wouldn't be able to deny they belonged together. Sated, his skin still tingling from the greatest sex he'd ever had, Niall was thinking life was pretty damn good.

The door to his office opened and a wide-eyed Frannie pushed through. She was adorably rumpled and wearing an old pair of sweats with the arms and legs cut off. A pair so mutilated he didn't remember owning them. "You lied to me!" she said, staring at the gold lettering on the glass door. "It says right here, 'Niall Keegan, Private Investigator'."

He folded his arms over his chest and sat on the edge of his desk. His body tensed in anticipation of another round with Frannie. "I wasn't kidding when I told you what I was."

She stalked over to him, color staining her cheeks. "You know very well I didn't have a clue what you were talking about. 'Dick' isn't in the vernacular these days. You deliberately deflected my question."

Niall took her proximity as an invitation and grabbed her hips, pulling her between his legs. "And it was so easy to do."

She reached behind her to shove away his hands, but he adjusted his grip downward to cup her lush buttocks instead.

"You're an asshole," she said, her chin jutting.

"But I'm also a damn good fuck, aren't I?" he growled.

"That word!" She moaned and pressed her belly against the open vee of his legs. "I feel like Pavlov's dog."

Niall lowered his head and kissed her, raising her on her toes to bring her up hard against his burgeoning desire. When he finally drew back, Frannie's eyes were closed and a smile curved her lips.

Niall thought he'd discovered the trick to defusing her anger — just kiss her silly.

Her eyes opened and she sighed. "So when do I start?" she asked.

"Looks like we already have. Question is whether you want it on the desk or where you're standin'?"

Frannie's eyes widened. "You're unbelievable! Do you think everything's about sex?"

Niall just stopped himself from nodding. Obviously, Frannie was looking for another answer. "Course not," he muttered.

She shoved at his chest until he let go. She backed out of reach. "I was talking about working. When do I start?"

"We talked about this a couple hours ago. Taxi driving is just a cover I use."

"So I'll learn to be a PI."

"I work alone."

"You just *made* yourself a partner," she said tapping her bare toe.

The frayed end of the sweats showed the top half of a logo. "Wait a second. What the hell are you wearin'?" he asked, his stomach plummeting.

"Just a pair of your old sweats. They have a drawstring so I can keep them up, but I had to cut the length. And I knew you wouldn't miss this old sweatshirt — it has a hole," she said, poking her finger through the seam on the side to prove her point.

Niall felt like his head was about ready to explode. "I love those sweatpants. I play basketball in them every Saturday night. And that sweatshirt is my lucky Yankees shirt. The Yanks have won every home game I ever wore that shirt to."

"Oh." Frannie dipped her head, uncertainty creasing her brow. "I'm sorry, but I needed something to wear. You ripped my dress to shreds. If you'd been there when I woke up—"

Niall took a deep, calming breath. "You can file."

Her head snapped up and her expression glowed. "Great! How do I do that?"

He gritted his teeth and turned his gaze to the ceiling. Damn, it was going to be a long time until morning.

* * * * *

Frannie hummed as she finished rearranging the last of the manila files in the battered metal cabinet. Niall would be impressed with everything she'd accomplished while he was gone. She glanced at the clock on the wall. He'd said he'd be home before four. There was still time to explore the inner sanctum of his private office.

He'd left strict instructions that she was to stay out of his office, but Frannie was dying of curiosity to see what a PI kept in his desk. Would she find personal notebooks with all the really juicy details about the things he'd seen? Or photographs from his latest stakeout?

She'd learned so much going through the files. They revealed an underside of life she'd thought only existed on the *Lifetime Movie* network. Husbands cheating on wives with younger women. Husbands cheating on wives with other men. Women meeting lovers in smarmy hotel rooms. Businessmen hiding cash from partners. Businessmen screwing their partners' wives.

She couldn't wait until she got her first case. Then she'd be an equal partner to Niall, and maybe he'd see her as more than a convenience. She didn't have any illusions concerning her importance in his life—he felt responsible for her. That they were compatible in bed was only an added bonus so far as he was concerned.

Frannie'd had it with being a mere convenience. She wanted to be someone's reason for existence—someone's whole life. If that someone weren't Niall, she'd just have to keep her eyes and her heart open. Although the thought of ever leaving Niall left her cold. How had he wormed his way into her heart so quickly? Vinnie had seduced her all through Catholic school and for years beyond before she ever gave him her virginity.

Taking a seat in Niall's leather chair, she rolled back and forth with a negligent kick of her foot, pondering where to begin her sleuthing. She turned the cards in his Rolodex, but didn't see anything that smelled of seamy secrets, and then pushed around the papers in his in-basket, finding nothing other than invoices and a few scribbled phone messages.

Then she pulled out the large drawer on the left pedestal of his desk and hit pay dirt—a whole new set of files marked "DVs".

"DVs? Delinquent Vouchers?" She pulled out a file and rifled through its contents. The photos and illegible notes seemed much like the contents of the files in the main office.

"Dumb villains, maybe?"

The door to the outer office creaked open and her heart skipped a beat. Niall couldn't find her snooping through his drawers. Frannie leapt from his chair and circled the desk, picking up the stack of invoices in his basket. Then she pretended not to hear his footsteps as he approached.

He reached around her and laid a folder in his basket. "I thought I told you this room was off-limits," he murmured.

"I finished filing," she said over her shoulder, "so I looked for more work I could do."

When he leaned down to kiss the side of her neck, she neatly sidestepped him and turned to give him a blinding smile.

His expression was cautious. She'd left him confused by her seemingly contradictory behavior. She'd had hours to think about her predicament. A little doubt would do him good.

She carried the stack of invoices into the main office, set them on the table next to the copy machine, and started running them through the feeder. "How did your stakeout go?" she asked nonchalantly, glancing over her shoulder.

Sighing, he straddled her vinyl-upholstered chair backwards. "It was a bust. Kowalski really was working late tonight."

"Sounds pretty boring."

"Deadly."

"I bet if you'd had company, time would have flown," she said, unable to resist the little dig.

"We've been through this, I work alone."

She shrugged as though his answer didn't matter. "I'm just saying I might have a better appreciation for what you do if I accompanied you once in a while."

"Uh-huh. Something could go wrong. I might be distracted."

Frannie faced him, keeping her face schooled in a serious expression. "No, you wouldn't. I'd be quiet as a mouse. I could take notes."

He smiled wryly. "If you haven't noticed, I can't seem to be in your company for longer than five seconds without getting hard. I'd say that's a pretty big distraction."

"Bragging?"

His eyebrows waggled wickedly.

Sensing a weakening on his part, Frannie walked toward him. "We could have sex before you start work—"

"We will anyway."

She raised one eyebrow. "Oh, we will? Or more to the point, will anyone else be with you other than yourself and George there?" she said, with a pointed glance at his groin.

Niall scratched his stubbling beard. "You're not goin' to leave this alone, are you?"

"Nope."

He took a deep breath. "All right, you win. *But* only if the case is routine, and only if you promise not to interfere."

Frannie grinned and drew a cross on her chest. "Cross my heart."

"The next time Mr. Kowalski steps out on his wife, I'll take you with me."

Frannie clasped her hands in front of her. "Really?"

He nodded.

"You won't be sorry."

"I already am," he muttered. He pulled a notebook from his inner jacket pocket and tore out a sheet. "I need to get this filed." He walked to the file cabinet, pulled out the upper drawer, and thumbed through the folders.

Frannie waited for his reaction.

"Where's the Kowalski file?"

"Under 'P'."

He glanced back at her. "Why 'P' and not 'K'?"

"'P's for Polish."

One dark eyebrow quirked upward. "You're filing by nationality?"

"Well, I started filing strictly alphabetically when you left, but there were so many 'S' names I decided we needed another subcategory."

He cleared his throat. "That was a...creative solution. But *I* don't need another subcategory, I need to find the file."

Frannie stepped beside him, pulled out the folder, and handed it to him.

Niall rested his arm on the top of the cabinet, and asked, "So where's Hughes?"

Guessing Niall wasn't too pleased with her ingenuity, Frannie squirmed beneath his stare. "Under 'G'," she said, her words clipped.

His face was starting to turn red. Frannie would never have figured him as a man so resistant to change.

"Why 'G'?"

Frannie folded her arms over her chest. "For Great Britain."

"His family's Irish."

"That's why it's in 'G'," she said, barely holding onto her temper.

"Ireland is not part of Great Britain!" he said from between gritted teeth.

"No need to get huffy," she said, retrieving the Hughes file. "I'll just put it under 'I'."

"And where will you put Mr. Rijik? He's from Iceland."

"Iceland? I thought he was Norwegian." Frannie began to see his point, and her shoulders slumped with dejection. "He's in the 'N's."

"Love, maybe you should stick to the alphabet."

"Fine." She walked over to him and leaned into his chest. "I don't think I'm much help in the office."

Niall wrapped his arms around her and kissed the top of her head. "Did you take any messages?"

"No. Your machine does a better job of that than I do." Frannie rested her head against his broad chest, drawing comfort from the sound of his steady heartbeat. She'd never convince him of her worth at this rate. "Maybe we should just go to bed."

Niall groaned, hugging her tight, and then pushed her away. "Not just yet. We need to retrieve your clothes from your old apartment, or next you'll destroy my favorite Knicks T-shirt."

She glanced up at his face. "Vinnie will be there."

His expression held no emotion — that in itself was a little unnerving. "Would you rather I go alone?"

Frannie's imagination leapt through every worse case scenario and she shook her head. "No. I need to say goodbye and tell him it's over."

"I imagine the bastard's already figured that one out."

* * * * *

Niall stood behind Frannie as she rang the doorbell, his shoulders bunched, ready for a fight.

The door opened a couple of inches and one side of Raeline Curtis's face peeked from the narrow space. Upon seeing who stood outside the door, her blue eye rounded. "Oh shit! Oh shit!"

Frannie gasped and stood stock-still.

"Hon, who's at the door?" Vinnie's shout sounded muffled and distant from within the apartment.

Niall bit back a triumphant grin. Vinnie'd already moved on.

As Raeline nervously removed the chain and opened the door wide for them to enter, Niall slipped his arm around Frannie's waist. Her back and shoulders were rigid. He had to nudge her to get her to move inside the room.

"I've come for my things," Frannie said flatly, never once glancing at Niall.

"I'll just get a suitcase," Raeline said, backing away from them, before hurrying to what Niall presumed was the bedroom door. "Everything's right where you left it." Raeline slipped through the door and closed it behind her.

"She was wearing my bathrobe," Frannie muttered.

Niall glanced around, curious to see Frannie's imprint on her former home. Creamy yellow walls and a plum-colored velvet sofa were clues to her vibrant, passionate nature. His own apartment seemed sterile and bland next to the color and energy of this room.

The door swung open a moment later and Vinnie stepped out, tucking a shirt into his pants.

"Here we are again," Niall whispered next to Frannie's ear and gave her waist a comforting squeeze before stepping away.

"Uh, Frannie! Jeez, you look great." Vinnie crossed his arms in front of his chest, and then dropped them. He stared, sweat popping out on his forehead. "Rae'll be out in a minute, she's packin' your clothes." He cleared his throat. "I know how all this looks, but—I thought you was dead."

Niall had to fight the urge to flex his muscle and give the scrawny, little wimp a scare. What the hell had a gutsy little firecracker like Frannie ever seen in this man?

"It's okay, Vinnie," Frannie said. "I was dead."

"It's just—" Vinnie paused, darting a nervous glance at Niall. "I don't want no bad feelings between us, hon."

"Don't worry, Vin. I'm not gonna bite you," Frannie said.

Niall couldn't resist staring at the open collar of the other man's shirt. He didn't want him getting too comfortable.

"I-I didn't think you was," Vinnie said, giving her a smile that looked a little strained. He gestured with his thumb back to the bedroom door. "About Rae, it was never nothin' serious. But she's been a gem, since you—"

"I'm happy for you Vinnie," Frannie said quietly.

Vinnie started to sweat in earnest. "Look, there's somethin' I gotta tell you. I didn't want you to hear it from no one else, seein' as how we was engaged and all..."

"You can tell me anything. I promise I won't get mad. I'm not the same person I was a few days ago."

"I'm glad to hear that," Vinnie said with a quick smile. Then his face froze. "Not that the way you were wasn't wonderful. You were—wonderful, that is!"

Frannie rolled her eyes. "Out with it, Vin."

"Yeah, well uh, you see, Rae and me are gettin' married tomorrow."

Niall caught Frannie just as she lunged at Vinnie. The other man's face blanched so pale, Niall feared he'd pass out again.

"You lousy, two-timing bastard!" Frannie screeched. "Three freaking years I waited for you to set a date."

"We gotta get married, Fran," Vinnie said, his voice approaching a whine.

"What? She's knocked up?"

The bedroom door swung open and Raeline dragged in a suitcase behind her. "Frannie, I know Vinnie didn't say it right." She set the suitcase at Frannie's feet and squared her shoulders.

Niall had to admire her courage. Frannie continued to fight his hold, wriggling like a worm on a hook. Rage had turned her face the color of her sofa.

"I found out I was pregnant after that night at the funeral home," Raeline said, wringing her hands. "I puked all over Vinnie's shoes on the ride back to my place."

Niall tightened his arms around Frannie and leaned down to whisper in her ear. "Are you mad because you loved him and he's a jerk? Or because you chose the wrong guy?"

All the fight went out of her, and she hung in his grasp like limp linguine.

"If I let you go, do you promise not to have another go at him?"

Frannie nodded, and Niall released her. Rubbing her arms, she scowled at Vinnie. "Niall, you still have that thing I told you I never wanted back?"

"It's in my wallet, sweetheart."

Frannie held out her hand. Niall slid his wallet from his jeans pocket and pulled the diamond ring from one of the credit card slots. When he placed it on her palm, she never once glanced at it. Instead, she handed it straight to Raeline. "A wedding gift. I don't hold any grudge against you, Raeline. I wish you luck. You're going to need it."

Raeline's eyes widened. "Th-thanks, Frannie. It's a gorgeous ring."

"Just remember, it's worth a few grand — you may want the money more some day." Without another word to Vinnie, Frannie grabbed the handle of her suitcase and rolled it out of the apartment.

Niall flexed his shoulders and arms and gave Vinnie the hardest, meanest look he had and winked at Raeline. Then he trailed after Frannie, whistling tunelessly as she stomped all the way out of the building.

All in all, he thought the visit with the ex had gone swimmingly.

Chapter Five

"Can you believe the nerve of that man?"

Niall paused mid-stroke and gritted his teeth. Once again, he was an inch from orgasm, but Frannie kept returning to the scene at Vinnie's apartment. "Can we do a play-by-play afterward, love?" He flexed his cock inside to remind her where they'd left off.

Frannie slid her legs from his waist. "I can't help it. I feel like such an idiot."

Sighing, he pulled out of her warm sheath and rolled off her body. He bunched a pillow beneath his head, prepared for another round of "What's-the-matter-with-Vinnie?" Reminding himself women had to talk their problems to death, he said, "Don't take it so hard. The one I feel bad for is Raeline. She has to deal with his tom-cattin' now."

Frannie sucked in a deep breath. "Wait a second!" She rose up on her elbow and stared at him like she'd never seen him before. "You seem to know an awful lot about Vinnie."

Niall cursed his loose tongue. "It's in his nature. Cheat one time—"

"Don't give me that horseshit." Frannie's eyes narrowed dangerously. "You weren't looking for a fare that night—you were on the job, weren't you?"

Niall raised his hands. "Now, Frannie—"

"And don't give me a line about you just happening to pass by on your way to the office."

Niall clamped his mouth shut. That was exactly what he'd intended to say.

"Lie one time..." She threw his words back in his face.

Niall pulled the sheet over his loins. He needed to keep his wits to dig his way out from a hole that was getting deeper by the second. "You're gonna chew on this until all the flavor's gone, aren't you?"

A frown drew her dark eyebrows together. "You had Vinnie staked out."

Niall felt a guilty flush heat his cheeks.

Her eyes glittered as she mulled over the problem. "Who hired you? Was it someone *connected*?"

Niall fell back on an age-old escape. "That's privileged information."

"Privileged schmivileged!" She sat up on the bed and reached for his robe. "I know, I'll just go through the files."

"You won't find anything there."

"Then I'll go through the ones stashed in your desk!"

"What the hell were you doin' going through my desk?" Niall stopped himself from going down that path. One problem at a time. "You won't find anythin' about Vinnie in there, either."

"Then I'll look through your bank records. Someone had to pay you a retainer for that piece of work."

She had him by the shorthairs. Niall grabbed her arm and pulled her down to the mattress. "There's something I've got to tell you."

"What? You've got more secrets? I'm so surprised."

"Look, Frannie," he said, trying one last time to get her to let go of this bone. "Knowin' the truth isn't gonna make you happy."

Frannie's eyes teared up. "I have to know who set this whole thing in motion. Don't you see?"

"Why? So you can pin the blame on that person? Or so you can thank them?" Her answer mattered. More than he was comfortable admitting.

Frannie shrugged. "I just have to know."

"All right. I'll tell you, but you can't go off half-cocked. She meant well, I'm sure."

"She?"

Niall drew in a deep breath. "Your mother."

Shock rendered her momentarily speechless. She opened and closed her mouth like a fish. "My mother hired you to spy on Vinnie?" she asked, her voice sounding a little strangled.

"Yeah, Donatella Valentine. Or Donna as she asked me to call her."

She bolted from the bed. "You call my mama, Donna?"

"Should I call her Mama Donna now?" he quipped, and then immediately wished he'd kept his attempt at mirth to himself.

Frannie's face grew red. Her chest puffed out with anger. "My mother had you follow Vinnie around?"

"I only just started working the case," he said, hoping a little lie would calm her down.

Frannie's hands balled into fists at her side. "How long?"

"A week—" Her frown had him revise his second white lie. "Three."

"Did you follow him around when he was with me?"

Niall held himself very still. "I had to learn his habits," he said quietly.

Her stare grew pointed. "Did you watch us?"

Niall squirmed. She wasn't going to like his answer. "Only when you were in public. I didn't wire your home."

"Did you watch us having sex?"

"Just once when you went down on him in his car after a movie."

Frannie blinked and her chin wobbled. "We saw 'The Chronicles of Riddick'. Vin Diesel always makes me horny."

He hated adding to her pain, but now that the truth was out, he had to tell her the rest. "And...when he fucked you in the bathroom stall at Benihana's."

Her tears spilled down her cheeks.

Niall's gut clenched. "I ducked in there when you both came down the hall. How was I to know he wasn't comin' in for a piss?"

"Did it turn you on—watching me?" she asked, her voice breaking.

Niall couldn't meet her gaze. "You're beautiful—and very sexy."

"Did you plan to turn me? Were you just waiting for an opportunity?"

"*No, never.* Never once did I even think it."

"You didn't once wonder what it would be like to have me, here like this?"

How the hell could he answer that question? He'd wanted her—dreamed about having her here in his bed. He sidestepped the question. "I never planned what happened. Do you think I put that bus there?"

Frannie collapsed on the side of the bed, like her legs wouldn't hold her up. "So what else did you learn about me?" she asked, wiping away her tears with the back of her hand.

"That you tried very hard to please him, but his neglect was driving you nuts."

"Were you following him or me that night?"

Niall's whole body tensed. This was the crux of the problem, wasn't it? The one truth he'd hoped she'd never learn. "I already knew what he was doing at the office that night. So I drove back to your apartment building. I arrived just in time to see you hail a cab."

Frannie wrapped her arms around her middle. "So you followed me."

"I was keeping watch over you. You looked like a woman with a bone to chew."

"But you broke the rules when you intervened between Vinnie and me, didn't you?"

"I was…concerned."

"You didn't have to stick around after you dropped me off. But you followed me into the bar."

"It was a rough place."

Her glare told him she didn't believe him.

"All right," he said, feeling defeat weigh on him. "I couldn't help myself. You looked upset."

"And you wanted to meet me." Frannie's voice was even, too quiet.

"Yeah," he said, not caring to varnish the truth at this point. Whatever he said would make him look like a jerk. "I wanted to meet you."

"Why? Because I'm the kind of girl who goes down on her boyfriend in a car?" Her voice rose at the end, fired by her anger.

"Because you fascinated me," he said truthfully. "Even then."

"I can't believe this. This whole thing—I thought it was coincidence. That maybe God meant this to happen to me. But it was all you—*and my mother*."

They stayed like that—her poised on the edge of the bed, him still as stone, afraid to move in case she bolted.

"So what are you going to do now?" he asked, wanting to reach out and stroke her back, needing to offer her any comfort she'd accept.

"What am I supposed to do? I make the most ridiculous decisions when it comes to men. My life's a mess."

"What do you want?"

"What I want can't even come into this discussion. I'll never have it."

Niall thought about the kids she'd said she hoped for, and his heart plummeted. That was something he'd never give her. Something he'd stolen from her forever. "Do you want to leave?"

Her breath gusted. "And go where?"

"You have a job. I'll advance you the rent, if that's what you really want."

Her gaze swung to his face. "You'd let me go—just like that?"

He gave her a smile he knew didn't look the least bit genuine. "If it will make you happy."

"And if I want to stay?"

His heart heard the poignant question in her voice. *Do you want me?* He rose on his elbow and reached for her hand. "You know you're welcome to stay as long as you want—and you don't have to share my bed, if that's what you'd prefer."

She tugged away her hand and shot off the bed. "And what am I supposed to do when I get hungry?" she shouted.

An inward smile broke over him, and he relaxed. Anger from Frannie was a good thing. "Order in?" he asked, stoking the fire.

"And what will I tell the restaurant—'Send me raw steak and a well-hung delivery boy'?"

Niall kicked off the sheet and sat up. "Oh, you're talking about *that* hunger. I guess I could accommodate you."

Frannie's glance swept downward. "You'd sacrifice yourself for me?"

"Baby, it's no sacrifice," he growled.

"Ooh!" Her hands fisted again and she paced. "I should be feeling really, really ashamed of myself. I've been used, manipulated, lied to—why does that feel familiar?"

Now his anger rose up to bite. "There's no comparison between what Vinnie did to you and what I—"

She halted and her head jerked up. "You're right. Vinnie never killed me."

Niall didn't react to that jab — he waited.

"I said, I *should* be feeling those things." Her shoulders slumped. "But I don't. Does that make me a weak person?"

"No. Just...adaptable."

Air hissed between her teeth.

"Pragmatic maybe?"

She faced him, hands on her hips. "What I feel right now is really, really hungry."

"Shall I order that takeout, love?"

Her expression grew crafty. "No, let's find an all-night diner and dine on the customers."

"Frannie?" he asked, worried he'd pushed her over the edge.

She shrugged. "I said I was hungry. We can leave a really big tip." Frannie gave him a saucy grin. "After I've filled my belly, I'll be really, really horny."

Catching on to her joke, he said, "God, I hope that's where I come in."

"Only if you play your cards right, buster."

Niall patted the mattress. "How about one for the road? Just to take off the edge?"

"I was thinking the same thing." Frannie crawled onto the bed, stalking him, not stopping until she lowered her body over him, her thighs sliding to either side of his cock for a mind-blowing caress.

Niall pushed her hair from her face. "There's still the little matter of your snooping in my desk."

She winced. "I was hoping that comment went right over your head."

"I think that infraction of the rules deserves a little punishment."

She bit her lip. "What are you going to do?"

"I did promise a little ass-fuckin'."

Her breath hitched. "You said we would wait until I'm ready."

"Aren't you?"

Her hips squirmed, tugging at his cock. "Niall?"

He rolled over, pinning her to the mattress. Looking down at her, Niall felt invincible. Frannie's wide-eyed gaze and slender form made him feel intensely male, like a conquering Roman crossing his Rubicon. Only his sword would sink into the softest flesh. He lowered his head and kissed her.

Frannie sighed into his mouth, and then their tongues mated, dueling for supremacy. Her nipples poked at his chest and hungry little moans broke in the back of her throat. She wriggled her hips, creating a heat between her thighs that threatened to unman him.

He stroked his cock between her legs, grazing her slick folds, and felt the first ripple of ecstasy shudder through her body. Just a little higher and he'd slide home.

Instead, he rose up, straddling her body. "There's that little matter of punishment." That was all the warning he gave her, before he flipped her onto her stomach. He leaned over her and whispered, "Give me the pillows."

Frannie grabbed blindly for the pillows and tossed them behind her.

Niall laughed and lifted her hips off the bed, sliding the pillows beneath her belly.

"This feels awkward," she said, her voice muffled in the bedding.

"Are you afraid?"

"You can see everything."

Niall pushed his knees between hers and encouraged her to widen them further with gentle shoves. "I can now."

In all their loving, he'd never once had her from behind. Her breasts were endlessly fascinating. But now he had a chance to admire her narrow waist, the gentle flare of her hips, and the lush, fleshy bottom that would cushion his strokes.

Niall closed his fist around his cock. God, he couldn't wait to bury himself inside her tight ass.

"Remind me, how does a little snooping offset your lying?" she said, her voice sounding a little thin.

Niall knew she was nervous. While all the blood in his body was rushing to his cock, he fought to keep his mind engaged. He needed Frannie to relax. "I didn't really lie." He started at her shoulders, massaging away the tension he found there with firm, squeezes and strokes.

"Mmm." Frannie sighed. "Didn't your mama ever tell you that omission is a form of lying?"

Never letting up, he worked his way slowly down her back. "Is that what Mama Donna told you?"

"I don't want to talk about my mama while you're doing this to me."

"Just what am I doing?"

"Looking at me. Touching me."

He ground the ball of his palm in the muscles on either side of her spine. "What do you think I see?"

"*Everything.*"

"Not quite. But maybe I need a closer look." Reaching her buttocks, he kneaded the rounded globes, spreading her cheeks for a peek between the creamy halves. Niall rubbed his cock against her bottom. "I love your ass, Frannie."

She clamped her hands over her ears. "Don't say that!"

His hands smoothed over her ass and down her thighs. "Why?"

"You don't have to make this more embarrassing than it already is. You're making me blush."

The word "ass" seemed to be a hot button. He rested his palms on her backside. "Your blush doesn't extend to your *ass*. Maybe I should do something to warm it up?"

"Like what?"

"I thought you didn't want me to tell you?"

She glanced over her shoulder. "Are you going to spank me?"

"It's your choice. I can spank your bottom or fuck it. Which is it to be?"

Frannie buried her face in the bedding again. "Stop saying that!"

The word "fuck" got an even bigger response. He swatted her. "Okay, I'll do both."

"No! Just...the ass thing," she said, her voice thin as the air.

"Which ass thing?" he asked, glad she couldn't see the grin curving his mouth.

"You know," she said, exasperation making her moan.

"Then a fucking, it is!" He squeezed her bottom. "But first, we need the magic lubricant."

Her head lifted. "What magic lubricant?"

"K-Y."

Her hands went back over her ears. "I don't want to hear any more."

"I'd hate for you to be afraid. I can explain every step, every penetration—"

"Just do it, damn you!"

"Back in a second." Niall bounded off the bed, but walking was hampered by his raging erection. When he returned, Frannie was in exactly the same position he'd left her, bent over the stack of pillows, her bottom in the air. But her breaths were shorter, and her fingers clutched the bedding. *Good!*

He climbed onto the bed, settling between her outspread legs. He laid the tube to the side, just within her range of vision.

Smoothing his hands up her inner thighs, he brought both thumbs to her plump labia and spread them open like the petals of a rose. "So, you want to know what I see?" he asked, dropping his voice to a purr. He leaned down to blow a gust of air over her heated, glistening flesh.

"Tell me."

"It's the most beautiful sight a man will ever behold — a woman's pussy, slicked with the cream of her arousal. Plump, rosy lips that guard a secret portal. When he spreads them wide, he finds a deep, dark secret, waiting for discovery." He pushed two fingers inside and twisted as he drove them deeper.

Frannie's buttocks tensed, and her knees dug into the mattress. "Tell me more!"

Niall bent closer and lapped the short space between her cunt and her tightly furled hole while he continued to finger-fuck her pussy. "Between the pale mountains of her bottom, is an arrow that points to a set of lips only the luckiest man will ever kiss." He tongued her ass, lapping with the flat of his tongue, then tunneling the tip into the hole.

Frannie shivered, but didn't protest. Mewls, soft as a baby kitten's, tore from her throat.

Niall noted a fresh release of moisture seeping from her cunt. She was almost there. He reached for the K-Y and squeezed a dollop onto the tip of one finger. Then he rubbed the finger around her anus until it glistened invitingly. "Shall I tell you how it feels for a man to dive into unexplored territory?"

"You're killing me, Niall," she said, her holding a hint of warning.

"If all goes well, you'll experience the 'little death'."

"You're enjoying this too much."

"Of course, I am." He kissed each glowing cheek. "I always love loving you, Frannie."

"No, you're making fun of me. I know I'm not very experienced —"

Niall gave her ass a squeeze. "I'm sorry if you thought I was making light of this, sweetheart. I was only trying to help you relax." He drew back. "I'll stop if you like."

"Don't you dare! I'm...ready for this." She glanced back, uncertainty shadowing her eyes. "But if I don't like it, will we have to do it again?"

He gave her a tender smile. "If you don't enjoy the hell out of it—it'll be my fault. And I won't ask it of you again."

Her hands tightened their grip on the bedding and she braced herself like she was preparing for a firing squad. "Then...then tell me what a man feels when he dives into unexplored territory."

Niall kissed her bottom again before proceeding. "If he has an ounce of caution in him, he learns as much about the area as he can." Niall pressed his thumb into her ass, his breath catching at the tightness of the muscles that resisted his penetration. His cock throbbed in empathy. "Sweet Jesus!" He gave a little moan, then got hold of himself. "Sometimes he has to take timid steps into the darkness, test the water with his toes." He withdrew and pressed two fingers inside, gently pulsing to ease the constriction.

Frannie groaned, her head thrashing on the bed.

So far, so good. She hadn't screamed bloody murder—yet. Niall pushed deeper and twisted his wrist, forcing the ring of muscle to loosen fractionally. *Christ*, she was tight. He had to be inside her now. He pulled out and reached for the tube again, spreading the gel on his cock, lubing himself like an axle.

Then Niall centered himself between her legs and spread her buttocks apart.

Frannie rose up on her arms, her shoulders rising and falling rapidly with her shallow breaths. "You aren't talking to me."

"I've lost the power of speech—*Jesus*, Frannie, I can't wait." Niall placed his cock at her opening and pressed his hips forward.

Frannie gasped. His cock inched inside, and she sobbed.

Niall closed his eyes. The sight of her trembling body was one sensory detail too many to take. He concentrated on the feel of her asshole, easing around his cock, allowing him to slide deeper. The muscles of her anus squeezed him, massaging his length, while never letting up the pressure. "Frannie—you're so damn tight. And hot! Baby, I have to move."

"Oh, God! Oh, God!" she moaned, as he started to pump gently in and out. "I've never felt so full. Move! Move!"

Niall gauged his thrusts, some shallow, some deep, but always sleek, gliding movements to gently introduce her to this new pleasure. Her body shuddered and her buttocks tensed, but she pushed back fractionally, telling him with her body how she enjoyed this fucking.

Ever mindful of her virgin flight, Niall gradually increased the depths of his deeper thrusts, plunging into her heat, angling slightly left and right to vary the sensation.

But Frannie grew impatient with his gentle tutoring; she slammed back against him sharply, encouraging him to increase the force of his thrusts.

Sweat broke on Niall's forehead and back as he strained to keep control, but Frannie made it impossible for him to keep his resolve to be gentle. He reached between her legs and cupped her pussy, grinding his palm into her cunt.

Frannie's bottom jerked and she cried out, flinging back her head to ride the storm breaking over her.

Niall shoved his fingers into her pussy and fucked her with his hand while his cock reamed her ass, harder and harder.

A keening scream erupted from Frannie and Niall felt her orgasm burn through her, as her vagina convulsed around his fingers and her ass constricted tightly around his cock.

Then he felt the change come over him. He'd fought the monster looming within him each time they'd made love, not wanting to frighten her or harm her with his brutish strength. That Frannie hadn't discovered the one inside herself was a testament to her gentle soul, but his body's need was growing beyond his control, overriding his better intentions.

The bones on his forehead crackled as they reshaped, his muscles bulged outward as the vampire inside him gained supremacy. His teeth slid from his gums and he opened his mouth wide in preparation for the bite.

Frannie moaned and jerked, her body erupting anew in response to his quickening. Niall leaned over her back, jerking his hips to continue his sensual assault while seeking the tender side of her neck.

Her head tilted to the side, and he bit deeply, suctioning through his teeth, drawing her life into his mouth. His body exploded.

Afterward, he closed the tiny wounds, withdrew his sex, and cradled Frannie's limp body in his arms. His rubbed his face on her shoulder to assure himself he no longer wore his monster's mask and gave a deep contented sigh.

Eventually, Frannie stirred and looked over shoulder to gift him with a brilliant smile. "Where did all that stuff come from?"

Niall stiffened. "What stuff?" Had she seen him?

"The things you said about me—down there. They were beautiful."

He managed a weak smile and said, "I'm Irish, we're all born with the poet gene."

She arched one fine brow. "Although, I'm not sure if I shouldn't be offended by you comparing my ass to a mountain."

"I assure you, love, you're more like the gently curved Appalachians than the Himalayans."

She covered his hands with hers and squeezed, wriggling her bottom against his groin until she was comfortable and he was not. "Then that's okay...I guess."

"Ready to go dine on diners?" he said, teasing her with her earlier threat.

"Can we order in instead?" She grinned. "I'm not sure I have the energy to get out of bed."

"Well-hung delivery boys will not be on the menu."

"Just one?" she asked in a wheedling tone.

"So long as the only one doing the biting is me."

Chapter Six

Frannie squinted at the row of letters appearing on the nice, neat labels in orderly succession on the word processor and sighed with satisfaction. The plastic files, free of grubby fingerprints, were almost ready for the drawer.

Fresh dividers were already done and propped between her coffee cup and the printer. "Poland", "Iceland", "Norway", "Scotland". Frannie didn't feel an ounce of guilt for not returning the files to their former, unimaginative order—besides, she figured Niall could never let her go if he couldn't find a thing in the cabinet.

A soft knock sounded on the office door and Frannie peered through the glass. Two women, dressed in black like a pair of crows, hovered outside.

Frannie waved at her mama and Zia Grazia and motioned for them to enter.

"Hello, Mama." She rushed over and bussed her cheek.

Donatella Valentine drew back warily and looked into her eyes. Then she relaxed and patted her cheek. "You need to eat more." She blanched instantly.

Frannie laughed and drew her to a chair and then fetched another for Zia Grazia, before taking her own seat. "I can't believe you're here."

"If the mountain won't come…" Zia Grazia leaned forward and stared at her. "You have the look, all right."

"What look is that?" Frannie said loudly, expecting another of Zia Grazia's rare but startlingly odd observations.

"Like you're in love."

Frannie smiled and stared at her elderly aunt. "You can tell from just one look?"

"I'm eighty-one," she said with a nod. "You learn a thing or two over time."

"I have a question to ask you, Zia Mia," Frannie said, using her childhood nickname for her dour, old aunt. "At the funeral home, I thought I heard you laughing when I was running away. How come you weren't afraid for me?"

"Have a cousin," Zia Grazia barked. "She got turned back in the Depression. Sends me birthday cards from Florida. Might go for a visit. The heat will be good for my bones."

"You knew I was a vampire?"

"You were dead—then you weren't." Another emphatic nod, then Zia Mia fell silent.

"She gave me this Niall's number," her mother said softly so her aunt couldn't hear.

"I don't understand."

"We were both worried about you. That Vinnie was no good. So when I said how I was thinking about hiring a man to follow Vinnie—she gives me his number." Her mother held up a finger next to her nose. "I wouldn't be at all surprised if she knew."

Frannie shook her head. She was over the blame game, but life sure was strange. Perhaps God had a sense of humor after all.

"So are you happy, honey?"

Worried by the shadows in her mama's eyes, Frannie gave her mother a hug. "I have a job, a new place to decorate—"

"And a man who puts roses in your cheeks?"

Frannie smiled brightly, ignoring the little twinge of sadness in her chest. Niall was good to her—playful, loving, giving—but he hadn't said he loved her. "I'm getting there, Mama."

"Good enough. Don't rush things—you have eternity to get it right." Donatella patted Frannie's knee. "So tell me, where's that vampire studmuffin of yours?"

Frannie's eyes widened at her mother's coarse comment.

Her mama winked. "I'm old—I'm not dead."

"Told her he was the man for the job," Zia Grazia shouted.

* * * * *

Frannie had just seen the women to their cab, when the phone rang. "Niall Keegan's office."

"Need to talk to Mr. Keegan," a man said, his voice barely audible.

"Mr. Keegan's not here, can I take a message?"

"Give me his beeper number."

Frannie didn't care for his furtive tone or the way he framed his demand. "I'm his...partner. Is there something I can do for you?"

"Tell him, Packie called. Got a make on Gunter Koch."

"Gunter Cock? Is he German?"

The man was silent for a moment. "Just tell Keegan, he's holed up in a hotel off Broadway. This is the address."

Frannie quickly jotted it down, her heart racing. "Cock" wasn't a name in the "regular" file cabinet. "I'll make sure he gets the message."

As soon as she hung up, Frannie dashed to Niall's office and sifted through the "DVs". "Gunter Koch" was in the center of them. She laid the message beside the folder and read the scant notes Niall had carefully filed away, then she held up the grainy photo. Gunter Koch was one handsome man, in a scary sort of way—blond, shoulder-length hair, a square jaw and piercing, dark eyes. But strangely she couldn't find a clue about the point of Niall's investigation. Just a list of names—names that were familiar to her from listening to Vinnie's one-sided calls with his "associates".

Frannie glanced at the clock. Niall wasn't due back until hours later. Chewing on her lip, she wondered whether she should beep him or…

She went to the large cabinet that held the tools of Niall's trade and found a camera with telescoping lens. She'd been practicing with it every night after Niall left on one of his cases.

Gathering a notepad and her purse, she quickly called a cab and hurried downstairs to meet it. If all went well, Niall wouldn't be able to deny her — if not a full partnership — an apprenticeship!

Francesca Valentine, Apprentice PI. She liked the ring of that.

Niall's steps lightened as he unlocked the office door. Frannie would be happy he was back early. More and more, he hated leaving her behind when he left for a job. He worried about her and longed for her company. Man, was he ever whipped — and loving it.

In fact, he was pretty sure he loved Frannie. Fiesty, nutty as a fruitcake Frannie. He couldn't even work up a good growl when he couldn't find a thing in that damn file cabinet. She'd have to stick around just to hunt down his case files.

Niall expected her to pop her head around the door to greet him, but the office was quiet. Too quiet. All his instincts told him she hadn't just run next door to the bathroom. He hurried into his office and saw the note and the open file on his desk.

Gunter Koch   Jesus, Mary, and Joseph! Frannie was trying to tail one of his DVs — Dangerous Vampires. He kept tabs on them, letting the Master's Council know whenever they pulled up stakes and moved location. Not that Frannie had a clue what sort of trouble she was heading into.

He had to stop her before Koch got wind that someone was spying on him. The man was volatile, moody, with business connections to two crime families — and his enemies had a way of disappearing.

* * * * *

Frannie was feeling very proud of herself. She'd finessed Koch's apartment number from the doorman, helping herself to a bite to help him forget. He'd also offered her the little tidbit that Koch was throwing a party.

Glad she'd opted for a black pantsuit, she left her jacket, purse and camera in a bundle behind a trashcan, unbuttoned her blouse to just between her breasts, and fluffed out her hair. Now she was ready to party crash. She'd beard the lion in his den — or at least find the scoop on him firsthand.

Letting herself in the front door, Frannie snuck a glass of champagne from an abandoned tray next to the foyer and pasted on a plastic smile. She rounded the corner and entered a smoke-filled room crammed with legitimate partygoers. Bobbing her head to the music blaring from a DJ's speakers, she studied the faces of each of the guests, searching for her mark.

"Do I know you?" a deep, harshly accented voice drawled from just behind her.

Frannie turned to find Gunter Koch standing right behind her. She smiled brightly, hoping he didn't see a flare of panic in her eyes. "Not yet. I was waiting to be introduced," she said smoothly.

"By whom?"

She drew in a nervous breath. "He's around here somewhere." She took a sip of the champagne and then gestured to the crowd. "It's some party you have here."

"I think you are not on the guest list."

Frannie's eyes widened at the hint of menace in his voice — her heart nearly stopped beating when his finger trailed along her cheek.

"But I can guess why you are here."

"Y-you can?"

"But of course. Every vamp Miss wants to taste the delights I offer."

"Delights? You have liver?"

He chuckled—a sound that did nothing to lessen the hysteria threatening to bubble from her throat.

"You're amusing—I think I will keep you for a while." His fingers closed around her upper arm and he pulled her behind him, through the crowd dancing in the large living room and down a darkened hallway. "You and I do not need the light, do we?'

He opened a door to a bedroom and pushed her inside. "Now, take off your clothes."

"I beg your pardon?"

"You are here, uninvited. There can be only one reason for your rude behavior."

"I want to take off my clothes?"

"But of course."

Frannie shook her head—Gunter was a very odd man indeed. No wonder Niall kept his file in his secret drawer. Creeps like this needed padded cells. "I-If it's all right with you, I'd like to keep my clothes for now."

He shrugged and quietly unbuttoned his cuffs. "I like a little modesty. Have you been at this for long?"

At what? She smiled weakly. "Not at all. A few days…"

"How delicious you are."

"Not really, I'm Italian—I eat lots of garlic."

He chuckled again. "Please, you must make yourself comfortable." He gestured toward the bed—a very large bed with the covers already turned back.

Frannie's eyes widened with alarm. "I'm—I have to pee," she said, her voice squeaking.

"I understand. You may use my bathroom," he said nodding behind her.

Frannie hurried to the door, wondering whether there was a lock, or if he'd lose interest if she made really disgusting noises from inside. She closed the door behind her and let out the breath she'd been holding.

She nearly shrieked when a hand closed over her mouth.

"Not one bloody, goddamned word," a voice whispered into her ear, and then he lowered his hand.

"Niall!" She whirled and flung her arms around his neck. "I'm so glad to see you. How did you get in here?" she hissed into his ear.

He nodded to an adjoining door opposite the one she'd entered.

"Well, what are we waiting for? Let's go."

"We can't leave that way, there's another couple inside. They came in after me."

"What are we going to do? Gunter's in the other room."

Niall's shoulders bunched beneath her hands. "We have to go through the window." He pushed her away and turned to raise the small window.

"Are you crazy? We're four floors up! And your shoulders will never fit through that postage stamp!"

He gave her a grin. "Do you trust me?"

"Always!" she said, nodding, wondering whether he was planning to stuff her through the window.

"Then close your eyes, and think light wispy thoughts."

"Huh?"

He shook his head and clucked. "You said you trusted me."

"I do!"

"Then close your eyes, love."

He was going to give her one last kiss before he crammed her through the window. She really ought to warn him, she didn't think her hips would fit. But she closed her eyes—at least partway.

Through her slitted eyelids, she saw Niall's body shimmer, then dissolve into mist. Shocked to her toes, Frannie slammed her eyes closed. *Think wispy thoughts!* Quicker than she could scream, her body grew light and she floated. Niall's essence tugged her through the window, and then she was wafting toward the sidewalk.

Once there, her body tingled, and she found herself facing him with both feet on the ground—and they were entirely naked!

He grabbed her hand. "Run for the cab!"

Frannie forgot how to work her feet and stumbled after him. "Niall, we just turned into smoke!"

"Mist, love, there's a difference."

"But that was the most amazing thing—do you do that a lot?"

"No! It takes too much energy." He ran faster, leaving her huffing in his wake. "We have to get home quick."

The cab was parked on the far side of the street, next to the corner farthest from the apartment doors. Frannie tried not to think about what her feet were stepping in—this was New York City after all.

"What I want to know," Niall shouted over his shoulder, "is what the hell were you thinkin' going off half-cocked into a vampire's den?"

"Half-cocked?" She stopped in the middle of the street, digging in her heels. "If you didn't notice—I almost got the whole Koch!"

He rounded on her. "Oh, I noticed all right, maybe you were wantin' to stay?"

"Of course, I wasn't! He gives me the wiggins."

"Then get to the damn cab."

A car sped by and honked. A shout sounded from across the street, "Hey, get a room!"

Frannie screeched and jogged to the gleaming, yellow taxi. "Niall Keegan, I'm going to kill you!"

* * * * *

Several weeks later, Niall Keegan reached out the window of his cab and adjusted the mirror. He couldn't miss Kowalski's exit from his mistress's apartment.

Satisfied with the angle, he sank lower in his seat and braced his feet on the floorboard.

"Did we miss him again?" Frannie asked, lifting her head from his lap.

Niall threaded his fingers through her hair and pushed her face back down. "No love, we've time."

Frannie's wicked mouth returned to her meal. She devoured his cock, lapping his shaft like a lollipop, sucking him like a vacuum until he orgasmed so strongly, he felt like she'd wrung it from his toes.

A shrill whistle sounded from outside, and Frannie jerked upright. "Fuck! That's him!" She turned the ignition, flicked on the headlights, and slammed the cab into gear. "You so owe me, buster."

"I promise I'll return the favor later."

She pulled a U-turn in the middle of the road and stomped on the gas, barely cutting off another cab to slide neatly in front of Edgar Kowalski and his girlfriend.

Frannie threw the man a cheeky smile. "Where do you folks wanna go?"

That's my girl! Niall smiled sleepily, still fighting the drugging effect of his orgasm.

"You familiar with the *Lizards 'n' Suds*?" Kowalski asked, as he slid across the seat.

Frannie cast Niall a wicked grin. "I know it well. It's where I met my husband."

"Yeah it was love at first sight," Niall said, slinging his arm over her shoulder.

"That's nice." Kowalksi's smile was more of a grimace— was he feeling a little guilty? "How long 'til we get there?"

"I'll have you there in a flash, sir," Frannie said, gunning the engine. In minutes, she pulled to a halt in front of the bar.

Niall glanced back at Kowalski and smothered a grin. The man was a little green around the gills. "That'll be ten bucks."

Kowalksi fished the cash out of his pocket and handed it to Niall. Then he and his girlfriend quickly exited the cab.

"Did you get that girl's license number?" Kowalksi said to the woman clinging to his arm. "She's a menace."

Niall shook his head. "It's a good thing you don't drive a cab for a living, love."

"I get where I'm going," she said smugly, turning off the meter and driving further down the street to park.

"That you do. Well, there's another case closed."

"Not until we have the pictures to prove it." She reached for the small duffel behind the seat and drew out a palm-sized camera. "Do you think our old seats are empty?"

"Feeling nostalgic?"

Frannie snorted and opened her door. "For that dive?"

He climbed out and followed her down the sidewalk, then froze when he realized where he was. Frannie stepped over the place on the pavement where she'd died without ever looking down. "Do you ever think about it?" he asked.

Frannie looked over her shoulder, and then down, appearing surprised to be standing on that exact spot. "All the time."

His hands curled into fists. "If I'd only acted quicker..."

She walked over to him and slid her arms around his waist. "If I hadn't followed Vinnie..."

Niall crushed her to his chest and hugged her with all his might. "I would have spared you the pain."

"What pain? You knocked me silly. I didn't feel a thing. Now this hug is another thing entirely."

Niall loosened his hold immediately. "Really? You didn't feel a thing?"

"Well, I felt your first bite."

"I'm sorry about that."

"I'm not. I died with that last delicious memory to carry me over." Frannie tilted her head. "What is it with you tonight?"

Niall cupped her cheek, stroking her lower lip with his thumb. His chest ached and his jaw tightened. "I guess, I just remembered I forgot to tell you I love you."

Frannie's eyes filled with tears and she laughed. "You think I didn't already figure that out? I'm a PI, remember?"

Niall felt moisture gather in his own eyes and smiled ruefully. "Oh, yeah? Then tell me what clued you in?"

Frannie leaned back in his arms and stared into his eyes. "When you told me you knew all about me before you ever met me—but you were still there to hold me when I needed you most."

Niall's heart clenched at the sweetness of her smile. "You think you're not easy to love?"

"I'm a pain in the ass, Keegan. Admit it!"

"That you are, Frannie Keegan." He gave her a cheeky smile. "But your ass is all mine."

About the author:

Delilah Devlin dated a Samoan, a Venezuelan, a Turk, a Cuban, and was engaged to a Greek before marrying her Irishman. She's lived in Saudi Arabia, Germany, and Ireland, but calls Texas home for now. Ever a risk taker, she lived in the Saudi Peninsula during the first Gulf War, thwarted an attempted abduction by white slave traders, and survived her children's juvenile delinquency.

Creating alter egos for herself in the pages of her books enables her to live new adventures. Since discovering the sinful pleasure of erotica, she writes to satisfy her need for variety—it keeps her from running away with the Indian working in the cubicle beside her!

In addition to writing erotica, she enjoys creating romantic comedies and suspense novels.

Delilah welcomes mail from readers. You can write to her c/o Ellora's Cave Publishing at 1337 Commerce Drive, #13, Stow, Ohio 44224.

Also by Delilah Devlin

Prisoner of Desire: Desire
All Hallows Heartbreaker: My Immortal Knight
Slave of Desire: Desire
Love Bites: My Immortal Knight
Garden of Desire: Desire
All Knight Long: My Immortal Knight
The Pleasure Bot
Relentless: My Immortal Knight
Ellora's Cavemen: Tales from the Temple III
Lion in the Shadows

Why an electronic book?

We live in the Information Age—an exciting time in the history of human civilization in which technology rules supreme and continues to progress in leaps and bounds every minute of every hour of every day. For a multitude of reasons, more and more avid literary fans are opting to purchase e-books instead of paperbacks. The question to those not yet initiated to the world of electronic reading is simply: *why?*

1. *Price.* An electronic title at Ellora's Cave Publishing runs anywhere from 40-75% less than the cover price of the <u>exact same title</u> in paperback format. Why? Cold mathematics. It is less expensive to publish an e book than it is to publish a paperback, so the savings are passed along to the consumer.

2. *Space.* Running out of room to house your paperback books? That is one worry you will never have with electronic novels. For a low one-time cost, you can purchase a handheld computer designed specifically for e-reading purposes. Many e-readers are larger than the average handheld, giving you plenty of screen room. Better yet, hundreds of titles can be stored within your new library—a single microchip. (Please note that Ellora's Cave does not endorse any specific brands. You can check our website at www.ellorascave.com for customer recommendations we make available to new consumers.)

3. *Mobility.* Because your new library now consists of only a microchip, your entire cache of books can be taken with you wherever you go.

4. *Personal preferences are accounted for.* Are the words you are currently reading too small? Too large?

Too...ANNOYING? Paperback books cannot be modified according to personal preferences, but e-books can.

5. *Innovation.* The way you read a book is not the only advancement the Information Age has gifted the literary community with. There is also the factor of what you can read. Ellora's Cave Publishing will be introducing a new line of interactive titles that are available in e-book format only.

6. *Instant gratification.* Is it the middle of the night and all the bookstores are closed? Are you tired of waiting days — sometimes weeks — for online and offline bookstores to ship the novels you bought? Ellora's Cave Publishing sells instantaneous downloads 24 hours a day, 7 days a week, 365 days a year. Our e-book delivery system is 100% automated, meaning your order is filled as soon as you pay for it.

Those are a few of the top reasons why electronic novels are displacing paperbacks for many an avid reader. As always, Ellora's Cave Publishing welcomes your questions and comments. We invite you to email us at service@ellorascave.com or write to us directly at: 1337 Commerce Drive, Suite 13, Stow OH 44224.

Printed in the United States
29810LVS00003B/52-537

9 781419 951435